TWO OF A KIND

SASHA COTTMAN

To Dean and Laura

Chapter One

London 1817
A crowded, dirty riverside tavern

"I'm getting married."

James Radley choked and spluttered on the large gulp of ale he had just taken into his mouth. Beer dripped down the front of his shirt and jacket.

"What the devil?!"

He wiped his lips with the back of his hand before looking dejectedly at the mess that was now his clothes.

Guy Dannon, his old school friend from Eton, met James's gaze. A wry grin sat on his face. It was obvious Guy knew exactly the sort of reaction his sudden announcement would provoke, and he was enjoying every moment of it. A friend he might be, but even James knew that Guy took particular delight in being a manipulative bastard when it suited him.

"Thought it was time for me to make a run for parliament. Everyone knows that a chap needs a wife in order to secure preselection for a safe seat. A couple of weeks ago, I went and spoke to someone with strong political connections, who not only agreed to help me get preselected, but who conveniently has a highly eligible daughter," replied Guy.

James carefully set his tankard of beer down on the table, not wishing to risk choking on another mouthful. It was bad enough that he now stank of beer.

He would put money on having never heard the words *Guy* and *wife* used in the same sentence before today.

"Things are already that far in motion?" replied James.

"Of course. Why do you think I went and bought a house and some land? It wasn't from a sudden need to display my grand wealth."

"I was wondering why you had done that. It makes sense that you would want one so as to entice a wife," said James.

Guy gave him a look of disgust. "I settled on a property because I cannot run for parliament if I am not a landowner. I have never had to do any sort of enticing when it comes to women, and I don't intend to start now. Especially not for a wife," said Guy.

James considered his ale.

I wonder if someone has slipped something into my drink.

Guy had always declared that marriage was for other men; it would never be for him.

"While I understand your political ambitions, Guy, even you would have to admit to being nothing more than an unashamed rake. You only see women as a means to sate your lust. You use them, then toss them aside," said James.

"And what has that to do with me getting married?" replied Guy. He seemed to find James's less-than-enthusiastic reaction to the news of his impending nuptials a little perplexing.

"How do you intend to be any sort of a decent husband and father when you think so little of the fairer sex?" said James.

Guy sat back in his seat and studied James. Slowly he shook his head, picked up his tankard and held it high toward James. "I know your family holds with foolish notions about love and fidelity, but I am a practical man. I have chosen a young lady from a politically connected family as my future spouse. She understands how these things work. Securing a seat for myself in parliament is what's important. Now drink up. We should be celebrating," Guy finally replied.

James didn't touch his drink. He knew enough about women to know that most held firm opinions on the subject of marriage. Given half a chance, a woman would not marry purely for the sake of political connections. It was love or nothing for many of them, and especially for the women in his extended family.

Instead of feeling elated over Guy's sudden announcement, he was filled with sadness over the news that some poor girl was about to be condemned to a cold, political union.

"So, who is this poor chit who is going to be saddled with you for the rest of her days?" he asked. If it was someone else the words might have been spoken in half jest, but when it came to Guy, James was deadly serious. His friend would make a terrible husband.

"Her name is Leah Shepherd and from what she has said, I think your sister Claire knows her."

James frowned. He had a vague recollection of perhaps having been introduced to her at some point but couldn't recall what Leah Shepherd actually looked like. He did, however, know of her father. Tobias Shepherd was a kingmaker in the lofty circles of English politics. "I can't place her, but there are always lots of young women coming and going from home. When do you intend to introduce her to your friends?"

"Tomorrow. You are going to meet Leah at a garden party in Richmond," replied Guy.

James leaned across the table and stared hard at his friend, unsure as to whether he had heard Guy correctly. Had he just said that they were going to a garden party? "I am not going to a bloody garden party. Those things are dangerous. Every unwed young miss in London will be in attendance, and they will all be on the hunt for one thing: a husband. Cupid will have his little sharp arrows trained on every bachelor's arse. Hell will freeze over before I set foot inside a garden party." James snorted.

The whole notion was preposterous. Garden parties were full of lovestruck couples making doe eyes at one another. He shuddered at the thought. Guy may well have his plans, but for James, marriage was not anywhere on the horizon.

Guy slowly smiled. "I'll tell you what, James. Let me buy us a large bottle of whisky and then we can discuss what you will or won't be doing tomorrow afternoon."

"Sounds like a plan," replied James.

Guy could buy all the whisky he wished; James Radley was not going to a garden party. Absolutely not.

Chapter Two

R ichmond, London
Hell has frozen over

As the carriage bounced along the road to the garden party, James roused from his monstrous hangover and shot Guy the filthiest look he could muster. "You are a dirty, rotten blackguard, Dannon. That was a low thing you did last night," he muttered, his voice rough.

"Stop whining, Radley. I didn't hear you complaining when I pressed any one of those ten glasses of whisky into your hand," snorted Guy.

"Ten? I thought it was only seven," replied James.

Guy chuckled. "Ten. It took that many before you finally agreed to come."

"As I recall, I was on my knees beside the River Thames at the time, and you refused to help me to my feet until I caved to your demands. Even then I didn't think you were serious about me going," said James.

Guy raised an eyebrow. "That would explain why you were not

ready when I arrived to collect you this morning. Trust me, James, I have never been more serious about anything in my life," replied Guy.

"But if you have already chosen this girl, why are we here?" asked James.

"To help seal the deal. I might not believe in love or any of that sentimental claptrap, but the *ton* likes to think it does. If a chap wishes to get hitched, he has to go through the motions of courting a young lady. Society expects me to pay Leah special attention and lavish pretty compliments on her before I make an official offer of marriage," replied Guy.

James silently chided himself. As his friend, Guy would expect him to be supportive of his efforts to secure a suitable marriage. Yet his conscience pricked at him. The way Guy was going about getting himself a wife was all too cold and dispassionate for his taste.

The stylish carriage pulled up at the end of a long line of similarly painted black ones outside an elegant country house. The younger adult members of London's social elite were all gathering for a pleasant Saturday afternoon, while James just wanted to go home and climb back into his bed until he felt more human.

With undisguised reluctance, he climbed out of the carriage after Guy. Then he stopped. He had been in a foul mood since Guy had appeared at his bedroom door earlier that morning and demanded that he promptly dress and make himself presentable. And as much as it had been Guy who had pressed glass after glass of whisky into his hand, James knew that he had no one to blame for his painful hangover than himself. A gentleman should learn to suffer for his sins in silence.

"Go on ahead. I shall catch up with you momentarily. I need a minute to find my good humor," said James.

"Suit yourself. I shall see you inside."

Guy headed toward the garden gate which was gaily decorated with bright yellow ribbons. Footmen in black and yellow livery lined either side of the entrance. This was one of the most highly sought-after party invitations in the final days of autumn. Soon it would be too cold to host outdoor events.

James glanced up at the sky. Fortunately, only small fluffy clouds dotted the blue heavens. Even the sun had made a welcome appearance. A man should be happy on such a fine day. But not James.

He frowned as he watched his friend depart. The prospect of Guy and Leah both willingly entering into a loveless union weighed heavily on his mind. He knew it was not his place to judge the decisions of others, but a marriage for political gain went against all that he had been taught to value in a lifelong union.

He pulled a cheroot out of his coat pocket and lit it. Leaning back against the side of Guy's town carriage, he drew back on the petite cigar.

Other carriages continued to make their way up the long drive and James watched with interest as various groups of young people and their chaperones alighted. There was laughter and smiles on everyone's faces. All except his.

He mustered a half-hearted wave to some new arrivals, then fixed a smile to his lips as an old university chum, Rupert Gill, began to make his way over to where James stood. Lots of his friends would be attending today and he knew he should make a better effort to be congenial.

"Radley. Didn't expect to see you here today," said Rupert.

James shrugged. "Guy Dannon got me drunk and made me come. He is courting a young lady who will be here today."

Rupert's eyebrows reached for the sky. "Guy Dannon is courting someone. Well I'll be damned. He is the last person I would expect to be hurrying into the arms of wedded bliss."

James took little comfort in the knowledge that he was not the only one to think that Guy and marriage were not suitable bedfellows.

"And what about yourself, James? Are you heading back to university soon?"

He rolled his eyes and shook his head. Going back to Cambridge was the last thing he wanted to do. Ill health had seen him abandon his studies in the previous year and he had not yet returned. If James had his way, he would never go back.

"At the moment, I am working as a clerk for my uncle, Charles Saunders, at his shipping office. A chap needs coin for beer and onion skins."

Rupert nodded. "Those are the important things in one's life. So, will you go back next term?"

"I don't want to, but according to my father, I have little choice. He thinks it is beneath my station to take up a full-time career as a clerk. He says I lack purpose and what I need to do is to establish myself on a path of progress and respectability. Oh, and of course to stick to it."

Rupert screwed up his face. "My father said a similar thing to me, which is why I am now attending these garden party shindys. I figure that there is no point in arguing the toss anymore. I should simply get on with the business of establishing myself and finding a nice girl to settle down with and raise a family."

James sighed. At least he was not the only young man in London having to deal with parental expectations. But unlike his friend, he was determined not to yield. His father was, in the main, right. Right in that as the son of the Bishop of London he should be aiming for a higher position than a mere shipping clerk. And he was also right in saying that James's life lacked purpose. But James baulked at the idea of setting out on the same path of respectability that his father had. If Hugh Radley had his way, James would soon be curate at one of London's major churches before taking up the role of a church minister and eventually becoming a bishop. A nice, predictable stepping-stone career. That had been Hugh's dream for himself, and he was living it.

And James knew that as far as his father was concerned, it was a foregone conclusion that James would be packing his travel trunk and heading back to university after Christmas. It wasn't the worst fate James could think of, but it didn't fill him with joy.

James could just imagine how his father would take the news that Guy Dannon had decided on a wife. Another lecture loomed.

"Well good luck with your future, James. I hope you and your father can come to an agreement which suits you both. I had better go inside," said Rupert.

They shook hands, and while Rupert headed toward the garden gate, James went back to leaning against the carriage and smoking his cheroot.

A short while later, another carriage drew up behind his and he glanced over. It bore the Saunders family crest. "Thank God," he muttered. His cousins were here. Caroline and Francis Saunders could be relied upon to display the right amount of disdain and utter disgust that this sort of event deserved. His day was saved.

"James!" cried Francis as he caught his eye. Caroline, wearing one of her trademark tight smiles, followed close behind as Francis jauntily headed over to join James.

Francis quickly slapped James on the arm with one hand, while at the same time, he reached out and stole the cheroot from James's fingers. It was a deft move which had Caroline laughing.

"James, darling, what heinous crime did you commit to be sentenced to an afternoon at a garden party?" she asked.

"Nothing and everything. But it is still better than staying at home on a Saturday afternoon while Papa polishes off his Sunday sermon. If he knows I am about the house he is likely to seek me out and start asking questions," he replied.

With the tense way things were between himself and his father, much as he hated to admit it, the party was the safer place for him to be. He was not, however, going to tell Guy that any time soon.

"Oh, you poor thing. We all know how much of a tyrant your father is," said Caroline.

Francis smiled. Everyone knew that Hugh Radley was a sweet and kindhearted man who only wanted the best for his children.

Fair-haired Caroline bent and gave her immaculately pressed skirts a brief once-over. They, of course, were impeccable. Her matching bonnet sat perfect on her head. Francis, meanwhile, removed his hat and ruffled his shock of pure white hair; he then drew back on the stolen cheroot. James resigned himself to the fact that he would not be getting his smoke back.

"Just remember the joy of the garden party when my father has you up to your eyeballs in shipping ledgers on Monday. Or worse, in the foul-stinking hold of one of the recently arrived ships, checking on cargo. There is one thing that a chap learns when he works for a living, and that is to treasure his Saturday afternoons," said Francis.

"So, why are the two of you here wasting your precious Saturday? I

9

thought you didn't particularly like these sorts of events," James replied.

Caroline and Francis shared a pained look.

"Our parents made us come. Mama says I have been moping about the house ever since Eve and Freddie eloped. Which, of course, is true, but I still wasn't keen on attending," said Caroline.

Poor Francis, as a dutiful brother, had no doubt had been compelled by their parents to squire his sister. None of them wanted to be here. What a fun threesome they made.

"Misery does love company," replied James.

"Speaking of which, I don't see either Claire or Maggie here today. Did you abandon your sisters?" asked Caroline.

James pushed away from the side of the carriage. While Guy had dragged him from his bed, it was to James's personal shame that he hadn't asked either of his sisters if they wished to attend. Claire at least would be angry with him when she found out. Maggie would likely have declined any invitation made. James made a silent promise to offer them both an apology once he got home. "No, I didn't bring them. I came with Guy Dannon. He has in mind to take up a career in politics and has decided he needs a wife. Apparently, he has found some poor chit who is prepared to accept him and all his failings," he said.

"Chit? James, that is not the way to describe a young woman." Caroline rolled her eyes at the use of the condescending word. Lord help the man who was foolish enough to describe Caroline as being a chit and dared to say it in her presence. He would soon learn just how razor sharp her tongue was as she cut him swiftly down to size. "Yes, Claire mentioned that he had set his marital sights on a friend of hers, Leah Shepherd. Do you know the girl well?"

James shook his head. "I barely know any of Claire's friends beyond a quick hello and goodbye. She tends to smuggle them in and out the house to avoid our father. He always wants to ask visitors their opinions of his most recent Sunday sermon."

Caroline and Francis exchanged a knowing look. All the Radley extended family had been the target of Hugh's friendly, but in-depth questioning of his Sunday sermons at some point or another. It was never a comfortable conversation.

Francis finished the last of James's cheroot and crushed the remains out with his boot. He straightened his jacket and turned to Caroline, who gave him a quick look-over before nodding her approval. She straightened his already immaculate cravat, then teased his hair so that it sat just right. James simply raked his fingers through his hair and left it at that.

Francis offered his sister his arm and turned to James. "Come on, dear cousin. Time, we went inside and faced the hordes. You cannot stay out here all afternoon skulking about."

With a resigned sigh, James followed his cousins into the garden party. He licked his lips. Hangover or no, he would kill for a glass of whisky right now.

Chapter Three

The moment he stepped into the party James was quickly reminded why he avoided them. As expected, the place was a sea of besotted couples. Passing through the crowd, he soon lost count of the number of 'darlings', 'sweethearts,' and 'dearests' that he heard young men offer up to their female companions. When one nearby gentleman told his lady friend that her smile was brighter than the sun, he was tempted to turn on his heel and head for the garden gate.

"James! Over here."

He turned and saw Guy waving to him.

His friend was standing in a section of the lawn which had been set up for a game of bowls. Beside him, but at an odd distance, stood a young woman dressed all in pink. From the proprietary way that Guy kept looking back to her, James deduced she must be Leah Shepherd.

"Here goes," he muttered.

At first glance, Leah Shepherd cast an attractive silhouette. Not that he would have expected Guy to have chosen a frumpy young woman for his future bride. With her pale golden hair tied up in a loose chignon, and partially hidden by a pink bonnet, she appeared to be much like any other young woman of London society. Her matching pink gown, which was offset with white gloves, made for an attractive enough outfit.

James knew how the inner workings of the *ton* operated. Miss Shepherd's outfit would have been put together with military precision. The right amount of innocence in the pink color of her gown, along with the fashionable cut of the bonnet, sent an exact message to all young men. She was in the market for a husband, but he had to be one who had enough blunt to be able to support a fashion-conscious young wife. Men without deep pockets need not apply.

Guy leaned in and spoke to her; the bonnet bobbed a touch. James made his way over, then waited for Guy to make formal introductions.

"Miss Leah Shepherd, may I introduce my closest friend, Mister James Radley. James is the son of the Bishop of London," said Guy.

Leah lifted her head just enough for James to catch a glimpse of her face before she looked down again. "Thank you, Mister Dannon. As I have mentioned before, I know Mister Radley's sister Claire. So, he and I have already met."

James flinched at the curt remark, but Guy did not react. The brief peek of Leah's face gave him no further clue as to whether he'd met her before or not.

"Miss Shepherd." James bowed. He noted she did not offer him her hand, which was just a little rude. In fact, she barely nodded her acknowledgement of him; it left James wondering how his normally rational sister had managed to make this unpleasant girl her friend.

Oddly, Guy didn't seem to either notice or care how Leah spoke to him or his friend. He appeared oblivious to his surroundings, almost as if he was an actor in a play just waiting for his cue to speak. He was going through the motions of courting Leah and nothing more.

"I was telling Miss Shepherd how wonderfully well you played lawn bowls," said Guy.

James froze. He couldn't recall the last time he had even picked up a lawn bowl let alone played the game. He frowned at Guy.

"Was that Miss Caroline Saunders I saw arriving with you just now? Perhaps we could make up a party of four and play a game," offered Guy.

Caroline and Francis had cleverly, and somewhat opportunely, disappeared the moment Guy had waved his hand in James's direction. James couldn't blame them for having abandoned him. Both his cousins appeared to be as averse to spending time with other guests as he was.

"Maybe a little later," he replied. Caroline would not thank him for asking her to come and play at lawn games. She would make him pay for it; of that he was certain.

"Well perhaps in the meantime I should get us some drinks. Miss Shepherd, would you like an orgeat?" said Guy.

James stifled a snort; just hearing Guy say the word *orgeat* hurt his ears. He would bet a pound that Guy had practiced the word on the journey over to Richmond.

"I would prefer a cup of tea, thank you, Mister Dannon," replied Leah.

Guy trotted off in the direction of the refreshment table, leaving James and Leah alone. James puffed out his cheeks. He knew that as a gentleman, it was up to him to make an effort at small talk. "I cannot recall exactly when you and I have met before, but we must have," he said.

She lifted her head, and he was graced with his first full look at her face. His gaze was immediately drawn to her blue eyes. Pale as the summer sky, they seemed to change to a darker hue as she moved her head in the sunlight. Gosh. A man could get lost in them.

Beneath those eyes was a soft, full mouth. Not perfect, mind you. It had a slight drop on one side. But that imperfection somehow seemed to make her even more attractive. How on earth could he have met her at another time and forgotten that lovely face or those enticing lips?

While those same lips were currently set in a straight, unimpressed line, he sensed that when the mood so took Leah, they would make for a heart-stopping smile.

What will it take to make you smile, Miss Shepherd?

Her mouth held the promise of tender kisses for the man who could find his way to her heart. James already had a sinking feeling that whoever that man was, it would never be Guy. Leah did not appear to be the least bit impressed with him, let alone behaving toward him in the manner expected of a future bride.

"I visited your family at Fulham Palace last spring. Your sister Claire had been ill, and I came to see her. You were recently returned from university, as I recall. We met only briefly, in the hallway as I was leaving. You were sitting on the stone flagging, patting your dog," Leah replied.

Her recollection of a brief meeting many months ago took James by surprise. Claire had been ill for a number of weeks, during which time she had received only a handful of visitors. People tended to stay away from patients who were suffering from anything other than a minor cold, and with good reason. However, the mention of him sitting on the floor with the family dog gave James a clue as to why he could not remember Leah. He was more than likely still half-foxed from the night before and using King as a means to shield himself from his mother's gaze.

"I must apologize. I had forgotten. It is nice to meet you again," he said.

His being in a drunken stupor was the only explanation for not having registered his previous encounter with Leah Shepherd. If he had been sober, he would have remembered her. There was something about Leah that was unforgettable.

She leaned in close and whispered, "I think you may have been under the weather at the time, so your brain might have been a little fuzzy."

A sharp whistle had them both turning and looking in the direction of the refreshment table. James frowned at the impolite way Guy had used to get his and Leah's attention. Guy was pointing at a plate of cakes while other guests stared at him, disbelief written on their faces. Beside him stood Caroline and Francis. They were staring daggers in James's direction.

"I think he wishes to know if you would like a cake, Miss Shepherd?" asked James.

When she replied. "No thank you," James shook his head at Guy.

He turned back to Leah and their gazes met. Her lips barely moved, but he could see that she was trying to force a smile. It looked painful, and the end result was that she held it for the barest of moments before her face went back to its previous neutral expression.

"Guy has obviously taken an interest in you," James said.

"Yes. He and my father have become quite close in recent times," she replied.

They watched as Guy picked up two glasses and started back across the lawn toward them.

The penny dropped for James. Guy wasn't courting Leah; he was courting her father. And both she and Guy knew it.

"Sorry, James, old chap, I couldn't carry a third drink," Guy said, upon his return.

James took one look at the cloudy concoction in the glass and was immediately grateful for that fact. Why people considered orgeat anything other than vile was beyond him. Going without was the better option. "You two enjoy."

To James's ongoing disquiet, Guy not only smiled but took a large sip of his drink. Leah took one look at the drink in her hand before setting it down untouched on a nearby garden table.

A sour-faced Caroline and Francis now appeared at his shoulder. Francis scowled at him, while Caroline looked fit to do murder. Guy had somehow managed to hunt down the Saunders siblings; there would be no escape for any of them.

"Miss Shepherd, may I introduce my cousins Caroline and Francis Saunders. Their mother, Lady Adelaide, is my paternal aunt," said James.

Caroline held out a hand in greeting. "A pleasure to meet you, Leah. I do so love your dress. You look stunning. You must tell me where you buy your gloves."

Francis gave a polite nod and added, "Charmed."

James watched with interest as Guy looked from Caroline to Leah and the expression on his face turned from bewildered to understanding.

"Yes, Miss Shepherd, you do look most pleasing in your gown," he said. His words sounded rehearsed and without care.

Leah matched his efforts with the tiniest nod. One blink and he would have missed it.

"Well since everyone is here, how about we set up for a game of bowls?" offered Guy.

"I shall sit this out, so you have an even number of players," said Francis. He headed over to one of the nearby garden chairs and took a seat.

As Guy went and collected the bowls, Caroline leaned in close to James and whispered in his ear. "Guy tried to make me take a glass of orgeat, even after I told him I never drink the foul stuff; he was quite insistent. Francis had to get firm with him. He might be your friend, James, but he has appalling manners."

James's gaze fell on Leah's untouched drink, and he recalled her having asked for a cup of tea in preference to it. Guy had obviously ignored her wishes too. He pursed his lips. If Guy was prepared to ride roughshod over the simple matter of a lady's request for refreshments, they could all be in for a very long afternoon.

Chapter Four

Leah watched Guy out of the corner of her eye as he bent down and aimed his bowl at the jack. After tossing it, he trotted behind the bowl, urging it on, a soft smile on his lips. The man was a chameleon, shifting the look on his face from a smile to a frown and back again, depending on who was watching.

At first glance, he appeared to be nice. He was handsome enough, especially when he smiled. His family were of a suitable social standing. Her father approved of him, which for most young women would have been an encouraging sign. But it was the fact that her father did approve of Guy Dannon that filled Leah with a deep sense of unease.

On face value, he should have been everything a young woman would want in a husband. Every morning for the past two weeks she had got out of bed and tried to convince herself that she should be perfectly content with Guy courting her. That when Guy proposed, and she knew he eventually would, she would accept his hand in marriage. And every time she thought about it, she felt a dull ache in her heart. Because no matter how hard she tried, she could not bring herself to like Guy.

She had counselled herself that this was not an unknown aspect of many marriages, that she should count her blessings and be content with him. But she just couldn't do it. When she looked at Guy, she saw her father. And knowing the misery that was her mother's lot, she knew if she married Guy, she too would be miserable for the rest of her days.

Her mother had suggested she wear the bright pink and white ensemble today, telling her that she was certain Guy would think it pretty. Leah wasn't so sure that men understood what the word pretty actually meant, but in the hope of avoiding yet another scolding from one of her parents, she'd gone along with it.

Guy's sole mention of her attire so far this afternoon was to tell her that her gown looked pleasing, or something to that end. She was sure as certain that he had only made mention of her clothing because Caroline Saunders had paid her a compliment. From the expression on his face as he spoke, it was clear that he was reciting something he had practiced. The dull, glazed look in his eyes as he spoke informed her that she could have been wearing a sack cloth and he would have said the exact same thing. Who knew if he had given any real thought to what she was wearing?

Their courtship thus far had seen him come to her family home on three separate occasions. He would then spend exactly one hour with her, during which he would tell her how lovely she was, sip some tea, and then leave. It was almost as if he didn't know how to converse with a young lady but had convinced himself that he could manage an hour of one-sided conversation in his attempt to woo her. On each and every visit to the Shepherd family home, he had never bothered asking her anything beyond questions about her health and how much butter she liked with her bread and cake.

She did, however, have her suspicions about Guy. She may be an innocent in the ways of love, but she was not a fool. Men such as Guy Dannon might behave as chameleons when it suited their purposes, but their reputations were not something they could change overnight. Leah was under no illusion about her potential husband; he was a rake. He was so much like her father, it made her feel ill.

"Huzzah!" Guy's victory cry stirred Leah from her thoughts. When she saw that his bowl had finally stopped within a foot or so of the jack, she politely applauded. Guy was cock-a-hoop with his efforts, proudly marching up and down between ends.

"Well played," said James. He turned to Leah and smiled. "Miss Shepherd, I believe it is your turn. Good luck."

She'd been immediately struck by James's easy smile and warm nature. It was in sharp contrast to Guy, but her appreciation of him was tempered by the fact that he and Guy were close friends. It left her wary. She had a lifetime's experience in dealing with duplicitous males; James Radley may just have been Guy Dannon in a different guise.

And just because he was the brother of a friend of hers, did not mean she would be lowering her guard with him any time soon.

She picked up her own bowl and walked to the front of the playing mat. Bending down, she delivered the bowl and let it run. She walked slowly behind it, remembering the lay of the green she had noted when they'd played from the other end. While the garden lawn appeared flat to the naked eye, it actually ran slightly downhill from left to right. It was a fraction of a slope, but it was enough to have Leah taking great care to not only ensure that the bowl landed in the right place, but that she put enough force into the throw.

When her bowl finally came to a halt, it was past Guy's and therefore closer to the jack.

"Yes!" she cried, throwing her arms up in the air in unrestrained glee.

James laughed, while Caroline applauded with a pleasing amount of vigor. When Leah lifted her gaze to where Guy stood, she caught sight of him glaring hard at her bowl. The soft smile he normally wore in her company was gone. In its place was a look of stony displeasure.

A chill of premonition slid down her spine. She knew that look, had seen it a thousand times on her father's face. It was the look of a man whom you did not cross. Lightness and humor were on display only when things were running their way, when it suited them. Silent, barely controlled rage was the order of the day when it was not. And when that fury was unleashed . . .

She shuddered and tried to force the thought away, telling herself that she should not judge Guy on the basis of one small look. He had not been unkind. *Yet.*

"Well played," he said, an edge of ice in his voice.

"Thank you. Luck, of course, played its part," she replied, in an effort to placate him.

He went to say something, but she saw him stop himself. A twitch in his jaw was the only sign that he was having to fight to bring his temper under control.

Leah be careful.

Guy walked from the bowling green to where the small party had left their belongings on a nearby garden table. The welcome autumn sun warmed the early afternoon air. She and Caroline had removed their bonnets, while the gentlemen had cast off their jackets. Beside Leah's bonnet sat the glass of orgeat, still untouched.

Guy picked up Leah's bonnet and strode over to her. Offering it, he said. "You should put this on."

She waved a hand in his direction and refused to take the bonnet.

He continued to hold it in front of her, giving it a little shake. "You wouldn't want to get freckles now, would you?"

Leah caught the tone of his voice and read the situation for what it really was, a power play. She already had a smattering of small freckles on her face courtesy of summers spent at her grandfather's estate in Cornwall; one or two extra freckles would not make a difference. Besides, she actually liked them. They gave her face a warm, friendly look.

"Thank you, Mister Dannon, but I am fine without the bonnet. It impedes my playing," she replied.

His countenance set hard, and she was certain she saw something pop in his jaw as he ground his teeth. A battle of wills ensued. Guy held out the bonnet, while Leah held his gaze and refused to take it.

"It's fine, Guy. I am not wearing a bonnet either. The sun is not that hot," said Caroline, coming to Leah's aid.

Guy kept his gaze fixed on Leah. She ventured a smile, but all the while her heart was beating hard in her chest. She knew this game well. Her focus was solely fixed on drawing the real Guy Dannon out. She wanted to see the man behind the polite façade of courtship. That version of Guy might be the one she woke beside every morning for the rest of her life, who would father her children. There was too much at stake for her to back down now.

He finally gave in, slapping the bonnet hard against his leg, after which he marched back over to the pile of belongings and threw it down. Silence hung in the air for a moment.

When Guy turned back to her, the angry look on his face was gone. He had managed to school his features into something socially acceptable. But his right hand was held in a tight fist, the whites of his knuckles clear from where she stood.

Leah blinked and looked to Caroline. "Your turn, I believe, Caroline," she said.

Caroline stepped past to take her place on the bowling mat. "Well done, Leah. You held your ground," she whispered.

I wonder how long my victory will last.

Caroline swung her arm back and the bowl flew out of her hand. It tore along the green and knocked Guy's bowl clear out of the way. Hers also went careening off the green and disappeared under a bush. She turned and gave a shrug, then gifted Guy with a beaming smile. "Oh dear. Sorry about that. I think I might have put a little too much into the throw."

Leah knew she should have held back on applauding Caroline's overzealous efforts, but the look of outrage and frustration which now shone on Guy's face was simply too much for her to resist. "Well done, Caroline! You killed Guy and yourself all in one foul swoop. We may need to mount a search party for your bowls."

James now stood at the end of the green and looked down at the bowl in his hand. Leah placed a silent bet with herself. She had her money on him putting too much into the delivery and having his bowl join both Caroline and Guy's past the jack and out of bounds. It would mean he lost, but it would placate Guy and his obviously bruised pride. James had said nothing while the battle of wills over the bonnet had taken place and Leah had him pegged as a people pleaser.

He bent, and taking what appeared to be careful aim, dropped the bowl into a smooth, clean delivery. It wasn't running fast and for a moment Leah worried that he had not put enough on the throw. But as

James slowly walked behind his bowl, faint hope began to build in her heart.

The bowl kept rolling, closer and closer to the jack. Closer to where Leah's shot had stopped. She dared not look at Guy, fearing that her growing sense of joy would show on her face. James was playing the game exactly as he should and was not pandering to Guy and his ill temper.

So, you do have a spine. Well done, Mister Radley.

A hush fell over the small group as the bowl inched its way nearer to the jack. When it finally came to a stop, it was almost touching Leah's bowl. For a moment, everyone froze.

James turned and, to Leah's surprise, cast a smile in her direction. When she caught the glint of mischief in his eye, her earlier opinion of him changed. Guy might think he was in charge of the day, but to her relief it seemed that James Radley was his own man.

"Well played, James," said Francis, who got to his feet and ambled over to where the two bowls lay on the green. He stood with his head tilted, studying them for a moment. "I can see we have a close game and as an impartial spectator, I am claiming the right to declare the winner."

James looked to Leah. "Are you happy for Mister Saunders to call the winner? I must, remind you of course, that as he is my cousin he may not be as impartial as he claims to be."

Francis gave Leah a cheeky wink. "Impartial, but not impeccable. I am open to all forms of bribes, including but not limited to money."

Caroline, James, and Leah all laughed at the outrageous remark. Guy, she noted, was too busy fiddling with his jacket to be paying much attention to the outcome of the match. It was clear that he had decided since he no longer had any skin in the game, he was not interested in its outcome.

James put a hand into the small pocket of his waistcoat and pulled out a single coin. With a grin and a flourish of his hand, he attempted to slip the coin into Francis's jacket pocket. Francis, meanwhile, kept his gaze fixed in the other direction. Caroline let out a gasp, then held her hands to her cheeks in mock horror. Leah found herself snorting with laughter at the silly pantomime.

When James cast another grin in her direction, Leah felt her heart skip a tiny beat. This was what a garden party should be like: fun, with a touch of flirting. Not tight arguments over the wearing of a bonnet.

She considered the situation for a moment. What could she offer to Francis that James had not already done? And what could she do that might give Guy reason to question whether she was actually the one for him?

It was worth the risk.

She walked over to where James and Francis were standing, still chuckling at one another in the middle of the bowling green. Upon reaching them, she stood in front of James.

"If this is the way you wish to play, Mister Radley, then so be it." She then turned to Francis and, rising up on her toes, placed a soft kiss on his cheek. "I hope that was payment enough, Mister Saunders," she whispered.

Francis, to his credit, showed neither surprise nor outrage at such flirtatious behavior. As she moved away, she caught the look of disapproval on James's face. She simply smiled back at him. She also ignored the loud, angry huff which emanated from Guy. Her message to both James and Guy was clear; she would be the judge of what was acceptable behavior.

Francis looked at Caroline, who nodded toward Leah. He raised an eyebrow in silent question, but Caroline nodded a second time.

"I declare Miss Leah Saunders the winner," he announced.

Victory tasted sweet, though Leah secretly wished that Francis would hand over James's coin as her prize. With her pin money running low, she could do with an extra coin.

She gave herself a moment to enjoy the applause from the other players. All, of course, except Guy. Her curmudgeon of a suitor refused to acknowledge her win. He simply waited until the others went to pick up their things before handing her the bonnet and saying, "Now put it on."

If she was honest, Leah didn't really care about the outcome of the game; her victory had come a little earlier when Guy Dannon had shown his true self. She had wondered as to how far beneath his veneer of polite and gentlemanlike behavior the devil lurked. She was certain she now knew.

The uneasy feeling, she had been carrying since he had asked for permission to court her finally settled like an unwelcome but familiar guest in her mind. Her instincts had *not* been wrong. He was nice when it suited his purposes. Nice when she was doing exactly what she was told. Once she dared to step over that line, his mask of civility fell.

Her mother had married for love only to discover she had chosen a man who controlled every aspect of her life. The females of the Shepherd family were told what to do and think.

Leah would be damned if she would make the same mistake. The sooner she could quietly sever all connections with Guy Dannon, the better.

Chapter Five

The following Monday saw James and Guy seated in the drawing room of Guy's recently acquired town house in Noel Street. During previous visits, they had utilized the smaller, warmer library. But as Guy was having the house redecorated and the painters were still working in there, they had been forced to change rooms.

With new curtains and floor coverings also evident about the place, it was clear Guy was sparing no expense when it came to his marriage preparations. The future mistress of this house would have the finest of everything.

"You are still going to go ahead and propose to Leah?" asked James.

"You mean after she was willful at the garden party? Of course. Girls like Leah think they are in control of matters. And while we are courting, it makes sense for me to permit her those little indulgences. She will, of course, see sense once we are married," replied Guy.

James frowned, unsure if he had heard Guy correctly. After the way Guy and Leah had interacted with one another at the garden party, he was not convinced that they would suit. "Do you even like her?" he asked.

"She is tolerable enough, which is sufficient for my purposes. I think she will make for a solid political asset. She is pretty in an average sort of way. I am sure I can train her for the bedroom and in other areas," said Guy.

James scratched his chin. While Guy appeared to be unfazed by his and Leah's complete lack of chemistry, she, on the other hand, had barely hidden her distaste for his friend. A woman in love with her potential fiancé would most certainly not have kissed another guest. It may have been on the cheek, but still, it was a kiss.

To James, it had been more than just a simple kiss. Watching as Leah's soft lips touched Francis's cheek had sparked something within him. In his mind, a voice had whispered one word. A word which had shaken him to the core.

Mine.

As he relived the memory of that moment, James gripped the arm of his chair and tried to calm his breathing.

Guy picked up his brandy and took a long sip, chuckling softly at James. "Relax, James. It is all part of the wooing process. Women like that sort of thing. Let them think that they are in charge. It makes them more pliable for marriage proposals."

From what he had seen of her, James did not think Leah was at all pliable. Yet despite what appeared to be clear signs of them not being suited to one another, Guy seemed determined to press on with courting and marrying her.

He had secretly enjoyed the sight of Leah defying Guy over her bonnet. She was an adult and capable of deciding whether to wear it or not. James liked women who had their own opinions, while he had less-than-kind thoughts about men who felt that only their views would hold sway. Guy had acted in an unchivalrous manner when trying to force Leah's hand. Only their friendship, and the worry of causing an embarrassing scene, had stopped James from stepping in and coming to Leah's aid.

Now that he had seen for himself the sort of behavior she was up against when it came to his friend, he was beginning to understand Leah's earlier rude greeting to him. The more he thought about it, the more he was certain that Leah Shepherd detested Guy Dannon. And that was no recipe for future happiness for anyone. "So, you think the two of you can make a go of this marriage lark?" he ventured.

"Of course. She was just a little out of sorts with me on Saturday, that is all. I plan to press ahead and speak to her father posthaste. It wouldn't look good on me if the chit suddenly got cold feet and the wedding didn't go ahead. Especially not after all the effort I have put into wooing her."

"It is your funeral," replied James.

Having seen enough of his cousins recently leap into the joyful arms of wedded bliss, James was convinced that Guy did not have an appreciation of the ingredients that went into making a successful marriage. For a start, all those other unions seemed to have had a great deal more mutual attraction and affection involved in them.

Caroline and Francis's sister, Eve, had recently eloped with the second son of a Viscount, with her parents' blessings. Even James, who wasn't the least bit interested in marriage, had been impressed with the amount of passion involved in that particular wooing. Hopefully Guy would take his time and not rush into offering for Leah's hand. "And when do you plan to speak to Mister Shepherd?" asked James.

"The day after tomorrow," replied Guy.

Any hope James had held for Leah and Guy to be spared a loveless union swiftly died.

"Damn, and double damn."

Her behavior at the garden party had not had the desired effect. Instead of Guy Dannon having second thoughts about courting her, he had decided to press his suit and speak to her father.

The party had been Saturday, and now it was Monday night. Her mother had excitedly announced to Leah earlier that Guy had made an appointment with Tobias Shepherd for this very Wednesday. Those words had filled her with dread.

"While I cannot say exactly what it is about, you should know it does not concern politics or business. I suggest you prepare yourself for some news, my dear girl."

Two days. It was not enough time for her to find a way out of the inevitable betrothal announcement. She could feign being sick, but her mother was a great one for purging and the laying on of leeches whenever someone in the house took ill. Memories of her last illness and the pain of the bloodsuckers were too fresh in her mind for Leah to seriously consider that drastic a measure. Besides, it would only delay the inevitable.

She and Guy would both be in attendance at a society ball on Tuesday night. It would be her last chance to help change his mind about offering for her hand.

As she sat up in bed, she wracked her brains. There had to be something she could do to scupper his plans to make her his wife. What would be enough to have a gentleman decide he no longer wished to marry a young miss?

She pushed away the obvious. Not even for Guy Dannon would she risk the scandal of being ruined. Besides, it would permanently put her marriage prospects in the river if she did do something that outrageous. Added to that would also be her father's swift and complete retribution.

It had to be something that would give Guy pause, but still keep her reputation intact. A deed which would get back to Guy and make him think twice about proposing marriage. She also needed this plan to involve someone whom Guy not only trusted, but who could be relied upon to immediately go to him and reveal all that she had done.

"And what if . . . oh."

What if Guy had a friend who could influence him enough to make him have serious reservations about marrying her? Even better if that someone already had their own concerns about the future union of his friend and a certain young lady. The look on James Radley's face after she had kissed Francis Saunders was not one of approval.

With Guy due to attend the ball tomorrow night, there was every chance that James Radley would also be in attendance. If James could be convinced of the folly of his friend offering for her, and of the need for him to do something about it, he might just be the solution to her problem.

"This could work," she whispered.

Leah slid down in the bed and huddled under the warm blankets and cover. Shadows from the flickering light of her bedside candle danced across the bed canopy. Lifting up the candle, she peered into the corner of the cream silk bed canopy, her gaze settling on a spider web.

A friendly spider had taken up residence there a week earlier and had created quite a clever web across the corner. She really should make mention of it to the household staff. No doubt her mother would be horrified that she hadn't, but she found the industrious labor of the spider to be fascinating. Every day, it worked at expanding and strengthening its web. Day after day, slowly but surely, its plans were being transformed into a masterful reality.

She should become more like the spider, planning a series of small incremental changes which, when complete, would lead to a different life. One that was in no way what her family had in mind for her.

James Radley was key to those plans.

Chapter Six

In his current state of career and life upheaval, James was not certain of many things. He was, however, sure of this: Guy was rushing with undue haste into an ill-suited union with Leah Shepherd. Guy was meeting with Tobias Shepherd on Wednesday afternoon, which meant that come suppertime tomorrow, his friend would have himself a fiancée.

Marriage wasn't something that one simply ticked off on a to-do list. But the way Guy was going about it, James suspected that in Guy's mind, it was. House, wife, and safe seat in parliament. It was all so cold and calculating in its execution.

"Did I tell you I am meeting with our local parliamentary selection committee at the end of the month?" said Guy.

"No. Why?"

A glint of something shone in Guy's eyes. "Because I am going to work my charm on them so that by this time next year, I will have a real shot at being preselected for a safe seat."

James stared at him. The hard-drinking, rakish Guy Dannon who he had known since Eton was fast disappearing. In his place was a man with steely determination. James wasn't certain that he liked this new version of Guy.

He picked at several dog hairs on the sleeve of his evening jacket and flicked them away. He really should not wrestle with King after he dressed for formal occasions such as tonight's ball—a furry dog was the enemy of the well-turned-out gentleman.

"Have you discussed any of this with Leah?" asked James.

Guy downed his brandy, then fixed James with a hard, almost mocking look. "Are you barking mad? Of course, I haven't discussed this with her. She is a slip of a girl. I've paid her sweet compliments each time I have visited at her parents' home, and foolishly fussed over her at a garden party. Not that being pleasant to her in public got me very far on Saturday. I was disappointed in both you and Francis over getting Leah all excited at the end of the game. She would not have kissed him if the two of you had not encouraged her with your foolish behavior."

James was not going to mention the minor detail of neither him nor his cousin being involved in Leah's sudden decision to plant a kiss on Francis's cheek. Nor was he going to say anything about his own reaction to *that* kiss. If Guy had any inkling that he wished he had been the one she'd kissed, their friendship may be called into question. James stirred from his personal musings. He really had to force himself to stop thinking about Leah. She was not for him. He just wished his nightly dreams were not full of images of her naked and in his arms. And those lips.

"Her father will tell her that she is to accept my suit. After that, she will do as I instruct," said Guy.

James closed his eyes for a second, while he absorbed the magnitude of Guy's words. Leah had no say in anything.

He rose from his chair, suddenly wishing he had not committed himself to attending this evening's ball. He would have cried off but considering the mood that Guy was in, he knew he would be made to pay for it. He had also promised Claire he would help her practice her waltz, and he didn't wish to disappoint his sister. If he could avoid spending more than the required polite amount of time in Leah's company, he might just make it through this evening with his heart still in one piece.

Guy followed him out to the cloakroom of White's club and

handed over his token to the attendant. Once they had retrieved their evening cloaks and hats, they walked the short distance from St James Street to King Street. While Guy took the lead, James lagged a step behind, his mind still concentrated on Guy's determination to press ahead and marry Leah.

Once inside the elegant mansion on King Street, he left Guy and went in search of his family. He found Claire and his mother in one of the anterooms. His other sister was nowhere to be seen. Disappointment at her absence added to his growing dark mood. If he could just get Maggie to attend more social events, she might be inclined to move on with her life. To find love once more.

"I was beginning to think you were not coming," said his mother.

James placed a dutiful kiss on Mary's cheek. He smiled at her soft, playful rebuke.

"I am always late, but never once have I failed to arrive," he replied.

Mary patted him gently on the cheek. "Cheeky boy."

"No Maggie this evening?" he asked.

His mother sighed. "She said she had letters to write. More plans for Robert's memorial. She wants to travel up to Coventry and meet with the local stonemason who is to make the statue."

He knew to leave his sister and her need to grieve over her late fiancé well enough alone. Some day he hoped she would find someone else to take the place of Robert in her heart. He had died at the battle of Waterloo more than two years ago. Their engagement had only been a brief one. Maggie was far too young to consign herself to a lifetime of widow's weeds.

Claire flicked open her fan and held it in front of her face. It was a subtle signal to move on with the discussion and not linger on the topic. James scowled at her, but she shook her head and mouthed the word 'later.'

"Is Guy here with you?" she asked.

Mary took a step back and waved them both a quick farewell. "I shall take that as my cue to go and find your father. Don't forget to pay your respects to the host before you leave. And, James, try not to drink too much tonight; your father is in one of his odd moods. I don't want him any grumpier and bear-like than he already is at the moment."

James raised an eyebrow at the thought of his father being bear-like. Hugh Radley was a cross hedgehog on his worst day. He was not one for raising his voice. His preferred method of disciplining his offspring was to have them come to their own realization that they had misbehaved, and then offer up a shamefaced apology.

"I promise not to drink too much this evening. Now go and have some fun," said James.

Mary Radley disappeared into the crush of party guests and was soon lost from sight.

"I came with Guy, but he headed toward the ballroom as soon as we arrived. I take it your friend Leah is here tonight?"

"Yes, she is in the ballroom. So, no prizes for guessing why Guy made a beeline for there as soon as you arrived. From the look of things, Leah and Guy appear to be moving at a rather hurried pace toward announcing a betrothal," said Claire.

James leaned in close. "And do you think that is a good thing? I am concerned that, as you say, things are moving a little too fast. He seems set on the match, but I have my doubts as to whether she feels the same eagerness to be wed."

"Yes, Caroline made mention of the odd goings on at the garden party on Saturday. And on the rare occasion that Leah has made mention of Guy, her words have not been kind. That does not augur well for a happy future for either of them. Though I doubt there is much which can be done even if she does not wish to marry him. From the moment Tobias Shepherd gave his blessing for Guy to court Leah, the wedding date was all but set."

Claire's words had James thinking once more about Leah. A young woman in the early and heady days of love would be sharing all manner of secrets with her friends. Her hopes and dreams for a marriage proposal should be the topic of every conversation. Yet from the sound of things, Leah was more than a little reluctant when it came to the topic of Guy Dannon.

Claire was right. That did not bode well.

෫

Leah's opinion of Guy wasn't something anyone in her family seemed to give a damn about. As soon as he arrived in the ballroom, her mother and older married sister were all over him like he was this month's copy of *La Belle Assemblée*. Leah, meanwhile, stood a step back from the tight gathering and watched with a sinking heart as her female relatives made pretty eyes at Guy.

Ugh.

It was some time before Guy finally tore himself away from the clutches of Mrs. Shepherd. Leah gritted her teeth as his gaze now fixed firmly on her.

"Miss Shepherd, Leah. How lovely you look this evening. Your gown matches your green eyes," he said.

She fixed a social smile to her face and nodded. "Mister Dannon. If you bothered to check, you would see that my eyes are blue." She wasn't going to grace him with the use of his Christian name in public. It was all a bit too familiar and encouraging for her liking. And Guy Dannon was not someone she had in mind to encourage in any way, shape, or form unless it was to encourage him to look elsewhere for a wife.

He raised a hand to her cheek and brushed his fingers gently across her skin. Her mother softly sighed as he did so.

"You have two new freckles on your face, Leah. You should have listened to me when I told you to wear your bonnet at the garden party," he said.

Her mother's sigh turned to a disapproving *tsk*. A reprimand would no doubt follow as soon as they got home. Pale, flawless skin was the ultimate fashion accessory for a young woman.

"I am sorry if you do not like a sprinkle of sunshine on a young lady's face," she replied.

"Leah, manners. Apologize this instant," hissed her mother.

A strange look came over Guy's face and he stepped back. "No, Mrs. Shepherd, it is I who should apologize. I overstepped the mark. I, as yet, have no right to be instructing Miss Shepherd on how she should dress or behave."

Guy bowed low before Leah. When he righted himself again, he met her gaze. His eyes held not a hint of warmth or sincerity. "Miss Shepherd, I offer my full and unreserved apology to you."

Caught between her mother's barely suppressed outrage and Guy's sleight of hand, Leah was left with no other option. "I shall accept your apology, Mister Dannon, if you will graciously accept mine. I should not have been so dismissive of your valuable opinion."

Mrs. Shepherd gave a slight nod at Leah's words. Guy held out his hand and a socially obliged Leah was forced to take it. His fingers felt hot and clammy.

"Mrs. Shepherd, would it be acceptable for me to accompany Leah and seek out some mutual friends of ours? Mister James Radley and Miss Claire Radley will be in attendance this evening. It might serve to lighten the mood if we were able to spend some time with them. I promise Leah will be in safe hands," said Guy.

His words were so typical of Guy—always working to twist the situation to his advantage. He would make the perfect politician.

"Of course, Mister Dannon," replied Mrs. Shepherd.

Reluctantly Leah took hold of Guy's offered arm and let him escort her from the ballroom.

"Now then, that wasn't so bad, was it? You will find that doing as I ask will make for a happy home," said Guy, gently patting her arm.

She gritted her teeth and forced herself to remember the spider and its web.

Her hope for salvation now rested in the hands of James Radley.

Chapter Seven

"Leah, come join us!" Claire waved to Leah and Guy as they walked arm in arm into the reception room which adjoined the ballroom.

James looked from his friend to Leah and back again. They were a study in opposite emotions. Guy had a self-satisfied smirk firmly plastered on his face, while Leah looked for all the world like she was going to meet the hangman's noose. Her posture was stiff, as if the only thing she had left was her dignity.

Guy held up a hand in acknowledgement of Claire before verily dragging Leah over to where she and James stood. At the sadness on Leah's face, James was sure something broke in his heart.

"So good to see you both again," said Guy.

Claire permitted Guy to kiss her hand. James bowed low to Leah, all the while wishing he could pull her into his arms and offer her comfort. Anything that would take away the pain.

To his surprise, she immediately slipped from Guy's arm and offered James her hand. "Mister Radley, how delightful to see you this evening."

He took her hand and placed a polite kiss on it. "Miss Shepherd, I trust you are well."

A hard smile spread across Leah's mouth. Unfortunately, it did not extend to the rest of her face. Her eyes still held pain within them. Instead of sparkling pools of aqua, they appeared as deep wells of dark emptiness.

She blinked, and he could have sworn he saw tears on her lower eyelashes. "Yes, I am well, thank you, James. And may I also thank you for the spirited game of lawn bowls at the garden party. I hope you have forgiven me for besting you," she replied.

He caught the look which Guy shot in Leah's direction. By the way that she studiously kept her gaze fixed on James, he suspected Guy had not appreciated her use of James's Christian name. There was something at play here, but he was at a loss as to what it was.

Guy loudly cleared his throat. "Leah, my dear, would you like a drink?"

She shook her head but didn't bother to look at Guy. It was clear that the war of wills James had witnessed at the garden party was still on.

Guy stopped a passing footman bearing a tray of drinks. He retrieved two glasses of orgeat which he handed with great flourish to the women. For James and himself, he then selected two brandies.

James caught the sour look on his sister's face as she took hold of her glass. He quietly sighed. He would be hearing about it in the carriage ride home. All the way back to Fulham Palace if he knew his sister. Claire was not one for having a gentleman treat her in such a patronizing manner.

His gaze now fell on Leah. She was holding her drink stiffly. Why Guy would think that Leah had suddenly developed a taste for it was beyond him.

"Would you prefer champagne?" James offered.

"Well, yes . . ." began Leah.

Guy took a sudden step closer to Leah and loomed over her. The move was so menacing that even James felt intimidated.

"Leah is fine with orgeat. It is a drink more becoming of a young unmarried miss than champagne. Of course, once she is married, then she will be permitted to partake in the odd glass of champagne. Drink up, Leah," said Guy.

Leah lifted the orgeat to her lips and took a sip. Guy remained standing over her. She took another long drink, her gaze locked on his. When she went to move the glass away from her lips, Guy lifted his hand and placed it under hers. "Finish it, my love."

As James watched the tense scene with growing unease, he felt the lightest of touches on his arm. His gaze met Claire's.

"Perhaps it is time we went to the ballroom and danced. James you could dance with Leah, while Guy and I can make up another pair," his sister said.

Guy took the now empty glass from Leah's hand and passed it to a nearby footman. He bowed to Claire. "What a capital idea."

Claire immediately handed her still untouched orgeat to James. A blaze of indignant anger burned in her eyes.

Bloody bastard.

Leah had begun building quite a collection of private insults for Guy, bastard being the latest.

She had tried. Her initial efforts at attempting to like him were not half-hearted in any way. But it was hard to like a person who treated you the way Guy treated Leah. The man was an overbearing pig.

He was just like her father. The first time she had looked deep into his eyes searching for any sense of connection, she had seen Tobias Shepherd staring straight back at her.

And now this. The battle over a glass of orgeat. From the moment Guy had handed her the drink, she'd known he was going to make her down every last drop. If there was one thing she knew about bullies, it was that they were nothing if not predictable. Whatever they did, it had to be with the long-term goal of eventually beating you down and winning. Guy, no doubt, would feel that by making her drink the foul, sweet liquid, he had won.

She felt sorry for Claire and James. Embarrassed for them to witness such behavior. From her knowledge of the Radley family, she suspected it was not something that they were used to seeing. Leah, meanwhile, had a lifetime's experience of it upon which she could call.

As Guy led Claire toward the entrance to the ballroom, Leah gave a small sigh of relief. She needed time to regroup her thoughts and steady herself for the next skirmish in the ongoing battle of wills. Guy might think himself the master of the game, but Leah was far from done.

"Are you alright, Leah?" asked James.

She gave him a bright smile. "Perfectly well, thank you. It is a lovely evening. Your sister dances well, so I am certain that Mister Dannon will appreciate her lightness of foot."

Leah bit down on her bottom lip. She was not going to make further mention of the incident with the drink. It was more important that she gather her wits and focus on the task at hand—that task being to get James Radley somewhere private.

"Shall we follow them?" he asked.

"In a moment. But before then, do you think we could go somewhere and talk?"

When his brows furrowed, she tapped him lightly on the arm, reassuring him. "Guy has already secured my father's approval to court me, and he has a second appointment at our home tomorrow. I'm not asking you to take me to your bedroom and ravish me. I just want five minutes of your time, James."

"Of course," he replied.

She offered him her arm and led him silently toward the hallway. Her heart was thumping a strong tattoo in her chest. James Radley may not like what she was about to do. She could only pray that Guy Dannon would hate it.

Chapter Eight

Much as he disapproved of the way Guy treated Leah, James still felt a strong sense of unease at allowing her to take him by the hand and lead him away from the main party. This was the sort of situation every young man was warned about. Going anywhere private with an unchaperoned, unmarried young woman was fraught with peril.

He was about to tell her that this was not wise, and that they should head back to the ballroom, when she stopped at an open door and quickly pulled him inside. This was madness.

"I think we should leave," he said.

"You agreed to five minutes. That is all I ask," she replied.

His gaze took in the room. From the large oak desk and towering shelves of books, it appeared to be the host's private study.

"This is the perfect place," she said. She let go of his hand and locked the door.

James swallowed a lump of nervousness. Leah was up to something, and every ounce of his good sense was screaming that whatever it was, he was in grave danger.

"For what?" he ventured.

The words had barely left his mouth before Leah took hold of the front of his evening jacket and pulled him hard toward her. With Leah gripping firmly onto his lapels, James had little choice but to bend. They came face-to-face, mere inches apart. He looked deep into her blue eyes, unable to pull away.

"This." And then she kissed him.

It was not just one kiss. Leah graced James with a blaze of hot, passionate kisses that took his breath away. Kiss after kiss, which soon had him seeing stars. When she opened her lips and her tongue darted into his mouth, James's cock went hard.

He should have resisted, should have pushed her away. But as the kiss deepened, he knew there was no hope of that happening. He was her willing captive. He kissed her right back.

His hand slipped around the back of her head, cupping the soft bun in which her hair had been set. She groaned. Every muscle in his body tensed. He wanted her. Their tongues tangled in a passionate encounter. Hot sexual need for this woman coursed through his veins.

He knew he should stop. This was wrong in so many ways. She and Guy might have their ongoing disagreements but by this time tomorrow, she would be his fiancée. James had to end this lunacy. But not yet.

Just a second longer. Just one more.

He finally managed to tear himself away, breaking the kiss. He stood, sucking in deep breaths. Ending the fierce embrace should have done the trick. But when he saw the glaze of passion in Leah's eyes, James reached for her once more and began to trail hot kisses down her neck. He was no longer in control of himself.

It was only when Leah patted her hand hard on his shoulder and murmured "enough" that the spell was finally broken. Without her intervention, he would have happily kept going.

She withdrew from his embrace, leaving only a cold space between them. "Thank you. Hopefully, that should do it."

Chapter Nine

There was an odd look on James's face as Leah took a step
back; it was a mixture of disappointment and confusion.

"Should do what?" he said.

She steeled herself, knowing her whole future depended on the
outcome of what she was about to say.

"That kiss should have you immediately seeking out Guy and
convincing him that he should cancel his meeting with my father
tomorrow. No man wants to marry a girl who his best friend has just
thoroughly kissed. A woman who is prepared to go into secluded
rooms with other men for secret trysts is not the sort of woman a man
asks to marry him." She looked down, suddenly unable to meet James's
gaze.

She had expected resistance, or at the very least a moment or two
of reluctance, but he had surprised her with his passionate response.
As far as first kisses went, she doubted it could be beaten. He really did
know how to make a woman's toes curl. His lips were so soft and
warm. The temptation to let him linger and play had been strong; the
touch of his hands on her body had sent shivers down her spine.

It was sad to think that she would never know the touch of this
man again. In another lifetime, she would have stayed in his arms and

let the kiss continue. In that other life, she would be his. It would be easy to give him her all and know no regrets. James and his alluring brown eyes would be what she saw every morning when she woke.

But it was not to be, and that bitter knowledge made her mind refocus. It forced her to remember why she had lured James to this room. She blinked, and as much as she wished otherwise, her gaze drifted back to his lips.

Those same lips were now tightly held in a thin line. On his lovely, handsome face was the stark story of realization. He had been used.

"I see. And here was I being foolish enough to feel pity for you. It would appear that you and Guy are better suited than I thought. Your weapons of choice are, of course, different, but you are both playing the game to win."

She shook her head slowly. His words of rebuke and regret stung. "No, James, you have it wrong. This is not a game. I am not playing at anything. I am fighting for my life."

The last remnants of the pleasant and heady pleasure of *that* kiss evaporated. "Please. Go and tell Guy that I dragged you into a room and kissed you. His pride will ensure that he doesn't tell anyone else, and I am certain that I can count on you to protect both your reputation and mine," she said.

Leah was desperately grasping for the fast-dwindling hope she still had in getting James to make Guy Dannon break ties with her.

"And what of the kiss? Are you going to stand there and tell me that you felt nothing? Because I can assure you my heart is still pounding hard in my chest," he replied.

He was right; it was better than anything she had expected. Not that she had gone into this encounter with any expectations other than seeking a way out of being with Guy.

Focus, Leah. You must focus on the outcome. Nothing else mattered.

"James, all I feel is fear. Fear that I will be bound to Guy for the rest of my life. I know he is your friend, but I cannot marry him. Please help me."

James had to understand that as distasteful as her actions may seem, she was using him to save her future. When he finally nodded, she let a slow breath of relief escape her lips.

He understood.

"I shall speak to Guy and let him know that you lured me into this room and attempted to kiss me. But remember this, Leah. You and I kissed, and there was a hell of a lot more happening between us in that moment than you are prepared to admit." He leaned in close to her. "Tell yourself all the lies you want, but we both know that you felt it too."

§♠.

Back in the ballroom, James discovered a less-than-happy Guy waiting.

After leaving the privacy of the study, Leah had headed off in the direction of the ladies retiring room. James, meanwhile, had found a footman bearing drinks and downed two large brandies in swift succession.

"Where the devil, have you been? And where is Leah? I thought the two of you were headed for the dance floor," grumbled Guy. He looked behind James's back as if expecting that the woman in question would suddenly appear.

James pointed toward the terrace doors. "You and I need to talk."

Guy huffed. He was clearly in a bad mood. What James was about to tell him would only make matters worse.

Outside on the terrace, he guided Guy over to a secluded spot away from the other party guests. He could only hope that Guy wouldn't risk losing his temper and creating a scene.

He had made a promise to Leah; he owed it to her to carry it through. Only a young woman with nothing left to lose would have made such a reckless gamble.

"What?" Guy asked.

"Leah lured me into a private room and before I knew what was happening, she was kissing me. She didn't hold back. I have serious concerns as to whether she is the right girl for you. Could you trust her as your wife if she is going to try that sort of thing with your friends?" James stilled; his gaze locked on Guy's face. He had basically just branded Leah as a tease or worse. A drip of cold sweat slid down his back. If Guy chose to punch him in the face here and now in front of other guests, there was nothing he could do about it.

One eyebrow raised then lowered. Guy looked away; his eyes fixed on the pot of flowers at the end of the terrace. Then a soft, knowing smile crept to his lips. It started small, before growing wide. A chuckle soon followed. He turned back to James; amusement written all over his face. "Did she now? The *little* minx."

James swayed on his feet, taken aback at Guy's reaction to his sordid confession.

Guy patted him on the shoulder and drew in close. "And was it good? She hasn't let me near her yet, so I am interested to know."

"Did you hear me? The girl you are courting lured me into a room and then kissed me. You can't possibly wish to marry her after that; she cannot be trusted. Your future wife will make a cuckold of you," replied James.

"Relax, James. I thought she might try something to dissuade me. Though I hadn't counted on her trying it with you. Of course, I am still going to offer for her. I am going to be a politician and I shall need a political wife. If sexually innocent Leah is prepared to kiss you before she is wed, imagine what she will do to further my cause once we are married."

"You cannot be serious," replied James.

"I am perfectly serious. Once she is well trained in bed, I shall instruct her as to which gentlemen she should lure to rooms at parties. Leah will make the perfect political wife."

James stood and stared at Guy dumbfounded. The man he had known at Eton was not the man who stood before him. This man was a stranger.

Guy shook his head. "You are so naïve, James, that at times I feel sorry for you. But don't worry about Leah trifling with you in the future. Once we are married, she will have plenty of other men to deal with. All you need to concern yourself with is writing your best man speech for the wedding breakfast and organizing my bachelor party."

Guy turned on his heel and headed back inside. Leah soon appeared in the ballroom and Guy quickly marched over to her before taking her firmly by the arm. James watched as Guy led Leah away, sadness filling his heart as she shook her head when Guy leaned in and spoke to her. He dreaded to think what Guy was saying now that he knew she had kissed James.

Not that the conversation really mattered. What did matter was that the woman whose kiss had rocked James's world was now destined to marry his best friend. A man who had revealed himself to be ruthless in his ambition.

And it was all his fault.

Chapter Ten

Mary Radley marched into the breakfast room and pushed *The Times* under James's nose.

She pointed her finger to an entry under the betrothal notices. "Well, it is official. Guy is getting married. I cannot begin to tell you how happy Mrs. Dannon is to finally know her son is taking on a wife. It was all she could talk about at the luncheon yesterday."

James managed the barest of smiles at his mother's news. Leah and Guy's betrothal was a fresh piece of hell for him. After Leah's plea for him to help her avoid marrying Guy, James felt heartsick. He had failed her.

He stuffed a hearty portion of scrambled eggs into his mouth before washing it down with a gulp of tea. It was a display of poor manners, but he needed to eat and leave the house soon. With his mother's arrival in the breakfast room, his father would not be far behind. James was keen on avoiding Hugh this morning. Today of all days, he did not need another lecture about his life choices.

"I won't be home for supper this evening, Mama. I am seeing Timothy Walters and Timothy Smith after I finish work. They are due to head off to Derbyshire shortly for a painting commission," he said.

His mother nodded but said nothing.

James was envious, but happy for his friends and their success. They had talent, and they both worked hard. The one thing he was prepared to admit being jealous of, was that their families had given them the opportunity to pursue their passion for painting. He could only dream of being able to paint and have patrons who supported his work.

Rising from his chair, he wiped his face on his napkin and made ready to make his escape. He got as far the breakfast room door before it swung open and his father marched in. Claire and Maggie followed close on Hugh's heels.

"Good morning, Radley family. Lovely to see you all here," said Hugh, clapping his hands loudly together. The Bishop of London was always a little too effusive in the morning for James's taste.

He made to step past his father and hurry from the room, but a smiling Hugh looked over his reading glasses at him. "Come now, James, you can spare a few minutes to break your fast with your family. Your Uncle Charles is not that much of a tyrant to expect you at your desk right on the crack of nine. And he would want you to arrive with a full stomach."

"I have already eaten," explained James.

Hugh gave a quick glance in the direction of James's unfinished plate of food, then pointed at it. "Wasted food is a sin. Now sit down, lad."

A reluctant James followed behind Hugh, Claire, and Maggie, and resumed his seat. The only bright side of being made to go back to the table was that he could finish the remainder of his breakfast.

"Claire, darling, Leah and Guy's betrothal notice is in today's *Times*," said Mary.

"Yes. Leah said Guy was at pains to have it announced as soon as possible," replied Claire.

"When is the wedding?" asked Mary. To James's quiet relief, the question was directed at Claire.

"A little over three weeks. It was the earliest they could get a booking at the church. Guy tried to talk Leah into an earlier date else-where, but she held fast on them getting married at St George's. You should see the long list of things that Leah wants me to help her with in the lead-up to the wedding," his sister replied.

Hugh nodded. "It is that time of the year when everyone is rushing to the altar. I have three weddings booked for this Saturday morning. As soon as one is over, the next will be coming up the steps of St Paul's. It will require precise timing to get them all done and dusted first thing. In my day, you got married as soon as the season was over. There was none of this waiting-until-late-autumn business."

James stabbed his fork into the sausage on his plate. He picked up his knife and after cutting the sausage in half, stuffed one portion into his mouth and sat chewing it slowly. All this talk of Guy and Leah's wedding had now made him lose interest in his breakfast. He held the other half of the sausage under the table, and King quickly snapped it out of his fingers.

James swallowed, feeling the sausage going down his throat in the same painful way that the news of the impending wedding had. He rued not having given the dog the whole thing.

Under the table, he balled his hands into tight fists. After the events of the garden party and the ball, his interest in Leah Shepherd had gone from barely thinking of her to spending more time than he knew he should, wondering where she was and what she was doing. Even his dreams had not been spared.

His nights were now filled with visions of her pale blue eyes staring up into his. Of her tender, pliant lips yielding to his kiss. The touch of her hair, so soft in his fingers. Worst of all, he had enjoyed long lust-filled dreams, at the center of which were those tiny brown sun-kissed freckles. He wanted to place a kiss on every single one of them. To count them all and then begin again. To still be kissing them as he rose over her and slid his hard cock home into her heated, willing body.

He picked up his cold tea and downed the rest of it in one inelegant mouthful, ignoring his mother's frown at his lack of table manners. He forced himself to think of work, of checking shipping manifests. He dared not risk trying to excuse himself from the breakfast table while his body was still in its hardened state.

He pushed some of the scrambled egg around on the plate, frustrated in the knowledge that he was completely besotted with Leah and there was not a thing he could do about it. The closest he would ever get to holding her in his arms again would be in his dreams.

"In other news of the *ton* this week, I hear the Dowager Countess Newhall is helping to arrange a country house party for her son," said Mary.

James sat up and forced his attention on listening to this less-than-interesting tidbit. Anything to get his mind away from Leah.

Claire snorted. "Who on earth would want to go all the way to Derbyshire? And it is getting a little late in the year for a house party. I hear from Cousin Lucy that the first snow has already fallen at Strathmore Castle."

"It snows all-year-round in Scotland, so I wouldn't be using that as any weather vane," replied Hugh.

"The former Countess Newhall is now the Countess of Lienz; she recently married the scoundrel she ran off with all those years ago. I know this because she sent a calling card yesterday. She is coming here later this week to discuss the possibility of you two attending the house party," said Mary. She looked from Claire to Maggie, giving them both a hopeful smile. "Who knows? One of my daughters might fall in love with an earl. Wouldn't that be lovely?"

Maggie shook her head.

Claire screwed up her nose. "No thank you, Mama. Lord Newhall and dear Cousin Caroline have had several nasty encounters of late. The man lacks manners. Besides, I shall have to stay in London to assist Leah with her wedding preparations; there is much to do."

And with that, the chance of either of the Radley sisters becoming the next Countess of Newhall died a swift death.

"Well then, your grace, we can forget about spending our summers at Newhall Castle, though I doubt that the Countess Lienz will take the news so graciously. She seems rather keen to have as many eligible girls in attendance as possible," said Mary.

"From what I know of the woman, all she will be looking for will be the girl with the largest dowry. Though from what William Saunders has told me, he wouldn't be surprised if Newhall holds out for a woman who has at least a degree of affection for him. No doubt the scandalous failure of his parents' marriage will have left its scars. And as I have always said, a marriage based on anything other than passion and mutual interests will surely falter," replied Hugh.

James caught the shared gentle smile between his parents. They were forever embarrassing their children with their stolen kisses and whispered words of endearment.

"Not that we are all granted the choice of whom we marry. It might sound unkind, but I think Leah and Guy's union is founded on her father's political connections rather than any degree of love. Her mother said it was a smart match and that Leah should be proud to have a possible future cabinet minister as her husband," said Claire.

His sister's words gave weight to Leah's reasons for not wishing to marry Guy. James now found himself in the unenviable situation of feeling sorry for Leah, while knowing he should be supporting his friend.

It was a little after seven in the morning and already he had heard enough about the impending wedding for one day.

"And with that, I am off to work. Those shipping ledgers will not complete themselves," James said, getting to his feet. He moved quickly out of the breakfast room, not bothering to look back. He didn't wish to catch his father's eye again in case he was asked to retake his seat. He had enough on his mind this morning without dealing with another argument over when he was going back to university.

His father's words about a marriage based on passion and love were foremost in his thoughts as he climbed into the Radley town carriage a short while later. That sort of marriage made sense in his world. His parents' marriage a prime example. A forced marriage, such as the one Leah Shepherd was about to endure, made a mockery of true love.

Having held her in his arms and for a brief, precious moment known the heat of her passion, James despaired at what now lay ahead for Leah.

She didn't deserve that fate.

Chapter Eleven

"I am so jealous. I am green with envy and am not ashamed to admit it," said James.

Timothy Walters picked up a blob of green paint with his brush and flicked it in James's direction. It fell short and landed with a splat to join the dozens of other paint spots which already dotted the dark wooden floor.

The attic at the top of the Walters's family town house in Bond Street, where the 'two Tims' worked wasn't overly large, but it was full of light. Timothy Walters' father had made his vast fortune in trade with the newly minted United States of America and had allowed his son to pursue his painting as a full-time career.

In addition to the two large easels at which the two Tim's worked, there was a small table where James sketched during his regular visits. The room was cramped but to James it was heaven. A private place in which to sketch, dream, and paint.

"When do you leave for Derbyshire?" he asked.

"Tomorrow. We have some final packing to do, and then we shall be heading off," replied Smith with a smile.

Walters added another daub of paint to his canvas and kept working. He didn't seem as happy about the impending journey north as much as his companion was. James looked at Smith, who shrugged.

"My friend here thinks himself in love. And from the miserable look on his face, I would say that the best place he could be right now is as far away from London and the young lady in question as possible."

"I expect you are right. She won't see me, so staying in London is torture," said Walters.

James frowned at the sad look on Walters' face. It was the same hopeless one that had stared back at him in the mirror earlier that morning.

"You really should come with us. Steal away from your parents and run off to Derbyshire. We all know you have the talent, James; you just need to be able to complete some paintings which you could then sell," offered Smith.

James snorted. The chances of his father allowing, let alone funding him to wander off to the Marchington Woodlands in order to paint, were somewhere between little and none.

"The position I currently hold at my uncle's shipping business is about as far as my father will allow me to stray from the path that he has chosen for me," he replied.

Smith dropped onto the chair opposite James at the table. "You need to speak to his grace. Tell him that this is the passion you want in your life. I never thought my father would agree, but he did."

James wasn't going to mention to his friend that having a father who was a well- known and successful musician had helped more than a little in that decision.

"When your father is the Bishop of London, there are certain expectations that society and family place upon you. It is expected of me that I shall follow in my father's footsteps. The way my life is panning out, my painting will be nothing more than a pastime," he replied.

Walters set down his paintbrush and turned to James. He held his hands softly together, almost as if he were saying a prayer. "Don't give up on your dreams. You never know—they might come true. I am still holding out for my love to realize that she and I are destined. This time apart from one another might be just what we need to bring her to her senses."

Smith gave his friend a dejected look. "Yes, but don't forget some dreams are that far out of our reach that we really should let them go. Not all dreams become reality."

"Who is the lady in question?" asked James.

"No one you know," replied Smith.

James got to his feet and wandered over to where Walters was standing at his easel.

"How did you go with getting Francis Saunders to ask the Prince Regent about our paintings?" asked Walters.

James shook his head. "Not good. One minute, Francis was keen to show him your work; the next thing, he decided he wasn't. I haven't been able to ask him why, but I shall have a word when I get a moment."

Francis had a strong personal connection with the prince and had initially offered to show the future king some of his friends' work. The Prince Regent was overseeing major renovations to the pavilion at Brighton and had spent a great deal of money acquiring artworks. James had hoped that through Francis, his friends may have been able to sell some of their pieces. But in the past week or so, he had sensed a distinct cooling in Francis's interest in putting their work in front of Prince George.

"It would be great for our careers if we could get some of our work displayed in the royal pavilion. It would certainly help to secure other patrons."

James considered the painting which Walters was working on. The subject was a wealthy looking gentleman. James tried not to screw up his nose.

Walters gave him a sideways glance. "Not the most exciting thing I have ever painted, grant you, but it pays good money. And my father does like to see me doing work for patrons in town. You might want to consider picking up some portrait commissions."

James shook his head. "There is no light or drama in painting people. I want to create major landscape pieces, ones that capture the imagination and have folk thinking they are standing seeing the real thing. No offence, Walters, but if I reach the point where I am painting portraits of ruddy-faced bankers and merchants, I may as well give up. I would rather walk away from my art than paint simply to pay the bills."

Walters dabbed his brush into the paint once more and leaned in close to the canvas.

"Someday, James, you may well eat those words."

Chapter Twelve

James had done his best to avoid Guy over the past few days, but the betrothal party loomed large. As best man, there was no chance of him being able to escape attending. The wedding preparations were moving ahead whether he liked it or not.

If it had just been himself attending the party this evening, he would have wished the betrothed couple all the happiness for their future, stayed for the speeches, and then left. But since Claire was one of Leah's friends, the whole Radley family had been invited. Even Maggie had removed herself from her usual place by the sitting room window and made the effort to attend.

"I hear everybody who is anybody is coming tonight. The Shepherds have gone all out," said Mary.

"Rumor has it that Guy will be pushing Tobias Shepherd to find him a nice safe seat as soon as he and Leah are married," replied Hugh.

"I expect once everyone sees Leah's gown, all talk of politics will cease. It is stunning. The fabric was the most expensive that the modiste had ever used. And you should see the material for her wedding gown. Why, it looks like something royalty would wear. Leah's parents and Guy are spending an eye-watering amount of money on the wedding," said Claire.

Her mother frowned at her. Money was a crass subject and should not be discussed in company.

"Is it true Guy has commissioned a special china dinner service for them? I heard it has over one hundred and twenty pieces and that is just for day-to-day use," said Maggie.

Claire nodded; her eyes wide.

The Radley family town carriage was a tight squeeze with Hugh, Mary, Claire, Maggie, and James all on board. They hadn't even arrived, and James was already in a foul mood. He grumbled as his father nudged him along on the seat.

"Come on then, lad, shift up and make some room," said Hugh.

James moved an inch or two over on the leather bench seat, earning him a hard stare from Hugh. Reluctantly, and with a decided lack of good grace, he moved again. He held his arms tight against himself and scowled at anyone who dared to look at him.

"I hope you are not going to be that much of a misery guts for the entire evening, James. This is supposed to be a happy occasion. Your best friend is getting married," said Mary.

"Yes, well since we are already going to the betrothal ball, do you think we could talk about something else on the way?" he replied.

He should have apologized to his mother over his behavior, but he couldn't shake himself out of his dour frame of mind.

"What is the matter with you, James? You have been in a black mood all week," observed Claire.

He knew full well why he was so out of sorts, but it wasn't exactly something he could share with them. His growing feelings for Leah were something he had to keep to himself. "I'm sorry. I am just a little at sea at the moment. The two Tims left for Derbyshire on Friday and I won't be seeing them for another month."

"Well then, with your friends out of town, now might be the right time to stop moping about the house and make some firm decisions about your future," said Hugh.

A frustrated James turned and looked out the carriage window. He had many things he would like to say in response to his father's words but decided that silence was the wisest option. That and a good half dozen glasses of something strong.

ཨ

"Oh, thank God," he muttered.

Caroline and Francis were standing on the footpath out the front of the Shepherd family home in Duke Street as James stepped down from the family carriage. He could have cried at the sight. These were the two people he could share an evening with and not get himself into trouble. He didn't want to hear any more about wedding gowns or extravagant dinner sets.

"Ah, my lovely niece and nephew," said Hugh.

"Uncle Hugh, it's good to see you. Mama sends her love," said Francis.

Hugh frowned. "Your parents are not in attendance tonight?"

Francis shook his head. "No. We have a new shipment arriving at the docks from the West Indies tomorrow morning, hence why I shall only be staying for a short while. And Mama is spending time with William and Hattie, helping them to set up the nursery."

William Saunders had recently returned from France, and to everyone's surprise, had taken himself a new wife. Hattie was with child and Adelaide Saunders was already a doting grandmother-in-waiting.

With family greetings quickly over, James held out an arm to Caroline. Francis accompanied Maggie and Claire up the front steps.

"Looking forward to this evening?" he asked.

Caroline screwed up her face. "Not particularly. But I am under instructions to attend tonight and to keep a low profile. I am not in my parents' good graces. I have received lectures from both my mother and father on the shortcomings of my behavior. Apparently, I am getting myself somewhat of an unwelcome reputation as a result of having one or two overly amorous admirers."

He winced, taking no joy in knowing that his cousin was also on the out with her family. Though for Caroline, it was not an uncommon occurrence. She had a prickly nature and did not suffer fools. Too many men had discovered to their great cost that beneath her stunning beauty lay a sharp mind. It would take a special kind of man to capture Caroline's imagination, let alone her heart.

"So, we both need a drink or three," he replied.

"Exactly."

Once inside the Shepherds' elegantly decorated reception hall, James hunted them down a drink. When the footman offered Caroline an orgeat and she recoiled in horror, James found himself laughing for the first time in days. He was still chuckling when he selected a glass of champagne and handed it to her.

Caroline sipped her drink while James nursed his wine. His bad mood and his father's reaction to it left him deciding that a simple French burgundy was the wisest choice for the evening. A glass too many of whisky might lead him to tell Guy a few home truths, and thereby ruin the evening.

"I hear you are off to Lord Newhall's house party in Derbyshire. I thought the two of you were enemies, so how did you manage to get saddled with that?" he asked.

She rolled her eyes. "Mama and Papa both think I need to get out of London for a time. Let things settle down with the populace of young unmarried men of the *ton,* or something to that effect. As far as I am aware, my trip to Newhall Castle is purely to make up the numbers. Francis is coming with me, so we are hoping to steal away from much of the festivities. Just don't let my parents find out the truth."

"Don't tell me the Ice Queen is thinking of abdicating," said James with a grin.

She swatted him on the arm. "Horrid beast. And don't say that too loudly in public; this country has laws against treason. I don't want the Prince Regent to hear that people have dubbed me a queen. Knowing how sensitive he is about titles; he might just have me arrested."

"Yes, and the Tower of London is not the most pleasant or warmest of places to spend your days," he replied.

"I hear from Cousin Claire that you are also in a bit of a funk at present. She asked if Francis and I could take you with us to Derbyshire. I said I would speak to you," said Caroline.

James put a finger to his lips and tapped them lightly. Now that was an idea he had not considered. Newhall Castle wasn't that far from Burton-on-Trent where the two Tims were basing themselves for the winter. If he accompanied Caroline and Francis to the house party, he could easily slip away for a few days and spend some time with his friends. He increasingly felt more comfortable in their company than he did with Guy. This was an unexpected, but possibly welcome change to James's plans.

"Are you serious about that? I mean, about me coming with you?" he asked.

Her face brightened and she smiled. "Absolutely. The three of us would have a lovely time together. Since I don't think I have any sort of shot at becoming the next Countess Newhall, we could have our own little private party in the middle of his," she replied.

Getting out of town for a week or so would mean James could avoid listening to Claire's almost constant updates about the wedding preparations. His head would be glad for the respite, though there was little he could do for his heart.

The offer was extremely appealing. And since he would be accompanying his cousins to Newhall Castle, his family-centric father would be unlikely to say no to him going. His mood lifted for the first time in days. It wasn't much, but he sorely needed it.

"If your father can spare both Francis and me for the time we are away, I could do it. I might be able to catch up with some friends who are undertaking a painting commission up at Burton-on-Trent. Hopefully Newhall won't mind if I slip away for a few days. You know Timothy Walters and Timothy Smith, don't you?"

He sensed a moment of hesitation from Caroline. "Yes, but since I plan to keep my visit to Derbyshire as low-key as possible, I don't think you should make mention of it to your friends."

He was about to ask her the reason for her guarded response when Francis suddenly appeared at his shoulder. Behind him stood Francis's friend Harry Menzies. At times, James wondered if the two of them were joined at the hip. Wherever Francis went, Harry followed.

Caroline gave Harry the merest nod before paying close attention to her champagne. Harry, in turn, greeted her with a bright smile.

James held out his hand to Harry in friendly greeting.

"Radley," said Harry, shaking his hand.

"Menzies. I didn't realize you knew the happy couple," replied James.

"I don't. But my father is trying to get Tobias Shepherd to find me a seat in the northern counties. Manchester needs a new local member and his aim is for it to be me. Not that I have the slightest interest in a political career, but Papa is insistent the family strengthen our ties with the area."

Harry's father had made his money in the textiles trade, and was no doubt looking to gain more traction for his family with the elite of England by getting his son into parliament.

Francis drew his sister to one side. "Excuse us for a moment, would you?"

Caroline nodded, before she and Francis walked a few feet away and began a private conversation.

Not wishing to appear rude by eavesdropping, James turned from his cousins and back to Harry Menzies. "Well you seem to have come to the right place if you are hoping to find a way to get into parliament. You just need to do as Guy Dannon is doing and get yourself a wife," said James.

James had been in jest with his remark, but the look that Harry gave in response, told him that Harry considered it to be no laughing matter. "I am working on that, Radley. Though I am aiming a touch higher than the Shepherd girl. With my family coming from trade, I need a wife with a more prestigious family name. Someone who comes from a traditional noble family," replied Harry. His gaze was fixed on Caroline as he spoke.

James felt a shudder of icy premonition chill his bones.

Leah sucked in a deep breath, straightened her shoulders, and stepped out of her room. As expected, her father was waiting for her on the landing. He offered her his arm. Their gazes met for an instant. The tight smile on his face almost matched perfectly to hers.

"You might want to summon a real smile for your guests and your fiancé. You know how people like to see a happy bride," he said.

"Yes, Papa," she replied.

Those two words had become her sole response to him over the past weeks. He had ignored her pleadings to refuse Guy's suit, telling her that it was a sensible marriage and that her future husband would make a fine politician. She was destined to follow in the footsteps of her mother and sister, so she should do as they had done and accept her lot.

Her father dragged her back into her bedroom and shut the door behind him, the familiar twitch of his mouth telling her that he was not the least bit happy. "You had better learn to fix your smile more naturally to your face if you are going to help Guy with his career. The sort of men you will be expected to grace with your sexual charms do not care for shy, simpering misses. They want a confident woman who knows how to please a man. Once you are married, you will have to earn your keep."

Leah blinked as realization dawned. Her own sire had refused her entreaty to call off the betrothal because he knew full well what Guy had in mind for his daughter. She had always known her father didn't love her, but now she understood that he saw her as nothing more than a pawn. A piece which could be moved about the board in the never-ending game of chess that was English politics.

She attempted a smile, but it faltered. Her father leaned in close.

"I shall give you this piece of advice Leah. Things will go easier for you with your husband if you learn comply."

He offered her his arm, and after she took it, he led her out of the room. They descended the stairs, with Leah carefully watching her every step. The hem and train of her cream silk gown was long. Guy had given clear instructions as to the exact color and length of gown Leah should wear for their betrothal party. It was elegant and beautiful; its fabric hugged her soft curves. A happily betrothed young woman would have felt like a princess in it, but Leah couldn't care less for the extravagant gown.

At the bottom of the stairs, Guy waited for her. "Ah, such a wonderous sight."

Her father took hold of Leah's hand and placed it in Guy's. She was already as good as married.

Hot tears stung her eyes as Guy leaned over and placed the briefest of kisses on her cheek. The prospect of becoming his wife filled her with heartbreaking pain. She would never love Guy. Her darkest fear was that she would soon have reason to loathe him.

"Our guests have begun to arrive," he said.

Much as her father demanded it of her, Leah was unable to summon a real smile. As Guy led her out to meet the family and friends who had gathered to wish them both congratulations, her lips remained in a tight line.

As soon as she set foot into the reception room, her gaze found James. He was standing next to Caroline. He appeared deep in thought. She stared at him for a moment, silently praying he would look up and see her.

When their gazes did finally meet, he closed his eyes for an instant and shook his head. He looked away. Without thinking, she clutched at Guy's arm for support.

"Don't be nervous, Leah. Just remember that in the very near future, I will expect you to charm powerful men and bring them under your control. Take this as the time to hone those special skills, my love. As soon as we are married, I will begin your education in the art of seduction. There are many men in this room I plan for you to fuck," Guy whispered.

At his words, a single tear began to trickle down Leah's cheek. She was doomed to live her worst nightmare.

Chapter Thirteen

etting out of London and heading to Derbyshire would solve some of James's problems, at least for the time being. By going to Newhall Castle with Caroline and Francis, he could find respite from the constant noise about Guy and Leah's wedding. He would be away from his father and the questions about what he had planned for his future. But most of all, it would allow him to slip away, meet up with the two Tims, and paint.

"Poor girl," sighed Caroline.

"What do you mean?" he replied, stirring from his plans.

Caroline tilted her head in the direction of the grand staircase. James moved in order to get a better look, and what he saw filled him with dismay.

Leah and Guy were standing at the bottom of the staircase, her hand placed stiffly on his arm. She wore a tight, forced smile. When hers and James's gazes met; he was filled with pity. Pity which quickly coalesced into anger. He fisted his hands as he tore his gaze from her.

If only I could beat someone to a bloody pulp.

When he turned back to look at her once more, Leah had a hand lifted to her face. She brushed something away, and he knew in his heart that it had been a tear.

A sharp pain tore at James's chest. If he didn't know better, he would have sworn he had just been stabbed.

Guy didn't appear to have noticed Leah's distress. He gave her a cold smile and pulled her closer to him in what could only be interpreted as an open display of possession. James wanted to seize his longtime friend by the throat and shake him violently.

The rest of the gathered guests had an entirely different reaction to the arrival of the newly engaged couple. A ripple of applause and soft gushes of "Look at her tears of happiness," and "What a wonderful couple they will make," were heard in the room.

He had to give Leah her dues. She blinked back her tears and went to greet her guests. She was already learning to control her emotions in public.

How long will it be until nothing of your true self remains?

He gritted his teeth. As he saw it, he had two choices before him. Either turn and walk out the front door, and deal with the repercussions of his actions, or stay and put his own private concerns about this impending marriage to one side.

Tearing himself away from them wouldn't do Leah any good. It may even make things worse. If Guy thought that James had severed their friendship because of his new bride, he may well blame her.

By remaining within the sphere of friendship, there was the remote chance that he may be able to temper Guy's treatment of his new bride, perhaps even be a positive influence. The Guy he thought he knew may not have been that far from the surface. A good friend may be just what the newlyweds needed. He could be that friend for both of them, but especially for Leah.

He felt something for her; he no longer doubted that fact. Yet he daren't entertain the possibility that it might be more than just a little crush. They barely knew one another, but every time he looked at Leah, his heart thumped in his chest and his mouth went dry.

Watching as the newly engaged couple made their way through the throng of well-wishers, he was torn as to what he should do. Turning back to Caroline, he studied her for a moment then did the one thing he knew he could. "About Derbyshire," he ventured.

"Yes?"

"I will speak to Uncle Charles first thing tomorrow. If he can spare me, then I will come with you and Francis to Newhall Castle."

"Excellent. Francis will be pleased. I think he was worried that he was going to be stuck with all the maiden aunts who are coming as chaperones for the other young ladies. Now at least we shall have a small group for hunting," replied Caroline.

As soon as he had spoken to Charles Saunders and hopefully gotten his blessing, he would stock up on paints and oils for the trip north. In the clear air of the English countryside, away from the hubbub of London, he would be able to paint and think. The soothing rhythm of brush on canvas had always given him clarity of mind. Right now, James badly needed to clear his head and make some hard decisions.

At the end of his time away from London, he promised himself he would have a settled on a position on the question of Leah. Either he would stand by her through trying to influence Guy, or he would sever all ties.

The sword of Damocles surely hung over his head. Should he do all he could to support the woman who had captured his heart? Or was it better to accept the situation and walk away? Either way he chose, he would be left with a broken heart.

Chapter Fourteen

❧

"**O**f course, I told him I will be back in time for the wedding."
Guy had not been the least bit happy with James upon
hearing that his best man was heading off to Derbyshire for
a week. They had exchanged brief but firm words; Guy only finally
being placated by James's solid reassurance that he would be back in
London in time to host Guy's debaucherously wild stag party.

"Guy cannot expect you to hang around London just because he is
getting married. Besides, most of the work is being done by the Shepherd family and friends. Lord knows I have been signed up for what
seems an endless number of tasks just because I am Leah's friend,"
replied Claire.

James was keen to avoid getting caught up any further in Guy's
wedding plans. The groom had given him a long list of entertainments
he expected to have laid out for him on the occasion of his pre-
wedding celebrations, several of which made James feel ill. There were
one or two on the list that he wasn't sure he could arrange without
getting arrested for crimes against the public good. As a stint in prison
would not go down well with his father, James had crossed them off.

His opinion of his friend had now officially reached its lowest
point. James could quite easily have ended his long friendship with

Guy at this stage and walked away without regret. He remained only because of his concern for Leah.

"Speaking of Leah, how is she holding up? She didn't appear very happy at the betrothal party," he replied.

Claire fell silent for a time. "She says it is just pre-wedding nerves. Her parents decided upon Guy as her future husband, and she told me that it is taking a little time to get things straight in her mind. That is all."

James wanted to press his sister further on the subject of Leah, but the arrival of a Fulham Palace servant in the doorway of the Radley family sitting room put paid to that notion.

"Miss Leah Shepherd," he announced.

Claire shot her brother a quick look. "Don't say anything about her being reluctant to marry Guy. She needs our support, not your sympathy."

Leah stepped into the room, stopping mid-stride when she saw James getting to his feet.

He bowed to her. "Good morning."

"Oh, I am sorry. Am I disturbing you?" she said.

James shook his head. "No, Claire and I were just discussing my plans to go to Derbyshire later this week. I am accompanying my cousins Caroline and Francis to Lord Newhall's house party."

"Yes, Guy made mention of it," Leah replied.

Claire rose from her seat on the comfy brown sofa. "I have those fabric samples you lent me earlier this week. Let me go and get them. I shan't be long."

Claire hurried from the room, leaving Leah and James alone.

"Please have a seat," he said.

Leah hesitated. Finding James in the sitting room had taken her by surprise. They hadn't been alone together since the night they had shared *that* kiss. At the betrothal party, she and James had exchanged a few polite words, all the while Guy had held her firmly by the arm.

She reluctantly took a seat, deciding it would be awkward for

Claire if she returned to find her brother and friend standing facing one another in uncomfortable silence. She removed her gloves and bonnet before placing them beside her on the sofa. "I was surprised to hear you were leaving town. I think Guy expected you to remain in London until the wedding."

"I know he was disappointed when I told him I was going away," replied James.

Leah silently chided herself for having made further mention of James's trip. James was wrong, Guy hadn't been disappointed when he'd told her of James's plans; he had been livid. The color of his face had been a deep red of barely suppressed rage.

While her fiancé had ranted about his best man going off into the wilds of Derbyshire "to paint like a child," she had sat, hands clasped softly in her lap, and waited for him to burn through his anger. She had borne witness to her father's tirades enough times to know that the best thing to do was to wait it out. One did nothing to enrage the beast.

"I think he will be happy when he knows you are back in town," she replied.

James glanced at the door. Claire had still not reappeared.

"About that night at the ball. I tried . . ."

Leah held up a hand. She didn't want to hear whatever James had to say about the aftermath of the kiss. Whatever he had said or done, it had made no difference because Guy had arrived at the Shepherd house on the Wednesday and asked for her hand in marriage. As far as everyone was concerned, the deal was done. There was nothing he could say or do to change that immutable fact. "Please don't," she said.

He sat forward in the chair and reached for her hand. She tried to move away but found herself unable.

"I'm sorry, Leah. So very sorry," he said.

His fingers brushed over her skin, his touch tender, caring. He was so unlike Guy that her heart broke just a little.

Leah finally summoned enough strength to pull away. She couldn't decide what was worse—the lifetime of cold indifference which she knew for certain lay ahead with Guy, or the faint memory of that night when she'd still held onto the hope that perhaps she could change her life. That she could find a future with a kind and loving man...like James.

"I . . . I have to go," she stammered. There was suddenly not enough air in the room. She got to her feet and grabbed her things. She rushed toward the door, knocking into Claire who had just stepped back into the room. The fabric samples in Claire's hands fell and scattered onto the floor, but Leah didn't stop.

"Leah?" said Claire.

She headed for the front door, breaking into a short run as soon as she was clear of the house. Her coachman barely had time to open the carriage door before she stumbled inside. Throwing herself onto the bench, Leah burst into tears.

Damn James Radley with his kind, foolish heart. He was not the hero she needed.

Chapter Fifteen

✿

I f James had hoped that the trip to Derbyshire would be the solution to his problems, he was quickly finding it to be nothing of the sort.

The Strathmore travel coach had been involved in an accident late at night on the road just outside Newhall Castle, and the driver's assistant had been badly injured. Caroline had then taken on the dangerous task of striking out in the dark and seeking help for the travelling party; in the process, she had sustained a nasty injury to her hand. Julian Palmer, Lord Newhall had used his war time experience to stitch her deep wound.

Added to that was the news that the day after James and his cousins left London, Julian's mother had put a rumor about town telling everyone that the house party had been cancelled. The former Countess Newhall's spiteful act had resulted in James, Francis, and Caroline being the sole house party guests at Newhall Castle. They had rallied around Julian and agreed to stay on and make the best of things.

However, it was only with the unexpected arrival several days later of Francis's friend Harry Menzies that James began to feel that matters were getting out of hand. There was something clearly wrong with Harry and the way he conducted himself around Caroline. As soon as he was able to get a moment alone with Francis, James intended to raise the issue of Harry's search for a wife.

Late in the evening on the third day after their arrival at Newhall Castle, James and Francis sat before the fireplace in one of the castle's sitting rooms. It had been a long time since they had been able to share a private moment and talk. With everyone else having gone to bed, now seemed the time to broach the subject of Harry Menzies.

James set his glass of brandy down and faced his cousin. There were enough disconcerting parallels between the situations of Caroline and Harry and that of Guy and Leah for him to continue to remain silent any longer.

"I know Harry is your friend, and he seems harmless enough, but I have a bad feeling about why he made the journey all the way from London to Derbyshire," said James.

Francis nodded. "Caroline is not happy that he is here. She says he makes her feel uncomfortable. To be honest, I don't fully understand what is going on."

Harry's words at the betrothal party had been rolling around in James's head all day. At no time did he find any comfort in them. "I think I may be able to shed some light on why Harry is here, and you are not going to like it. I spoke to him at Guy and Leah's betrothal party and he told me he was looking for a wife. I got the distinct impression that Harry has set his sights on marrying Caroline," replied James.

Francis stilled. "That would be an unwise thing for Harry to attempt."

Caroline would never accept a marriage proposal from Harry, and the last thing James wanted was to be dealing with another woman having to face an unwelcome suitor. He could only pray that Harry was not as determined as Guy had been in forcing the issue.

"I will speak to Harry after breakfast tomorrow and give him a gentle nudge. I am sure he will understand the need for him to return to London," said Francis.

"And if he doesn't?"

"I will pack him up and take him back myself."

Chapter Sixteen

Leah didn't have to suck in her stomach as the modiste pulled on the tight bindings of the wedding gown. She held up her hand. "It is still too loose, but I don't want it taken in again," she said.

She met her mother's gaze in the reflection of the dressing room mirror. "You have to stop losing weight, Leah. You already look drawn and pale. You don't want Guy thinking he is marrying a stick creature now do you? And we can't have society matrons making remarks about how sickly the bride looks," said her mother. Mrs. Shepherd reached over and gave Leah's cheeks a hard pinch. A small amount of color appeared on them before they returned to their dull pallor.

Unable to keep food down most days, she had lost significant weight since the betrothal announcement. What Guy thought of his future bride's sudden weight loss, she really didn't care. He had made it clear on more than one occasion that he wasn't marrying her for her beauty.

"The matrons of the *ton* can say what they like. As long as I turn up at the church on the wedding day, I am sure Guy will still marry me," Leah replied.

Her mother snorted. The mornings of having new gowns fitted, followed by shopping for all manner of items to set up her new home, were beginning to meld into a never-ending torture for Leah. But Mrs. Shepherd was determined that her youngest daughter was turned out with not only a full trousseau, but all the linen and china she would likely need for the first years of marriage. And since Guy was footing the bill, no expense was being spared.

A full dining setting, including cutlery for twenty guests, had arrived at the Shepherd house earlier that week and it had taken three hours to unpack the boxes. Rather than simply having it delivered to his own home, Guy seemed at pains to show his future in-laws that he was a man of means. When her mother and sister finally left Leah alone with the stunning chinoiserie green dinner set, from Wedgwood and Byerley, she had sat at the end of the long dining table and simply stared at it.

Once they were married, Guy expected her to be the hostess of many dinner parties and private soirees, all of which would be designed to aid in his efforts to become not only a member of parliament, but at some future point, a member of the Prime Minister's inner circle. Guy had his sights set on a cabinet post.

The modiste gave Mrs. Shepherd a questioning look.

"Should I take the gown in again, madam?"

Mrs. Shepherd huffed. "No. Leave it as it is. I shall have our cook add more potatoes to my daughter's evening meal."

"You have to eat Leah. Guy will be expecting you to provide him with a child as soon as possible, and for that you will need your health," said her mother.

Leah swallowed the lump in her throat. The thought of sharing Guy's bed made her feel nauseous. She had experienced enough of his hard kisses to know that he was likely to be the only one enjoying sexual activities in their bedroom. Her place was to learn what pleasured a man and then use it in order to seduce other men. All to further her husband's political ambitions.

Mrs. Shepherd brushed a hand over the back of Leah's neck and whispered into her ear. "Just do as he asks, and all will be well. Give him a few children and he will then do as most men do and find his pleasures elsewhere."

Leah rallied and gave her mother a soft smile, but the tired eyes and sunken cheeks staring back at her in the mirror betrayed her deep unhappiness. She turned away for a moment, schooling her features into a socially acceptable bland expression.

Two more weeks of trying to hold her nerves steady would test her resolve to its limit, but she held onto the promise she had made herself at the betrothal party. Amid all the congratulations and warm wishes for the future, she had come to a fateful decision.

The fittings and shopping for the forthcoming wedding would continue. But she would not be marrying Guy. Her inspections of the decorating work underway at Guy's house in Noel Street would go on. But she would not be marrying Guy. She would attend all the 'at homes' and lady's mornings as directed by her mother. But she would not be marrying Guy.

The wedding gown was a stunning piece of elegant artistry. As with their betrothal party, Guy had insisted on his bride wearing a garment which would be the talk of the town. All eyes would be upon her at the wedding; she could just imagine what the guests would think of the opulent statement Guy Dannon was making with his money. Not a penny was being spared on this wedding. And for that Leah was grateful. Some of those pennies were now being directed to another cause. She had saved a coin here and put a farthing away there. Slowly, she was building a secret stash of money. Money she would use to escape.

And day after day, as the wedding drew closer, she repeated over and over again the same words in her mind: *she would not be marrying Guy.*

❧

"How are you today?"

Leah shrugged. Her moods these days vacillated between despair and numbness. She was visiting Claire Radley at Fulham Palace, relieved to have a rare afternoon's respite from her mother.

Mrs. Shepherd had put more planning into her daughter's wedding and new home than Wellington had done to overthrow Napoleon. Why, only yesterday she had spent the better part of the day going from drapery to drapery across London in order to find the perfect curtain fabric which would match the green dining setting. Leah had followed, forcing herself to show the suitable amount of interest when it was required.

Today she could at least walk the grounds of the Bishop of London's home and not have to worry about the minutiae of curtain fabrics and dinner plates. It was a blessed relief.

"I'm just content to be out in the fresh air and away from the whole wedding palaver. Guy has decided that we are to attend a ball or a party every night, right up to the week of the wedding. Between him and my mother, I am utterly exhausted," Leah replied.

Claire gave her a look of sympathy. "I wish there was something I could do to help you. I thought perhaps at the beginning of all this that you were just a little shy of the idea of marrying Guy. But I have come to the realization that you don't want to marry him."

Leah stopped. She turned and looked back toward the main palace building.

Fulham Palace dated back many centuries, with the main structure having been built during the Tudor period. While Leah loved the grand residence, it was the famous walled garden that had won her heart. Privacy and peace could be found among the stunning collection of trees, shrubs, and flowers. Privacy which she now valued.

"Tell me, Claire. Are you serious in wishing to help me or was that just a kindness you offered?" she asked. The last thing she wanted was to put her faith in another of the Radley siblings and have them fail her. She caught the scowl on Claire's face and shook her head. "I should not have asked. Forgive me."

"I am serious. This must be such a trial for you. Leah dearest, I cannot remember the last time I saw you smile," replied Claire.

Over the past weeks, she had kept her own counsel, not daring to trust anyone with her secret. And while Claire Radley was her friend, and a young woman with a mind of her own, it remained to be seen if she could be trusted to help with her plan. There would be a real risk to Claire's reputation if things went awry.

Leah faltered for a moment, unsure of her next step.

Claire, meanwhile, remained close. "If your heart is not in this marriage, then tell me what I can do to help. It is torture watching you suffer. Whatever you need, you only have to ask."

"Give me your hand."

Claire offered her hand and Leah took it in hers. She then placed it over her own heart. A solemn vow between friends.

"If I am discovered, I swear to keep your name out of this. Nothing of my plans will ever be linked to you or your family. I shall take all knowledge of it to my grave. Will you make the same pledge?" she said.

Claire nodded slowly. There was a wariness on her face which gave Leah hope. Her friend understood that the plan was not without danger. Leah was not just experiencing a case of pre-wedding jitters.

"My father is forcing me to marry Guy, but I have decided to run away. I am going to seek refuge with my grandfather, Sir Geoffrey Sydell, in Cornwall. He is the only man I know who is brave enough to take a stand against my father. The only one with the willpower to put a stop to this marriage," confessed Leah.

Sir Geoffrey had long been an outspoken critic of his son-in-law. Something which had eventually seen the end of visits to Mopus Manor by the Shepherd family. It had been over two years since Leah had last been with her grandfather. Her father had forbidden her to write to him in the intervening period; and only the occasional message relayed through family friends had kept her informed of his life and health.

"Alright, so what do you need from me? I will do all I can," said Claire.

Leah sighed. It was such a relief to finally be able to share her plans with someone else. She could trust Claire. Now it just remained as to whether her friend could actually render her any real form of assistance.

Leah knew where the greatest risk lay in her attempt to escape. Keeping it secret from her father and Guy was paramount. "I need money to buy a ticket on the mail coach to Truro. I also need to know exactly where the coach leaves from and at what time. My family and Guy are watching me like hawks. Even the coachman who brought me here today will be questioned as to where we travelled, once I return home," she said.

Claire nodded.

"I have some of my allowance set aside for Christmas gifts. And, of course, I was going to buy you a wedding present. So, I have that money as well. Now don't take this the wrong way, but I must ask, have you thought this through? I mean really thought it through," replied Claire.

Had she thought it through? It was all Leah could think of from the time she woke each morning to the moment she blew out the bedside candle at night. Her whole existence consisted of devising ways she could escape from the clutches of her father and Guy Dannon.

In defying her father, she was risking everything. If she succeeded, there was every chance that he would never let her set foot in her home again—that she would be forever an outcast from her family. Leah had no illusions as to her likely fate. For refusing to yield to his command, Tobias Shepherd would sever all ties with his youngest daughter.

She had considered every possible option that had come to her mind, from the unlikely to the insane. Fleeing to her beloved grandfather was the only one with any real merit. "Believe me, if there were another way out of this marriage, I would take it," replied Leah.

"First thing tomorrow, I am going to make discreet enquiries about the mail coach. It's a good thing James is out of town. I can move about without the worry of him wanting to accompany me. Though we shall have to move fast; he is coming back from Derbyshire early next week in time for the wedding," said Claire.

It was music to her ears to hear that James was still out of town. The last thing she needed was for him to discover her scheme and offer his assistance. Knowing how well his first attempt at helping her had gone, she was better off him not knowing anything about her arrangements.

Because if anyone could throw her plans into disarray, it was James.

Chapter Seventeen

Leah was being careful in whom she placed her trust. For all her kind thoughts and deeds, even Claire was only permitted to know parts of the escape plan. If things did go awry, Leah could not bear the thought of her friend suffering any sort of repercussions that might follow. She was in no doubt that Tobias Shepherd would find a sly way to make even the daughter of the Bishop of London pay for attempting to meddle in his affairs.

"The coach leaves midmorning from the Gloucester Coffee House in Piccadilly. If you are able to make your way there, you will only have to hide for a short period until the coach leaves. The ticket office assured me that the coach to Salisbury is never full so you should have no problems in securing a seat," said Claire.

The two young women were in Leah's bedroom a few days later, allegedly looking at fabric samples for redecorating Guy's house, but in truth they were working on Leah's plans to escape.

Claire handed Leah a copy of the mail coach timetable for the west country. Leah read it; and after having memorized the pertinent details, handed it back to Claire. She couldn't risk her parents discovering it if her father decided to search her room.

The only time she could be certain of making her escape was on the morning of the wedding. While her parents and Guy were inside the vestry at St George's, attending to the final wedding paperwork, she would make her move. She would have to hope that her precise planning and a healthy dose of luck would see her make good on her getaway.

"The time between you leaving the church and when the mail coach departs is the most dangerous. You cannot risk being discovered, so you must disguise yourself as soon as you can after making your way out of St George's. I brought this with me. I thought it would help."

After a quick glance toward the door of Leah's bedroom, Claire looked at the box she had brought with her. She opened the lid.

Inside were the fabric samples and trims which they were supposedly discussing. Claire rummaged around in the box, then pulled out a piece of folded black cloth. She quickly handed it to Leah.

"Hide this somewhere," she said.

Leah frowned. "What is it?"

"One of my mother's old woolen cloaks. I found it in the back of a wardrobe. It has a large hood which you can use to hide your hair and face. People will take less notice of a woman in a black cloak than they will a young woman in a wedding gown," replied Claire.

Leah was momentarily lost for words. It was comforting to know that someone else was trying to help cover all contingencies. She crossed to her bed and lifted the mattress, before stuffing the cloak as far toward the middle of the bed as she could. If her luck held, her maid would not discover it while making up the room.

"Thank you. I shall return it as soon as possible," said Leah.

Claire held out her arms, and the two young women embraced. When Claire pulled back and met Leah's gaze, Leah saw the tight smile which sat on her lips.

"Don't worry about getting the cloak back to me. Just you worry about making it in one piece to Cornwall. Until you are safely at your grandfather's house, you must not take any sort of unavoidable risks. Leah, it is not worth it," replied Claire.

Leah nodded. The wedding was mere days away. Between now and when she arrived at St George's, she had to hold her nerve. "Thank you. Thank you for everything you have done for me. I hope someday I can repay the favor," she said.

Claire smiled. "Your happiness will be all the payment I shall ever need."

Chapter Eighteen

J ames was up just after dawn. As he finished washing and shaving for the day, he stared at his reflection in the mirror. While the man who looked back at him had a smile on his face, inside, he was a just little ashamed of himself.

Every other day so far during his stay at Newhall Castle, he had been reluctant to drag his often hungover self from bed much before the hour of ten. This morning, with the trip to Burton-on-Trent foremost in his mind, he was up and about well before he heard the early morning footsteps of the castle servants.

James's suspicions about Harry's behavior had been proven right, and he took no pleasure in that bitter fact. Harry Menzies had indeed ventured to Newhall Castle in an effort to force Caroline into accepting his suit. To no one's surprise, other than Harry's, she had refused him.

Within hours, a furious Francis had packed Harry and himself back off to London, leaving James to stay on at Newhall Castle as Caroline's chaperone.

Fortunately, Caroline was coping well in the aftermath of Harry's unwelcome marriage proposal and was still insistent that James go and spend time with his friends and his sketchbook. In a serendipitous but happy coincidence, the two Tims had sent word that they would be in town on market day and were eager to meet up with James. A small buzz of what could only be described as excitement sat in his stomach. When was the last time he had felt cheerful about anything?

His box of paints and brushes lay on his bed. He had opened it late the previous night, standing and smiling at them as he'd pictured being able to set brush to canvas and create a new piece of work. The sight of them, along with his sketchbook, made him want to take that giant leap and grasp the future that his heart so desperately craved.

Through the pure luck of having been born into a wealthy family, he had been gifted with the sort of life choices that many others could only dare to dream about. By dithering over making a decision of what he should be doing with his life, he was wasting that gift. It was an insult to all those less fortunate.

He slipped his jacket on and headed for the bedroom door. A hearty breakfast was in order to ward off the winter chill. He had woken with a determined heart; he would go to the woodlands to sketch. Julian's aunt, Lady Margaret, could be asked to stand in his place as chaperone for Caroline. Not that she particularly needed one this far from the prying eyes of London society. And he would only be gone for a day or two.

An hour after breakfast, Julian, Caroline, James, and Lady Margaret set out for the weekly market at Burton-on-Trent. Lady Margaret sat with a happy smile on her face, but both Julian and Caroline appeared more subdued.

There was little conversation in the carriage for the first part of the journey. Guilt over his earlier, at times, taciturn behavior finally spurred James into making a start. "I hope you don't mind me going to see my friends while we are at the market. I must confess that it is purely a selfish thing I am doing in making the trip over to Burton."

Julian waved his concerns away. "I would be a terrible host if I kept you from seeing your friends. Do they live in Burton?"

"No. They are undertaking a series of paintings of the local area. They have a patron who is moving overseas and wishes to take some memories of their home county with them. My friends sent word yesterday informing me that they will be at The Union Inn in the town square this morning," he replied.

Caroline turned from the window and nodded at Julian. "James is a skilled painter in his own right. I am certain that if he was not destined to follow my uncle into the senior ranks of the Church of England, he too would be treading the path of the artist."

"Caroline, did you know that Francis had been interested in some of the smaller paintings from my friends and that he had expressed a desire to purchase one or two of them? He was going to show them to the prince of Wales," asked James.

"Yes."

Her single word reply did not fill him with confidence. He had been hoping that Caroline could shed more light on why Francis had suddenly changed his mind about championing the work of the two Tims to the Prince Regent.

"So, would you know why he changed his mind about buying them? I only ask because he went from being keen on them one day to refusing to discuss anything about them the very next," said James.

Caroline's gaze drifted to him. Her face was not one of happiness. Perhaps she had developed second thoughts about his going off into the wilds to sketch. "I expect Francis has his reasons. He may not appreciate all your friends the same way you do. Just because they are your chums does not mean that they are his, or mine, for that matter," she replied.

While her words were a little cryptic, James was perceptive enough to pick up on the underlying meaning of them. Her remark had him wondering about Timothy Walters. Walters was a member of Caroline's court of admirers. He was another man who appeared to be always at her beck and call at parties. More than once, James had seen him standing close to Harry Menzies as they'd jostled over who was going to present Caroline with her next glass of champagne. If Walters was on the out with Caroline, he had not made mention of it.

Meanwhile, Caroline began to rummage in her reticule. It was another unspoken signal from her. It told him to leave things well alone. He took his cue and let the matter rest. As soon as he got an opportune moment to speak to Caroline alone, he would raise the matter again.

Once they reached Burton-on-Trent, James's thoughts moved to the question of finding his friends. The town was bigger and more crowded than he had expected. Not long after they'd arrived in the main street, they were forced to alight from the carriage. Walking the short distance into the town square, they were greeted with the sight of row upon row of market stalls, all selling local produce.

"I didn't realize it would be this big," James said, taking in the view. He chanced a glance at Caroline, but she was looking elsewhere. He noticed a subtle change in her black mood. She had gone from being quiet and distracted, to being on edge.

Julian pointed toward a small double-story public house which stood on the corner of the square. A sign was hanging above the doorway of the whitewashed building. The Union Inn.

He turned back to Julian who, after looking briefly in Caroline's direction, nodded toward the tavern. His message was clear; Caroline would be safe with him and Lady Margaret. James hesitated, torn between his need to support his cousin and the burning desire to seize his future.

He took hold of Caroline's arm and she looked up at him. The sadness in her eyes was heartbreaking.

"There is The Union Inn. Are you still alright for me to go and see my friends?" he said.

Caroline muttered a low, "Yes. You need to do this, James."

"Caroline will be fine with Lady Margaret and myself. There is plenty to see and do here at the market," said Julian.

"Thank you. I shan't be long," said James. With more haste than he knew was polite, he made a hurried dash across the square.

He would gauge Caroline's mood once he returned, and if she was still amenable to his spending a day or so with his friends in the wilds of Derbyshire, he would leave Burton with the two Tims rather than return to Newhall Castle. In the meantime, he could only hope that

Julian was able to work his magic and bring Caroline out of her funk. But as soon as he opened the door of the inn and saw his friends waiting for him, all doubt fled.

By day's end, he would be somewhere in the Marchington Woodlands.

Chapter Nineteen

James hadn't counted on the bitter, biting wind which greeted him upon arrival in the Marchington Woodlands. The tiny stone cottage which his friends occupied had an even smaller fireplace than the one in their attic in London. It didn't take him long to understand why neither of his friends removed their coats even when they were inside.

"I thought all those Christmases and New Year's at Strathmore Castle in Scotland would have hardened me up for this, but I must confess—I am absolutely freezing," he said.

Smith chuckled. "I take it Newhall and his drafty castle don't seem as bad as you thought now?"

"No. Actually it has been a good stay. Newhall, it turns out, is quite a decent chap. His home is warm and inviting. I shall be loath to leave when the time comes," he replied.

Walters frowned. There had been an awkward meeting between the two parties in the middle of the market at Burton. Upon seeing Caroline, Timothy Walters had pushed Julian aside before gushing and fawning over Caroline. She had not seemed the least bit happy to see Walters. James had felt embarrassed for both his cousin and his friend.

"How long is Caroline staying at Newhall Castle? Perhaps we could all travel over to visit. We didn't get much of an opportunity to spend time with her today," said Walters.

Out of the corner of his eye, James caught the slight shake of Smith's head and a silently mouthed "no." He gave a touch of a nod in reply.

"Lord Newhall may not take kindly to unannounced visitors. Radley, how about you and I go and get some more wood for the fire? I think tonight is going to be a cold one," said Smith.

As soon as the two of them were outside, Smith took hold of James's arm and pulled him close. He looked back to the door of the cottage, but their mutual friend remained inside.

"You need to keep him away from your cousin. He has it set in his mind to marry her. He ignored her wishes and went to see her father. Charles Saunders rightly refused him, but Walters did not take it well. She is all he ever talks about. And from the look on Newhall's face today, I was left with the distinct impression that Caroline is about to become the next Countess Newhall," said Smith.

The pieces of the puzzle now fell into place for James. Little wonder Francis had backed out of getting the Prince Regent to buy any of the two Tims' paintings. If Timothy Walters was an unwelcome suitor for his sister, Francis was not going to want to have anything to do with them.

What was it with some men? Here was yet another stubborn male who had decided that what he wanted carried more weight than the stated wishes of a young woman. First Guy, then Harry, now Timothy.

At least Caroline had the support of her family when it came to suitors. Unlike Leah, she would not be pressured into marrying a man she did not love.

"Thank you. It explains a lot, replied James.

Smith bent and picked up a log, then piled several more into his arms. James followed suit. It would look odd if they returned to the cottage empty-handed.

When they were inside, he didn't say anything to Walters about what Smith had revealed regarding Caroline, and he was careful not to make mention of her again. A headache threatened just at the prospect of yet another male trying to force his marital intentions on a young woman against her wishes.

His thoughts turned to Leah. He quickly chided himself for his selfishness. An awkward conversion with Smith and a headache was nothing compared to what she was facing.

He grabbed his sketchbook and headed back outside, hopeful that the cold, clear air would be a balm for his worried mind.

After an earlier walk through the woods and down to the nearby river, James had decided that he would attempt to create two distinct, but thematically linked landscape paintings. The trees which overhung the water provided the perfect backdrop for his first landscape, while the woodland canopy behind the cottage would give him the framework, he needed for the second.

The *Derbyshire Twins*, as he'd named them, would form the main pieces in his portfolio. Two large paintings designed to be hung in the same space, thus, giving the illusion of the viewer standing within the woodlands themselves. He had never attempted to paint anything on this scale before, but he knew preliminary sketches were vital.

After taking a seat by the edge of the water, he began to create his own version of the landscape which he saw before him. His sketches would not be exact replicas of the place. He would use them as the inspiration for his creations. Once he had the composition clear, he would then stand before an easel and seek to put the light and balance he saw in his mind's eye onto canvas.

It was late by the time he finally closed his sketchbook. In the fading light of the afternoon, he returned through the woods to the cottage. In the book were pages of partially drawn trees and the swirling waters of the river. They were rough impressions; only half complete. But in his heart, James knew he now had what it would take to make those sketches come alive.

James slept on a short, narrow bed for the night. The two Tims had been left to share the other bed, which from the grumbles he heard, was not the most comfortable of arrangements.

Not wishing to overstay his welcome, he rose as soon as the sun was up and stoked the fire. He had slept fully clothed, the cottage being little more than four thin walls against the might of the winter winds.

Today he would continue to work on more of the sketches from the previous day. He opened his sketchbook and checked his drawings, nodding his pleasure at how well things were progressing.

Walters wandered out from the bedroom, his hair, and clothes in post-sleep disarray. He came and stood next to James watching as he turned the pages of the sketchbook. When James got to the work which he had started the previous afternoon, he stopped.

"What do you think of these? I am planning to paint two large landscapes," said James.

"I like what you have done so far. There is a nice symmetry about the rough outlines. I can just imagine what the two of them would look like hanging side by side as completed paintings. Though you may need more time to fully develop the pieces," he said, tapping his finger on the page.

James considered the sketches. Walters was right. They were a long way from being finished. With Guy and Leah's wedding taking place soon, he wouldn't have time to finish them before he had to return to London.

Perhaps a return trip to Derbyshire was in order. Being away from London was not such a bad thing. While he thought constantly about Leah, he knew there was nothing he could do about the impending wedding. At least through his art, he could do something to mold his future into one that was his own. If he was able to focus his time and energy into bringing the *Derbyshire Twins* to life, he might be able to make himself enough of a name to carve out his own place in the world of English painters.

Still, a small voice of doubt whispered in his mind. Was he good enough?

"Do you really think I could do this? I mean, make a career out of my painting. I am just not sure if I have enough talent to succeed. Please be honest with me. Am I good or am I deluding myself?" replied James.

Walters raked his fingers through his tussled hair. "James, you have more talent in your little finger than I do in the whole of my body. You need to get these sketches finished, and then get painting. You live in a bloody palace so you should be able to find a room which you can commandeer for your work."

Fulham Palace had plenty of rooms in which James could paint. And if his father did not allow it, then he could rent rooms in town. The money he earned from working at his uncle's shipping office would be enough to keep the proverbial wolf from the door while he established his career. He could do this, but he would need his father's approval. He also wanted Hugh's support.

"So, what you are saying is that I need to stop dithering and go and paint?"

Smith appeared from the door of the bedroom and wandered over to stand alongside them. He looked down at the sketches and nodded. "Have we managed to convince you yet? If not, I don't know what else we can do. James you could be one of the greats of English landscape painting. You just have to stop listening to your father and start listening to yourself," he said.

A grin which felt a mile wide formed on James's lips. His heart swelled at the thought of what he could accomplish. He then made a decision. He would spend today putting the finishing touches to the preliminary sketches, then head back to Newhall Castle and tell Caroline that they were leaving for London.

"Yes, you are right. I've ignored my own instincts for too long. I have to tell my father that I will not be following him into the church. This is my life, and I am going to be a painter."

His friends slapped him vigorously on the back.

"About bloody time, James," said Smith.

Chapter Twenty

A matter of days later, James found himself standing on the seashore at Brighton having just witnessed Julian and Caroline's wedding. After sharing a celebratory glass of champagne, the madly-in-love newlyweds had abandoned the rest of the small wedding party and gone back across the road to their hotel. Francis had polished off most of a bottle of his father's best champagne and was snoozing on the beach.

James had rolled up his trousers and was now seated next to his father on the soft sand. He had spent the best part of the last hour staring out to sea, trying to think of the right words.

On the journey home from Derbyshire, he had composed a suitably compelling speech to present to his father. He had a list of good reasons why he did not intend to go back to university, nor to follow Hugh into the Church of England. But as he looked across at his father, he knew he didn't need a grand speech.

"I made a decision while I was in Derbyshire. I want to pursue a full-time career as a painter. I know if it came down to it, that the final choice would be mine, but it would mean the world to me if you would give me your blessing."

James watched as Hugh's shoulders slumped. He knew he had

disappointed his father, finally putting an end to his long-held dream of his son following him into the church, but James was at peace with his decision.

Hugh looked up at him. A soft smile sat on his lips as he nodded. "You have my blessing, but it does come with a proviso. Your mother and I will support you financially for the next six months. But if you have not succeeded in selling a single painting by the end of March, and I don't mean to family and friends, then you agree to go back to Cambridge next autumn and complete your degree. After that, we can discuss other career options outside of the church."

James considered the offer for a moment. If his father supported him financially for the next six months, he would have time to complete not only the two large *Derbyshire Twins*, but also a number of smaller works. Having money would mean he did not need to work for Charles Saunders during the day. He could invest all his time and energy into his painting. It was a tempting offer. Very tempting.

He decided to push his luck. "Would that offer also extend to me being able to go back to Derbyshire to work for some of that time? It would help me to complete my current pieces."

His early sketches were a long way to being finished. And there was something about being able to absorb the light and color of the landscape which he knew he would not be able to do if he tried to complete the major paintings while based in London.

"Yes, alright, I understand. The Lord says that a good shepherd is one who gets out among his flock. I expect a painter needs to see the landscape if he is going to paint," replied Hugh.

James blinked back tears. "Thank you. I really appreciate your support. I know this is not what you had in mind for me, but I need to at least try and make this work. If I fail, I promise it won't be through lack of effort."

Hugh placed a hand on his shoulder. "I have never doubted your work ethic, James. I had just hoped that someday you and I would be able to work alongside one another. I realize now that perhaps I need to let the Lord do his work and not stand in your way."

"I am sorry that I have not been able to find the same passion for the church that you have, but I hope that through my painting I can show the beauty of God's creation. You have a gift for reaching people through your sermons, while I believe I can speak to them with art. And I hope that is enough for you," James said earnestly.

"Whatever you do will be enough for your mother and me. We are always proud of you. Now, be a good lad and go and retrieve that bottle of champagne from Francis. You and I have something to celebrate."

James collected the half-empty bottle from beside his sleeping cousin. He handed it to his father. He knew he should be overjoyed at being given the opportunity to pursue his life's passion, but as he watched Hugh drink from the bottle, James felt a sense of emptiness inside.

Leah and Guy's wedding was a matter of five days away. While he had been granted the chance to change his own future, the woman he loved was still fated to marry the wrong man.

Knowing the miserable future which lay ahead for Leah, James's victory suddenly felt bitter and hollow.

Chapter Twenty-One

J ames raced downstairs from his room at Fulham Palace. He had a long list of errands to complete this morning. Guy and Leah's wedding was only a day away, and as best man. he had a celebratory party to organize for this evening. Out of respect for the bride, he had decided that while it would be a drunken mess of a stag party; it would not be the debauched orgy that Guy had requested.

Stepping out into the main courtyard of the palace, he saw a carriage drawn up to one side. Visitors were always coming and going from Fulham Palace, so James didn't pay it much notice at first. But when he saw the face of the young woman who alighted from the carriage, all thoughts of his plans for the day vanished.

It was Leah.

He swayed on his feet. If he had thought that a little time and distance would cool his ardor for her, his heart swiftly told him otherwise.

Her head lifted and their gazes met. Despair punched him hard in the chest. He took a faltering step back. Instead of the loving smile that she had always gifted him in his lustful dreams of her, the real Leah gave him barely a scant nod.

He hurried over, hoping to catch at least a moment alone with her before Claire appeared from the family residence.

He bowed. "Miss Shepherd, how lovely to see you again."

At this close distance, he got a better look at Leah, and what he saw filled him with dismay.

In the time since he had last seen her, she had lost a considerable amount of weight. Her cheeks were slightly sunken. The delightful curves which had set his teeth on edge at the garden party were now almost gone. She barely made an impression on the bustline of her gown. Just how much weight she had lost since the betrothal party he feared to guess. Leah was only a pound or so away from becoming a wraith.

"Mister Radley. I see you are returned from Derbyshire," she replied.

The sadness in her eyes nearly brought him undone. His heart protested. This would not do; he couldn't just stand there and make polite conversation with Leah, knowing that it might well be the last chance he got to speak to her before the wedding.

"Yes, I returned a few days ago. I am sorry I have not seen you since then." He stood for a moment, struggling to find the right words to say. This encounter was so confronting, so bloody awful. When she went to step past him, James reached out and took a hold of Leah's arm. "Whatever I can do for you in the future, you only have to ask."

She looked down at his hand and frowned. Her body language told him his touch was unwelcome. "Why would I need your help, James? I shall have a husband this time tomorrow. He shall provide for me. Now kindly remove your hand."

The sound of footsteps on the stone path had him looking back toward the front door. Claire was making her way over to them. He frowned at the less than happy look on his sister's face.

He leaned in close. "I know this marriage is going to be a trial for you. So please, Leah, let me be your friend. When it comes to Guy, I could try and intercede on your behalf."

She shook her head slowly.

"I hardly think Guy will thank you for attempting to meddle in our marriage. He has already told me he does not trust you when it comes to me, so I would suggest that there is little chance of him listening to your counsel even if you chose to offer it. Thank you, James, but once again you have fallen short when it comes to playing at being my hero."

Claire came and stood by his side, she glared at him. "James is there something you need? If not then please leave Leah alone, she is not here to see you."

He stirred from his sister's harsh rebuff and muttered, "No. I was just saying hello."

"Good. Come on, Leah. We have things to do. Say goodbye, James," said Claire. His sister slipped her arm into Leah's and they began to walk away, no doubt headed for the comfortable sitting room upstairs to discuss final wedding preparations.

James stood and watched them. Leah might be putting on a brave face for her impending nuptials, but the way she barely fit her clothes spoke volumes for her state of mind. Even her manner of walking was stilted.

But it was her final heartbreaking words which threatened to bring James to his knees. Leah no longer cared to hear what he had to say. She had resigned herself to her fate.

He was not her hero.

Chapter Twenty-Two

The icy midnight air greeted Leah as she opened the door leading into the rear garden of her family home. She wrapped her shawl around her before giving one last furtive glance back toward the main entrance. She was alone. With her travel bag in one hand and a small lantern in the other, she stole out into the darkness.

Her family had kept a close eye on her the past few days; she was rarely left alone. While she had made every effort not to show any sign of her reluctance to marry Guy Dannon, she knew her father would not be taking chances. There would be no sudden crying off on her part.

Not for the first time did she send a prayer of thanks to heaven for having confided in Claire Radley. Leah had continued to recite the schedule for all mail coaches leaving for the west country over the past few days, hoping she had memorized it correctly.

In the bag, there was a small coin purse with enough money in it for her to be able to buy a ticket through to Truro. The extent of the coins she and Claire had managed to cobble together would permit her to purchase one meal a day en route. The journey west would be a trying one, but she was prepared to endure anything rather than marry Guy.

Leah barely fit any of her clothes now, the stress of the past weeks having seen her struggle to keep food down. Guy's only comment about her rapid weight loss was to coldly remind her that she had better have enough energy for their wedding night. The thought made Leah feel ill.

As soon as she reached her grandfather, she would make herself at home in the kitchen and not leave until his cook had fattened her back up to a normal size. She *must* reach Sir Geoffrey's home in Cornwall.

Now on the eve of her wedding, hiding in the dark of the garden, she faced down her fears. What if her family suspected she was attempting to run? What if her mother decided she needed to stay close to her daughter on the morning of the wedding? And what if her father . . . no. She had to put those thoughts to the back of her mind. She had to trust herself and her determination not to accept the fate they had chosen for her. She could do this. The price of failure was unthinkable.

Hidden by the black shadows of the house, she made her way over to the small potting shed. It was situated just inside the garden gate which led from the rear laneway into the mews and stables. The Shepherd family gardener and his assistant were the only people who ever set foot inside the brick and stone building.

There was a gentle creak of hinges as she pushed the door open. In the still night air, the noise was enough to set her nerves on edge. She prayed the stable boy, who slept upstairs in the nearby loft, was a sound sleeper. Her being caught in the garden at this hour with a travel bag in hand would take more than a little explaining.

She set the lantern on the floor and lay the shawl over the top of the glass. It gave only the barest of light for her work, but she dared not risk making it any brighter.

The travel bag fitted neatly beneath the potting bench. She pushed it farther under the bench, tucking it out of sight. The bag contained a few old items of clothing she had stolen out of the house including a pair of sturdy boots, and some small personal possessions which she could not bear to part with. She couldn't risk attempting to take any of her new clothes with her. Her mother would no doubt notice their absence.

The three plain day-gowns she had retrieved from under the mattress of her bed were warm and functional, perfect for the chill sea winds of Cornwall. At the top of the bag lay that last, vital piece of clothing: Mary Radley's long black woolen cloak with a fitted hood. If she did indeed make it all the way to her grandfather's house, Claire's help would have played an important part in her success.

Timing was one thing she had to control in her plans to escape, but deception was just as crucial. The cloak would help her to hide from her family until she was safely on board the coach and headed out of London.

Her heart raced. She stood and looked at the potting bench; the bag was well out of sight. She took in a slow, calming breath. Tomorrow, she would need steady nerves and a clear mind.

"You can do this Leah," she whispered.

The sound of boots shuffling on the stone step outside the kitchen had her dropping quickly to her knees. She pulled open the glass door of the lantern and blew out the candle. The potting shed was immediately thrown into darkness.

She poked her head out the door and saw that the family cook had taken a spot on the top step at the back door. Leah knew that if the woman was true to habit, she would be holding a roughly rolled fag in her hand, having lit it over the kitchen stove. As the cook lifted her hand to her face, Leah's suspicions were confirmed. Apart from the hint of the moon from behind some thick clouds, the golden glow of the burning tobacco was the only source of light in the gloomy garden.

Damn.

Leah sat back and drew her knees up to her chest. She wrapped her shawl once more about her and waited. Much as she was freezing in her thin nightgown and woolen shawl, she dared not make a move. She had been patient up to this point, everything diligently prepared. Now was not the time to lose her nerve.

Come tomorrow, if her luck held, all the plans that she and Claire had so carefully put together would come to fruition. All that she had suffered at the hands of her father and Guy Dannon over the past few weeks would have been worth it.

She refused to even consider what would become of her if she failed.

Chapter Twenty-Three

J ames threw the last of his shirts into his travel trunk before closing it up. He had packed the warmest of his shirts, jackets, and trousers. Derbyshire had been cold enough when he left, but with winter now closing in, he knew it would be freezing.

He packed up his paintbrushes and put them carefully into their travel box. After treating himself to a visit to Ackermann's on the Strand the previous day, he was in possession of fresh oil paints. The paints were wrapped in their pig's bladders and stored in an airtight tin at the bottom of his travel trunk. As soon as he got to Burton-on-Trent, he would seek out rooms which were large enough to accommodate the easels and canvasses of his planned *Derbyshire Twins*.

Whenever he needed to check on the colors and shading of the landscapes, he would make the trip back out to the Marchington Woodlands before returning to his room to paint. The awkward situation with regard to Timothy Walters and Caroline had made him decide on not staying a second time with the two Tims in their tiny cottage.

After standing up as best man for Guy while he married Leah, James knew he was going to need every calming balm under heaven to ease his troubled soul. He had to get away. The look of hopelessness on

Leah's face, and the sight of her gaunt figure when she'd stood in the courtyard at Fulham Palace, had haunted his dreams during what little sleep he had managed to get after returning home from Guy's stag party in the early hours.

"Get through the service, then out the front door," he muttered.

After the previous evening of saluting his best friend and wishing him every happiness with his new bride—all the while fighting the nearly overwhelming urge to punch Guy in the face—James knew he did not have the strength to maintain his composure for the wedding breakfast. The sight of the best man in tears while the groom made his thank you speech would raise too many uncomfortable questions.

The one saving grace this morning was that the rest of the Radley family had left early for the wedding. His mother and sisters had accompanied his father into town. The Bishop of London was due to conduct the wedding service at St George's.

Time alone at home was a precious respite for James before the impending agony of the wedding.

"Yes, just get through the service."

By the time he left the house, those words were constantly on his lips. The more he said them, the more he hoped they would help to keep his emotions in check.

Standing next to the groom at the front of the church would mean he was in the center of much of the attention. He owed it to Guy not to reveal his true feelings in front of several hundred guests. He also owed it to Leah not to make what he could only imagine would be the worst day of her life any more difficult. Neither he nor Leah wanted this wedding, but both were bound by social expectations and commitments.

His sudden disappearance from London immediately following the marriage service would be a touch awkward to explain. Hopefully Guy would be too concerned with securing his preselection for parliament to give much thought to the odd timing of James's departure for Derbyshire.

He promised himself that once he was back in London, he would see how things were settling between Leah and Guy before deciding on how best he could support her. If what she had said was right, and

Guy no longer trusted him around her, he would have to tread carefully.

He sighed. Why did loving someone have to be so damn hard and life so bloody complicated? In another lifetime, they would have met, fallen in love, and married. They would have been happy. Leah would have been his. And in that other life, he knew she would have loved him.

"Oh, don't be a fool, James. There is nothing you can do to stop this wedding. Just get on with. Get through the service, then leave," he muttered.

After one last check of his jacket and bronze-colored waistcoat, he picked up his travel bag and headed downstairs. In his luggage was a hip flask full of the finest French brandy from one of his Uncle Charles's recent shipments. The travel trunk was already loaded onto the roof of the coach. Everything was in readiness for his swift departure from town.

After the wedding, he intended to make short work of the contents of the hip flask, then get started on the first of the three bottles of brandy he had stowed inside the travel coach. The bottom of a brandy bottle seemed a very good place for him to be right now.

By the time the coach did leave the cobbled streets of London and make its way onto the Great North Road, he intended to be well into that first bottle and on his way to drunken oblivion.

After climbing aboard the coach, he checked his pockets. He had enough money from his father to last a good month in Derbyshire. The next few weeks, he would concentrate his time and efforts on getting the *Derbyshire Twins* underway, then he would return to London and speak privately to Leah and make sure she was alright. When it came to be helping her, James was powerless. He could at least offer her a sympathetic ear.

The journey from Fulham Palace to St George's Church should have taken less than an hour, but James was in no particular hurry this day. Several times he rapped on the roof of the travel coach and asked for the driver to slow down. He knew it was foolish of him to try and delay the inevitable, but still, he did.

The coach was travelling at little more than a snail's pace when it finally drew up outside the front of the church in St George Street. His heart was beating so hard in his chest that he was tempted to ask the driver to take a second turn around the block while he tried to calm himself. He looked down at his hand. It was shaking. He curled it into a tight fist.

"For God's sake, man, pull yourself together," he muttered.

Time and tide waited for no man. The wedding would be going ahead whether he made it up the front steps or not. It was poor form for the best man to be late, which he was, and today of all days he did not want to test anyone's patience.

With one last resigned sigh, he opened the coach door and stepped out. He lifted his gaze to the driver and his mate who were seated on the top of the coach.

"I won't be more than an hour. Then we can start the journey north. And I promise that when we leave, you can set the pace," he said.

The two men gave a tip of their hats in reply. James was grateful for the patience of long-time family servants. The men knew him well enough to accept him and his odd foibles.

He clenched his fist once more and gave a small pump in the air. He could do this; he owed it to his father not to make a scene in the church.

After a quick look left and right, he dashed across St George Street and turned left, heading in the direction of the entrance to the church. He had just set foot on the pavement when a flash of white caught his eye.

Down the church steps raced a figure dressed all in white, a large bouquet of white lilies in her hand. As she reached the bottom of the steps, she stopped and threw the flowers back in the direction from where she had come. A hand reached up and ripped the coronet of flowers from her pale fair hair. She tossed it after the bouquet. Then, picking up her skirts, she fled down St George Street.

For a moment James stood rooted to the spot, his mind struggling to process what his eyes had just witnessed. His feet started moving before he had a chance to think. He broke into a full run. "Leah!"

Stepping into the street, she hailed a hack and after opening the door, leapt inside. As soon as the door had closed, the driver sped away, not sparing the horses.

Wedding guests raced out of the church. Fortunately, Guy was not one of them. When he caught the eye of one of the other guests, James quickly pointed in the opposite direction to the one Leah had taken. He held his breath, praying that his misdirection worked.

"Thank god," he muttered, as several male guests ran off up St George Street.

James turned and waved wildly to the driver of his travel coach. He was not going to wait for Guy Dannon or Tobias Shepherd to appear out the front door too. As best man, they would expect him to go chasing after the bride. While, he fully intended to do just that, James was also determined that he would be the only one following in the direction that Leah had taken.

Fortunately for him, the driver and his mate were still seated on the top of the coach. They had witnessed the whole scene. The driver flicked the reins and the coach started forward. James ran up alongside and grabbed hold of the door.

"Follow that hack, and don't lose it!" he bellowed.

He swung up into the coach and slammed the door behind him. Then, pulling the glass window down, he put his head out, watching as the hack in front turned into Little Brooke Street. He gripped tightly onto the doorframe as the coach tilted when it followed the hack into a sharp right turn at New Bond Street.

"Hurry!" he cried.

Where are you going, Leah? Where are you going?

They met a body of traffic as they reached the main thoroughfare at Oxford Street. The coach stopped, waiting for a gap in the flow of carriages and coaches, before it could make the turn. The hack, which was a smaller and nimbler vehicle, made it around without any trouble. James screwed up his face in frustration. He was going to lose her. "Fuck!"

When his coach was finally able to turn onto Oxford Street, the hack containing Leah was already out of sight. A panicked James was forced to risk a throw of the dice.

"Duke Street! Turn left at Duke Street!" he cried.

If Leah was attempting to flee her own wedding, there was every chance she was headed for home. It wasn't the best place for her to go, but he doubted she had many other options. He had to trust to his instincts. He could only pray they were right.

As the coach pulled up out the front of the Shepherd family home in Duke Street, James slapped himself on the head. Of course, she wouldn't have gone to the front door.

"The laneway! Try around at the back of the house."

His heart was beating a thousand miles an hour in his chest. His mouth was dry with the rush of adrenaline as it coursed through his body.

As his coach pulled into the rear laneway, James caught a glimpse of Leah climbing back into the hack. She had a brown travel bag in her hand.

He pulled his head back inside the coach. From the look of it, she had not seen him. The hack now pulled away from the rear of the Shepherds' house at a more sedate pace. He turned and looked out the rear window of the coach. No one else was following. He was the only one in pursuit.

They followed the hack down to Piccadilly, where it pulled into the courtyard of the Gloucester Coffee House.

"Where are you going?" he muttered.

The Radley family travel coach slowed and pulled in a little way behind the hack. James waited. He did not wish to startle his quarry.

He delayed stepping from the coach until Leah had climbed out of the hack and walked toward the door of the coffee house. He sighed with relief when she didn't look back. If she had, she would have seen the Strathmore crest emblazoned on the side of his coach. The game would have been up.

After she had gone inside, James took the opportunity to check the mews. The coffee house was a well-known staging place for the mail coaches travelling to the west country of England. Next to the stables at the back of the building stood one solitary mail coach. It was being loaded with boxes and bags.

The driver from his own coach climbed down and hurried over to James.

"If that young lady is doing a flit, then it looks like she is taking that coach. It is the only coach ready to leave the yard. The other mail coaches usually go late at night so that the mail can be delivered early in the morning. Do you want me to go inside and take a look?" he said.

All of James's plans to go to Derbyshire and take up his new career as a painter came to a sudden halt. Before him stood his very last chance to come to Leah's aid, to show her what she really meant to him.

She may well have succeeded in fleeing the church, but she was now alone. And she was still in great danger. Any moment now, someone could come into the yard looking for her. And if that someone was Tobias Shepherd, he would seize his daughter and drag her back to the church. Her father would force her to marry a man she detested.

Here and now, James would do what he should have done all along. He would stand up for the woman he loved. He would protect her. Today, he would become the hero she needed.

Nothing else mattered.

James nodded. It was too great a risk for him to venture inside. It was critical at this moment for him to be slow and steady with his moves. Leah had to think she had escaped undetected, all the while he would be standing guard just in case one of her family members came looking for her.

He dug into his coat pocket and pulled out his leather coin pouch, handing it over to the coach driver.

"If you can find out where Miss Shepherd is travelling to and then purchase me a ticket for the same coach trip, I would be most grateful. Your discretion, of course, would be appreciated," he said.

The driver raised an eyebrow, then nodded.

At that moment, the trip to Derbyshire evaporated.

While the driver headed inside, James and the driver's mate pulled his travel trunk down from the roof of the Radley family coach. They set it down on the other side of the coach out of sight. If Leah did happen to come back outside, James did not want her to spot his trunk also with its Strathmore coat of arms emblazoned on the side.

With the collar of his coat turned up to hide his face, James stood in front of the door of the coach and covered the Strathmore crest from view.

The driver returned within a few minutes. "She is booked on the Salisbury mail coach, which is the one over there," he said, nodding in the direction of the partially laden coach. He handed James a ticket and his coin purse. "That was the last ticket. The coach leaves at the quarter of the hour, so we had better hurry if we are to get your things onboard without the young lady seeing you."

James grabbed his travel bag, while the driver and his mate hauled his travel trunk across to the Salisbury mail coach. Once his luggage was lifted onto the roof, the next problem presented itself. How to get onboard the coach and keep his identity secret from Leah for as long as possible. She had to think she had made clean her escape. Only then could he confront her and get to the bottom of what was going on. To help her with her plans.

"Could you please take the coach back to Fulham Palace and when my father returns home, let him know that I have had a change of plans. I must find out what is happening with regard to Miss Shepherd. I fear she is in grave danger."

He quietly slipped both men a handful of coins. They were well enough paid by his father, but he wanted to thank them personally for helping him. No one made mention that he was also buying their silence.

With the Radley family coach now gone, James climbed aboard the Salisbury mail coach. There was little to reveal his identity with the collar of his coat turned up, a scarf wrapped around his head, topped off with his hat, and finally a book strategically placed in front of his face. He would just have to pray that Leah was too busy with her own concerns to be bothered attempting to make small talk with the other passengers. If she was half as clever as he hoped she was, she would be endeavoring to keep a very low profile.

In the meantime, he would wait. Keeping her safe from a distance. Then once they were far enough away from London, he would remove his disguise.

James continually checked his pocket watch as he waited for Leah to arrive with the rest of the passengers and board the mail coach. His hand nervously tapped out a fierce beat on his knee. Time seemed to pass at an endless, slow pace. Every second that ticked by, he kept a watchful eye on the entrance to the yard. If Tobias Shepherd or Guy Dannon suddenly appeared, James was ready to leap out of the coach and race to Leah's side.

His friendship with Guy had once been important to him, but now, protecting Leah was his everything.

Chapter Twenty-Four

L eah sat quietly in the passenger waiting room of the Gloucester Coffee House, her head lowered but her gaze fixed firmly on the door. Mary Radley's cloak covered her fair hair and wedding gown.

Every time the little bell above the door tinkled as it opened, she gave a start. Until she was safely on board the mail coach and bound for Salisbury, there was the real chance that someone from her family would come looking for her.

Knowing Guy and his truculent pride, she doubted he would lower himself to the grubby task of hunting down his wayward fiancée and trying to convince her to marry him. He would leave that up to her father. And if Tobias Shepherd did indeed march through the door, it would be with the sole intent of finding his daughter, dragging her out of the coffee house, and hauling her back to St George's church, where he would then stand over her and make certain she signed the wedding register.

Her hopes now lay in the false clues she had left behind at the family home. She prayed that they would be enough to throw her father off the scent and have him looking elsewhere while she made her initial escape. Her luck just had to hold; she remained hidden from view in an out-of-the-way corner of the room just in case it didn't.

When the driver for the mail coach came inside the waiting room and rang his hand bell, crying, "All aboard for the Salisbury coach!" Leah could have wept. She slowly rose from the long wooden waiting room bench, careful not to make any sudden movements lest she attract unwanted attention.

With the cloak still covering much of her head, she followed the three other Salisbury-bound passengers outside into the yard. Her steps were measured and unhurried. Her group of fellow passengers consisted of an elderly couple who seemed more concerned about the box of cakes they were carrying than actually speaking to anyone else, and a young naval officer who had been busy studying a book of naval flag signals while he sat inside the coffee house. Leah was pleased; they seemed the perfect passengers to her mind. All three were busy with their own concerns and therefore unlikely to remember a young woman in a black cloak who kept to herself.

When she caught sight of the mail coach standing in the yard, her heart sank. It was a very small coach. Boxes and trunks were piled high on its roof. She had travelled some distance from London in her life, but usually it was in a private travel coach with room to spare. With four passengers onboard, it was going to be a very cramped journey to the west country. She quietly consoled herself. If she could make it all the way to her grandfather's estate, the discomfort would be well worth it.

Climbing aboard, she noted a fifth passenger was already seated. The unexpected presence of another body in the small space had her flinching as she stepped inside. Her nerves were still very much on edge.

This new passenger had claimed the nearest corner on the left-hand side of the coach and had his nose already firmly in a book. He made no sign of acknowledging the other passengers as they took up their respective seats. Instinctively, Leah headed for the corner diagonally opposite to him and took her own seat. Drawing the hood of her cloak fully down over her face, she made it look as if she was intending to go to sleep.

While the mail coach driver and his mate busied themselves with tying down the last of the load, Leah sat quietly, taking in long, slow breaths. When the coach finally pulled out of the yard and turned onto Piccadilly, she put a hand to her face and wiped away a tear. The constant fear and self-doubt she had endured over the past weeks now fell away. In their place now sat quiet determination.

She had done it.

Chapter Twenty-Five

Trying to remain incognito and spy on Leah at the same time was proving more difficult than James had first imagined. The cramped conditions in the mail coach didn't help matters. They were seated a matter of feet away from one another—too close for a casual study of her.

The young naval officer who sat shoulder to shoulder with James looked up and around the carriage every so often before going back to his study of naval signals. James was grateful that he did not attempt to engage him in conversation.

When his arm eventually tired from holding the book up in front of his face, James pulled his hat down as far as he could in order to maintain his disguise. He ventured a sneak peek at Leah at one point, but she still had the hood of her cloak drawn over her face. It was like they were both playing a game of hide and seek.

His nerves remained on edge. His brain constantly churned with the question of not why she had fled the wedding—he could easily answer that one—but where she was headed. From the moment he had seen her flee the church and leap into the waiting carriage, it was clear to him that Leah had a plan in place.

He wanted to help her with that plan. But in order to do so, he had to find a way to gain her trust and get her to bring him into her confidence. That was easier said than done. He had already failed her once before.

The Salisbury-bound coach stopped briefly several times on the way out of greater London, picking up and offloading parcels and letters. Each time, the passengers remained onboard. At the call of each stop, James made a mental note of how far they were from London.

At some point, they would be far enough that he could risk revealing his identity. But as the miles grew, he remained hidden, unsure of what he should say to Leah when he eventually approached her.

In the wildest of his imaginings, he had never thought he would experience this. Had never thought that his prayers for a miracle to help change her future would actually be answered.

A good fifteen miles from London, the coach stopped to change horses. The passengers all alighted. Some of the little group went in to the nearby coaching inn and availed themselves of the facilities.

James bought himself a hot beef pie and a small tankard of ale while keeping an eye out for any sign of Leah venturing in from the stable yard. From the window, he could see her standing close to the coach, her cloak still covering most of her face. She boarded the coach as soon as the fresh horses had been hitched into place. She wasn't taking any unnecessary risks.

He was proud of her for having planned beyond the mere detail of buying a coach ticket. It was obvious that she had put some thought into the problem of where dangers still lurked even this far from London. If she ventured into the coaching inn, people would see her. And if someone was to enquire, the people who worked at the coaching inn might even recall seeing a young woman in a long black cloak who appeared to be travelling on her own. They may even remember which mail coach she had been a passenger onboard, and where it was headed.

Finally, at Basingstoke, some fifty miles west of London, James decided it was time he spoke to Leah. He would have been content to have remained hidden for a few more miles. The greater the distance from London, the less chance she would panic and flee from him. But the worry that she had not appeared to have eaten or drunk anything since they left town some eight hours earlier now gave him cause for concern.

The mail coach pulled into the mews of the main coaching inn at Basingstoke, and all the passengers alighted. To his relief, and no doubt hers, Leah made her way over to the outhouse.

While she was gone, James went inside and purchased two cold pork pies. Uncertain of what Leah would drink, he also bought a large tankard of watered down cider. He then headed out into the mews.

She was wisely standing to one side of the stable yard, the hood of her cloak partly pulled back. Her gaze shifted constantly as she observed the hive of activity which buzzed around her. There was a steady stream of mail coaches arriving and departing, many of them at a fast clip. In the fading light of the late afternoon, it was a dangerous place for anyone to be wandering about and not paying full attention.

With the scarf still hiding much of his face, James walked calmly over to her. She glanced in his direction. She nodded, then turned away. He was pleased that she was still being cautious.

Standing next to her, her offered her one of the pies. While she looked down at the food, James took the opportunity to remove his scarf and reveal his face.

"Leah, you need to eat," he said.

Her hand, which was part way to reaching for the pie, suddenly stilled. It was as if she had turned to stone.

❧

James. James Radley. But how?

"Please, Leah. Have something to eat and drink. Then we can talk," he said.

She lifted her head and looked either side of him, frantically searching for any sign of her father or Guy. All this time she had thought she was making good on her escape, and James had been sitting a mere five feet away!

"Who are you with?" she asked, her voice quivering as panic gripped her.

He shook his head. "No one. And no one but me knows where you are."

Her hand dropped to her side; the pie forgotten. What was it with this man? He was always crashing into her life when she didn't expect it. On this occasion, she could only think of one reason why he would be here. He was trying to win back Guy's trust.

"I can't marry Guy. I'm sorry, James. I know he is your friend. I beg of you, please don't make me go back to London. I would rather die than marry that man," she pleaded.

He laid a hand gently on her arm. "It's all right, Leah. I am not here to make you do anything you do not wish. I promise, I am not going to send you back to London. The last thing I want in this world is for you to marry Guy."

She looked at him, unsure as to whether she had heard him correctly. He didn't want her to marry Guy. If that was the case, then why had he followed her all the way from London?

"Please take the pie," he insisted.

Her empty stomach growled a second time and she relented. Hunger won. She accepted the pie and took a bite. She rejoiced as the taste of the soft flaky pastry and cold pork meat hit her taste buds. It tasted like heaven. When she had finished the first mouthful, James offered her a large tankard.

"Drink this; you must be parched. I haven't seen you drink anything since we left London."

She accepted the tankard and took a sip. Sweet cider kissed her dry lips. She then took a long drink. After taking a second bite of the pie and chewing it, she washed it down with more of the cider. Eventually the pie and a good amount of the cider was gone.

"Thank you. I was absolutely famished. I've been sneaking looks at that box of cakes which that elderly gentleman has been nursing on his lap all this time," she said.

She handed him back the tankard. James drank some more of the cider, before passing it to a nearby stable boy who then wandered off toward the inn, downing the last of the drink as he went.

They were now alone in the stable yard; the driver of their mail coach and his assistant were still inside the inn, along with the rest of the Salisbury-bound passengers. Now was the time for her to ask James the first of a number of pertinent questions. That first question being, how the devil had he come to be on the mail coach with her?

"You were already on the coach when I climbed aboard in London. How did that happen?" she asked.

"I was arriving at St George's when I saw you coming out of the church. I followed you. I got one of my servants to go into the Gloucester Coffee House and find out where you were headed. Once he knew where you were going, he purchased a ticket for me. I had to hide out on the coach just to be certain you would not recognize me and get spooked," said James.

That explained *how* James had come to be standing next to her in the middle of a coaching inn some fifty miles from London. The reason *why*, she suspected, was something else.

The rest of the passengers for the mail coach appeared from out of the inn and headed in their direction.

"But why?" she asked.

James leaned in close. "I was serious when we spoke yesterday. I want to help you, Leah. We have another thirty miles to go until we reach Salisbury. I suggest we both stick to our established routine within the confines of the coach until then. It might draw undue attention to us if we were to suddenly start talking to one another. At Salisbury, we can continue our discussion and then make some decisions. Does that meet with your approval?"

She nodded, slowly. They both knew she had little option but to do as he asked. Attempting to escape from James would only draw attention to them both, and her plans did not include her being stranded in the middle of Basingstoke with only a handful of coins to her name.

They both climbed back into the mail coach. Leah did as James requested, and put the hood of her cloak over her head once more. She immediately discovered that there were new benefits to be had from hiding under it. With the pie and cider now settling comfortably in her stomach, she could close her eyes and grab some sleep. And with her line of sight to James blocked by the heavy woolen hood, it also meant she couldn't fall prey to the ongoing temptation of chancing a look at him.

In the darkness of the hood, just before she closed her eyes, one more question crept into her mind. If James was prepared to betray his best friend, then there had to be more of a reason for him doing so than simply wishing to help her.

What was he up to?

Chapter Twenty-Six

T hey kept to the plan for the next change of horses, neither making a move to speak to the other. James bought an oat biscuit at the coaching inn and handed Leah half of it as he passed her on the way back to the coach. He ventured a smile in her direction—a smile which made her blush. She had forgotten his lovely smile. It was a pity she could never forget that kiss.

In the late hours of the evening, the mail coach reached its final destination for the night. The ancient town of Salisbury. To her surprise, James not only had a small travel bag with him, but a full travel trunk which was unloaded from the top of the coach and carried into the inn by two porters. The sight of the travel trunk immediately raised questions in her mind.

It was as if he had read her thoughts and packed to make the journey with her all along. But that didn't make sense. The only other person who knew of her plans to flee London was Claire, and she had sworn an oath that she would never tell anyone. Had her trust in Claire been misplaced? Had Claire broken her vow of silence and confided in her brother? She hoped she was wrong.

He caught her staring at his trunk, and no doubt he observed the worried look on her face. He shrugged. "I was leaving for Derbyshire at the end of the wedding service and was already packed; it is purely a coincidence that I had my things with me." James held out a hand to her. "Come."

She looked at his outstretched hand, unsure as to whether she should trust him. Her worry about Claire and whether she had revealed their secret to James sat uneasy in her mind. Added to that was the fact that she and James had never actually been friends. True they had kissed, but that had been purely an attempt on her part to get him to convince Guy of her lack of suitability as a wife. Much as she had enjoyed the kiss, she wasn't certain he even liked her.

Yet here he was, being kind to her. Buying her food and drink and offering his help. She looked at his outstretched hand, still hesitant as to whether she should take it.

He may well have provided her with badly needed sustenance, but she still didn't trust him. When it came down to it, he was first and foremost Guy's friend. Who was to say that he was not simply keeping an eye on her while waiting for Guy and her father to catch up with them during the night?

That made far more sense than what James had told her. His story of having seen her leave the church and already being packed for a trip to the countryside was too convenient for her liking. The notion that Claire had caved on keeping their secret and confided in her brother on the morning of the wedding, and that James had been waiting at the coaching inn for her to arrive made more sense.

Claire was a lovely girl who had been raised in a family where trust was easily given. Her friend was well meaning, but at times she could be a little too naïve when it came to the true nature of people. It hurt to think she may have betrayed Leah's trust, but there was nothing to be done about it. James was here. She would just have to deal with whatever came next.

The real worry, of course, was whether she would be able to make it all the way to Cornwall. There was still some two hundred miles to go before she could reach the safety of her grandfather's house. Who knew what could happen between her and James on the road between Salisbury and Truro?

James scowled at her continued refusal to take his arm. His

response was not entirely unexpected. Men. They always thought they could tell a woman what to do; and when she didn't immediately comply, their pride got in the way.

She was tired and out of sorts. It was the end of what felt like the longest day of her life. She was many miles from home, and in the company of a man she did not entirely trust. And she had just discovered that her best friend had more than likely broken their sacred promise.

"Come on inside, and out of the cold, Leah. We can get some hot supper before retiring for the night," he said.

She straightened her spine and met his gaze full on. "I am fine by myself, thank you very much, Mister Radley. I did have some of this planned before your unexpected arrival," she finally replied.

She began to walk away, but when he took a firm grip of her cloak, she was forced to take a hurried step back.

James had dealt with stubborn females all his life. His sisters had minds of their own, and his recent experience of time spent with his cousin Caroline reminded him that it ran in the family. While it was good to see that Leah was capable of making her own decisions, her picking an argument with him in the middle of the yard of a coaching inn in remote Salisbury at this time of the night was not, in his opinion, the wisest course of action. It was likely to draw unwanted attention to them both.

They were well away from London and the protection of her family. Whether Leah liked it or not, he had a responsibility to ensure her safety. Polite society would demand that he take care of her; his lovestruck heart begged him to.

"I am perfectly aware that you are an intelligent young woman, capable of many things. But I am not leaving you here alone in a coaching inn, end of discussion," he replied.

Blue eyes blazing with defiance stared back at him. What he would give to haul her into his arms and kiss her senseless right now. If Leah thought that by being willful with him, she was taking a stand and making him angry, his hardening body would have to disagree.

"I wouldn't be alone. I am going to sit and wait downstairs in the ticket office until the coach for Exeter leaves at first light, the night porter will keep me company," she said.

Damn. While he had been quietly congratulating himself on being one step ahead of her, she had been making other plans. He hadn't seen that coming. And he didn't have a ticket to travel on to Exeter. He would need to dip once more into the money his father had given him for the trip to Derbyshire. And who was in Exeter that she was travelling to meet? His mind began to formulate possible answers, most of which he found unsettling.

Did Leah have a secret paramour in the west country? Was that the real reason behind her reluctance to marry Guy? The sudden thought that she had already given her heart over to another man pulled him up sharp.

"What is at Exeter?" he asked, trying to hide his concern.

"Nothing. It is just a stop. I have a ticket right through to Bodmin with the mail coach, after which I will take the local coach to Truro, after which I shall wait for the cart to take me to Mopus Passage, after which I shall walk," she replied deadpan.

James blinked at the long list of place names as Leah rattled them off. Mopus Passage. What sort of a name was that for a town? He had never heard of it. He could only pray it was not some small out-of-the-way fishing village where Leah intended to take a boat from England. He held fast to her cloak, steeling himself for the answer to his next question.

"What is in Mopus Passage and who is waiting for you there?" he asked.

She huffed. "Mopus Passage is the hamlet near where my maternal grandfather, Sir Geoffrey Sydell, has his estate. His home is at Mopus Manor. He will give me sanctuary."

Thank God. Leah had an actual plan. She wasn't running blindly from London or into the arms of another man; she was headed to the safety of family. He smiled with relief.

The journey west would take several more days. Truro was a long way from London, if memories of his schoolboy English geography lessons served James right. But if Leah's plans included sitting up each night and not taking a room at the various inns along the route, it meant she must be low on funds. Her reluctance to spend money on food and drink on the journey from London now made sense.

It also gave James the perfect opening.

"I am going to take lodgings here at the inn tonight. You may as well come up to my room and sit in a safe place, away from prying eyes. Just think, Leah; if I was able to follow you, who is to say that someone else didn't see you get onboard the coach in London? Your father could be arriving here at any moment," he said.

It was a dirty trick, and he promised himself that he would feel shame about it later. There was also a grain of truth to it. If someone in London had bothered to ask at the Gloucester Coffee House about a young fair-haired woman travelling on her own, it wouldn't have taken much to discover where Leah had gone. He was as keen as she was to avoid the two of them being discovered.

"Please," he added.

To his relief, her shoulders relaxed. A brief nod of her head saw him let go of her cloak.

"Thank you, Leah," he said.

After securing a room for the night, they followed the coaching inn porters with James's travel trunk up the narrow flight of wooden stairs. When they stepped into the tiny room, the porters had to squeeze past both James and Leah in order to make it back out and onto the landing.

The room itself could only have been described as tiny. *Small* would have been too generous a word. The roof was so low that it barely cleared James's head once he had stepped through the door. Apart from a double bed and a small chair and table which sat by the fire, there was no other furniture. James's travel trunk was squeezed in between the bed and the barely-there window.

"Could we please have some supper sent up? Whatever is on the menu. Also, some cider or ale," James said to the head porter. Once the two porters had gone back down the narrow staircase, James closed the door.

Leah stood and surveyed the room. "This is very cozy; I think my wardrobe at home is bigger than this. There might be more space downstairs in the waiting room after all," she noted.

His gaze followed hers around the room. She was right; it was little more than an oversized cupboard. "Yes, but you are not sitting in public view up here and there is a lock on that door. While you remain hidden, I stand a chance at being able to protect you. Leah we can make it work. We shall just have to make allowances for one another tonight. I will do everything in my power to see you safely to your grandfather. In return, all I ask is that you trust me."

Leah looked utterly exhausted. James could only imagine what today had been like for her and the toll it must have taken on her nerves. He craved for her to now let him bear that worry.

"Alright," she replied.

As she slumped down onto the bed, her whole body seemed to crumple in defeat. Her chin dropped and she began to cry. Big, fat tears rolled down her cheeks and a mournful sob escaped her lips.

"Oh, Leah." James sat down next to her, placing a comforting arm around her shoulder. At that moment, nothing else mattered. His stupid lovestruck heart wasn't important, and nor were Guy Dannon and Tobias Shepherd. All that mattered was that Leah was safe, and she knew someone gave a damn about her.

His chin rested gently on the top of Leah's hair. The scent of her perfume made his heart ache. Today had been one of the most challenging days of his life, so full of twists and turns that at times he had struggled to keep up. Yet sitting here, holding her in his arms, he knew without a single doubt that he was exactly where fate had decided he should be.

They sat for a time, the only sound in the room being Leah's soft sobs. James stroked his hand gently up and down her back. Leah slipped a hand around his waist.

Today had been hard enough for him; for her, it had been life-changing. A day where she had cut the very ties which bound her to her family and home. After today, her old life would be forever behind her. She could never go back.

She pulled a handkerchief from out of her cloak pocket and wiped her face. "I expect that whatever your reasons were for following me from the church this morning, you thought they were the right thing to do. But considering our somewhat checkered past, you cannot be surprised that I am not willing to place my trust fully in you at this moment. I don't know you well enough, James."

"I understand. I hope over the next few days that you and I will get to know one another better. I wish with all my heart that you willingly come to place your trust in me. Leah, I care about you. I shall do whatever I can to keep you safe," he replied.

Now was not the time to get into a discussion about how he truly felt for her. In fact, that time may never come. On the road to her grandfather, he would make sure she slept in a warm bed every night, and that whatever Leah needed, she would have. And if in the end that was the only way he could show her his love, then so be it.

The hint of a wry smile appeared on her lips. She didn't believe him. "I used you to try and convince Guy not to offer for me. I lured you into a room and then kissed you with the sole intent of making you go and tell him that I was not suited to be his wife. You obviously decided I was a foolish chit who did not know what she wanted. I wonder if you even told him about the kiss."

"I tell him about the kiss, but it clearly made no difference. And I have never thought you a foolish chit. How about we put the worry of what we think of one another aside for the time being. All of those conversations can wait. First, we need to eat. Then we should discuss what is to be done tomorrow," he said.

She released her other arm from about his waist. James felt the pang of regret as Leah moved away.

"What is happening tomorrow is that I am getting onboard the coach for Exeter," she said. She rose from the bed, and after crossing the floor, took a seat in the small fireside chair. "I shall sleep here tonight," she said. Her fingers tapped the hard arms of the chair. She softly nodded, looking for all the world like she was totally convinced she could actually sleep in such an uncomfortable place. There was little chance she would get any rest there.

James shook his head. "If anyone is going to sleep in the chair, it is me. My mother would have my guts for garters if I left a young lady to sit in a chair all night."

He suspected they could argue that particular topic for hours if he allowed himself to get dragged into it. But sleeping arrangements were not important at this moment. Before they sat down to supper, he wanted to know more of Leah's plans. To decide how best he could help her. "Where exactly is Mopus Passage?"

"Mopus Passage is a tiny village on the Tresillian River, right where it meets the Truro River. When I say village, I mean it is a collection of houses and a tavern—nothing more. Truro is the nearest town, some two miles away," she replied.

"Won't your family know to look for you there?" he said, stating the obvious.

She nodded. "No doubt they will eventually, but my grandfather is a powerful man. My father hates him, not the least because he knows Sir Geoffrey has the wealth and political connections to be able to stand up to him. I am certain that my grandfather will do everything he can in order to save me from having to go back to London and face my father's wrath."

Her words were heartbreaking. While James had been concerned about her family pressuring Leah to return to London and marry Guy, she was more concerned with the threat of retribution from her own father. It was truly awful.

Leah sat with her head bowed, her gaze cast down to the floor. When she looked up at James, more tears filled her eyes. "You think that I jilted Guy because I didn't love him. That is only part of the truth. Did you know that he planned to use me to seduce his political allies and opponents? The fact that my father knew of his intentions only serves to make it that more repulsive."

"Leah, I am so sorry. I was aware that Guy planned to use you to further his political ambitions, but I had no idea he intended to corrupt you. I tried to talk him out of marrying you because I thought the two of you were ill suited. But he simply wouldn't listen. I cannot believe that your father approved the marriage. I only wish I had done more to save you."

Leah shrugged. "My father was complicit in Guy's plans, so there was nothing you could have done. My mother was no better. She told me to accept my lot and submit to Guy's wishes," she replied.

James was close to tears, his body shaking with barely suppressed fury. He had abandoned her. While he had been with his cousins in Derbyshire and worrying about his own future, Leah had been fighting a battle for her soul.

How could he profess to love her when the truth of Guy's plans for Leah had been staring him straight in the face all along?

You failed her.

"I must admit to having been more than a little shocked when I saw you after I returned to London. I was a fool in thinking that you were resigned to your fate. I failed you, Leah, and for that I shall always be sorry. But I swear that from now on, I shall protect you. No one will take you back to London against your will," he said.

"Don't make promises you cannot keep, James. My father has ways to make people suffer long after they think they have gotten the better of him. He specializes in revenge."

James got to his feet. It was another three or so days of travel to the west country—time during which Tobias Shepherd could catch up with them and attempt to snatch his daughter back. James had to concentrate his mind and efforts into keeping Leah safe.

A knock at the door tore him from his thoughts. He motioned for Leah to hide on the floor on the other side of the bed. Once she was hidden from view, he opened the door.

"Ah, food. Good, thank you," he said.

A maid carried a tray into the room and set it down on the table. The heady smell of hot stew and freshly baked bread filled the cramped space. The maid looked down at Leah where she lay on the floor and raised an eyebrow.

"Have you found it, dearest?" asked James.

"Not yet, but I am certain I dropped it over here somewhere," replied Leah.

The ruse worked and the maid gave a bob of a curtsey, then left the room. Leah climbed up off the floor and hurried over to the food. Picking up the knife which had come with their supper tray, she began to cut the half-loaf of bread into generous slices. She handed James a piece, then dipped her own slice into one of the bowls of stew. She stood with her back against the wall while she quietly ate.

James offered her the single chair to sit and eat, but she waved him away. "I have been sitting down all day. I need to walk or at least stand," she replied.

James followed suit with the food, standing to eat. While he ate, he pondered the situation which they now both faced.

He had to get Leah to her grandfather without her family discovering where she was. The risk with staying at the coaching inns and travelling by way of the main roads was that it left them exposed to being discovered. They needed a way to get to Mopus Passage without being found by the Shepherd family.

And then he had an idea.

"I shall be back shortly. In the meantime, lock the door after I am gone and don't open it unless you hear my voice," he said.

"Where are you going?" she asked.

"To secure us a means of private transport."

Leah may well have her concerns about travelling with him, but James was under no illusion as to what he would do if Tobias Shepherd intercepted them en route to Cornwall and tried to take Leah back. With that thought foremost in his mind, he was determined to do all he could to avoid Leah's father.

Once downstairs, he had a quiet word with the innkeeper, who promptly pointed him in the direction of the nearest gunsmiths.

As soon as James was gone, Leah attacked her wedding gown. She tore at the laces with the sharp knife, not bothering to spare either the fabric or the bindings. She found a lose thread and pulled on it hard. The gown was left in satisfying shreds within minutes. When she was finally free of the hideously expensive dress, she rolled it up into a tight ball and stuffed it into her bag, vowing to never wear it again. She retrieved one of her simple day gowns and put it on.

Leah then sat and finished the rest of her stew in her warm, comfortable attire. She washed it down with the half tankard of ale.

The ale was bitter and not something she was used to drinking. Its effect, however, was most welcome. By the time James finally returned to the room, she had just enough energy left to unlock the door and let him back in before she lay down on the bed and promptly fell asleep.

Sometime in the middle of the night, she woke with a start and sat up. Panic gripped her before she managed to focus her gaze on the fireplace. In the chair by the fire, James was stretched out fast asleep, snoring softly. When she saw him, Leah smiled; James had draped his mother's woolen cloak about himself.

She lay in the dark, allowing her mind to ponder the events of the day. This was not the wedding night she had imagined, thank God. But lying listening to James's heavy breathing, her heart told her that not only was she exactly where she should be, she was also with the right man.

Chapter Twenty-Seven

"**D**o you think it is wise for us to take so long to travel to Mopus Passage? What if my father has followed me and is waiting for us when we reach my grandfather's house?"

Leah's question was a sensible one, and it had kept James awake late into the night. They needed a plan.

He had sworn a silent vow to do everything in his power to protect her from the rest of the Shepherd family. He was not by nature a violent man, but when faced with tyranny, even good men would take up arms. The pistol he had purchased the previous evening lay hidden in the pocket of his coat. He could only hope that he wouldn't have cause to use it.

But he was determined that Leah should have the right to choose whom she married. He knew that there was more than a small amount of self-interest in that promise. While Leah remained unwed, there was still a flicker of hope for his heart to be granted its greatest desire.

For her to love him. For her to choose him.

James's plan involved him driving the private carriage he had hired last night. They would travel the main road during the day, but instead of staying at the coaching inns en route at night, they would find lodgings at smaller out-of-the-way villages.

It would mean they would take longer to reach Mopus Passage. James had weighed up the options and decided that it was the overnight stops where the greatest risk of Tobias Shepherd trying to reclaim Leah lay. Leah's father could call upon the services of the innkeeper and his staff to help secure the release of his wayward daughter from the blackguard who had spirited her away from her lawful guardian. If that situation eventuated, he would be powerless to do anything to help her.

Leah took a sip of her tea before setting the cup down. James could tell she was not convinced of the merit of his plan. In the cold light of morning, she seemed less at ease than she had the night before. "I'm sorry," she said.

James looked across at her. "What are you apologizing for?" If anyone should be offering up an apology, he knew it was him. Every day he should be telling her how sorry he was for leaving her to face Guy and her father alone.

"For doubting you. You have had ample opportunities in the past day to tie me up and force me onboard a London-bound coach. All you have done instead is to feed me and give me somewhere safe to sleep. And you have listened," she said.

He shook his head. He was not going to accept her apology for not trusting him. Until now, he had given her no reason as to why she should place her trust in him. "How about we both apologize, and agree to be friends? That way, we leave here today with a fresh start," he said.

The word *friends* didn't roll off James's tongue as easily as it should. That same tongue now felt the pressure of his teeth as he forced himself not to say anything more on the subject, fearing that if he did, he would say too much.

He wanted Leah to see that he was more than just someone feeling an obligation to keep her safe. He wanted her to be happy. He ached to be a part of her life, for her to see him beyond being merely Guy's friend. As far as James was concerned, his bond with Guy was already irretrievably broken.

"You wish to be friends?" she asked.

"Yes."

"Alright, we can be friends. But you must understand that friends don't keep secrets from one another. Which means you have an obligation to tell me not only why you chose to betray Guy, but also why you are helping me." Leah reached out a hand and they locked fingers. "Please, James, help me understand. I want to trust you, but I need to know the truth."

"When I saw you run out of the church, I didn't stop to think about whether I was betraying Guy or not. I saw a young woman who had chosen to flee her wedding and I knew you needed my help. The last thing I was going to do was to grab you and drag you back inside St Georges. I sent some of the wedding guests in the wrong direction, then followed you," he replied.

"Guy will never speak to you again after what you have done. I hope for both our sakes that you are prepared for the impact of losing that friendship," said Leah.

"I understand what yesterday will have cost me. But you mean more to me that he does," replied James.

James really didn't want to have this conversation so early in their journey west. He wanted them to spend time together so that when he felt it was right to declare himself, Leah would have had the opportunity to get to know him a little better. For them to have strengthened their friendship, and hopefully, for the first buds of genuine affection for him to have formed in her heart. It was not to be.

"Why?" she asked.

"What can I say? I care more deeply for you than a mere friend should. When we kissed that night at the ball, you stole a piece of my heart. I want to spend time with you to not only see you safely to your grandfather, but also for you to see the real me."

Leah squeezed his hand. "Thank you for your honesty, James. But could we agree to start our journey together with just being friends? I am not sure what else I am capable of feeling right now."

He nodded. "Of course."

She gave him a shy smile. "James Radley, you are full of surprises."

They agreed to set out later that morning on the road to Exeter. By leaving later each day, they would avoid the early morning mail coaches as they came thundering through on the main road.

Breakfast would be taken in the secure privacy of their room, with Leah remaining out of sight as much as possible. At day's end, they would find lodgings at an inn in one of the villages off the main London-to-Exeter coach route.

It was comforting to know that someone else had her best interests at heart. James may have failed her by not getting Guy to give up on his marriage proposal, but he appeared to be doing everything he could to make amends. However, his confession of having feelings for her beyond that of mere friends left her wary. She was still undecided as to how much she could trust him.

The carriage James had hired the previous night was only big enough for his travel trunk and their bags to fit inside, leaving both he and Leah with no option but to ride upfront behind the horse. His profuse apologies over the size of the barouche were touching. She'd politely refused his offer to hire a bigger carriage with a driver. She didn't want to take any more of his money.

"This could be fun without a driver. Who knows? You might even let me hold the reins at some point," she said.

A single raised eyebrow was the only response she got from James. Leah stifled a grin. She recalled the game of lawn bowls and his silly hijinks with his cousin Francis. James was in possession of a pleasing sense of humor.

She found herself wanting to get to know him better, to understand the man behind the easy smile. Apart from the odd comment that Claire had shared about her brother, Leah didn't know much about James Radley at all. She knew him to be a caring man, one who was prepared to race after a fleeing bride and ensure that she spent her failed wedding night under his protection in a warm, comfortable bed, with a belly full of hearty stew and spicy ale. There was a lot to be said about that sort of man.

While James and two of the porters wrangled his trunk into the back of the barouche, Leah stood to one side and studied him. She appreciated what she saw. Strong muscular arms and broad shoulders spoke of a life which extended beyond the mere social pastimes of the *ton*. Her gaze settled on his well-formed rear and she softly smiled.

She turned away quickly from her private observation of him when he reached down and picked up her travel bag. In the cool air of the morning, she felt the heat of embarrassment burning on her cheeks. Her study of James Radley had not been with the right amount of cool, detached interest that society would demand of a young unmarried woman. Leah had broken so many rules over the past day, she doubted she would ever be able to follow the strictures of polite society again. She would live the rest of her life on her own terms. This morning she had woken the same as she had for all her life, a spinster, and for that she was thankful.

"Are you ready to leave?" James asked.

Praying that the heat on her cheeks had faded, Leah took a step forward. Yesterday had been a day when she had played out a long-rehearsed scenario. Everything had been planned down to the last detail.

Today, however, would be different.

Instead of taking the mail coach alone onto Exeter at first light, she was about to embark on an adventure with the beguiling James Radley. A bubble of excitement sat in her stomach. The fear she had felt during most of the previous week, and especially in the early hours of yesterday morning, was mostly gone. James made her feel if not completely safe, then at least protected.

James held out his hand. It was a high step into the driver's seat. Gathering her skirts, Leah looked for a suitable foothold. It would require an inelegant move for her to make it all the way up there.

"It might be easier if you would permit me to lift you," he said.

The notion of him placing his hands on her waist and lifting her into the carriage was more than a little outrageous. The thought had her mouth suddenly going dry. It wasn't the first time that James had touched her. Memories of *that* kiss still lingered in her mind. The scent of his cologne had been heady enough. The moment their lips touched; her mind had gone utterly blank. He had held her prisoner in his sensual embrace, their tongues dancing over one another. The taste of his brandy had been a sharp, but welcome . . . *oh*.

The sensation of heat racing down her spine, along with other secret parts of her body becoming suddenly warm, had her breathing hard. Her peaked nipples lay flush against the bodice of her gown. She had never been so affected by a man before. Just the thought of his strong hands on her body had her quivering with anticipation.

She looked at James with his arms held out. It was beyond proper behavior for her to even be considering what he was suggesting. But then again, for all intents and purposes she was already ruined. She had shared a room with him the previous night; them both being fully clothed mattered little in the story of her fall from grace.

If her father didn't come chasing after her, he would make damn certain she would never be able to make a suitable marriage. She decided that she may as well enjoy her downfall. A girl could only fall once and if it was going to happen to her, she couldn't think of a more handsome man to crash to earth with.

With a nod of approval, she turned her back to him and James placed his hands about her waist. Just before he lifted her, she caught the now familiar scent of his cologne. If her flight to Cornwall ended with her living out the rest of her days as a spinster, then the memory of his manly smell and strong hands would be one she would treasure in the years to come. She would take comfort in the knowledge that for one brief moment, she had been with a man who made her feel alive. A man who made her believe she could be free.

"Place your feet on the running board, and grab hold of the bar," he instructed. He firmed his hold on her and lifted her up. Leah placed one foot on the board and reached for the bar. When she began to fall back, James slipped his hands from her waist and pushed hard against her backside. His fingers spread firmly over her buttocks and gripped tight.

"Oh!" she squealed as she was lifted high into the air. She dropped down onto the softly padded seat with an inelegant "oomph." Reaching for the handrail, she quickly steadied herself. Only when she finally managed to get her feet settled on the wooden runner and had her hands on the rail did her heart begin to slow its fast beat.

The sound of raucous laughter filled her ears. She looked down at James. The saucy devil was doubled over. His shoulders shook. When he eventually managed to look up at her, she caught the sparkle of delighted mirth in his eyes.

Leah giggled; James's laugh was infectious.

"Oh, I am so sorry. I am . . . bah ha!" He walked around to the other side of the carriage, still chuckling. She watched him place his boot on the side of the barouche and step up with ease to take the driver's seat. They exchanged a foolish grin as he plopped down beside her.

"I can go and hire a driver," he finally said after several more snorts of laughter.

Leah shook her head. This was much more fun than they would have with a driver. James was beyond handsome when he laughed, and she wanted to keep seeing his smiling face. She already looked forward to the next time he would have to help her into the carriage.

"We shall manage," she replied.

The journey through to Exeter from Salisbury would take them several days longer than if they had travelled by the fast-moving mail coach. Ninety miles was a long way in a barouche which at top speed would hit somewhere around five miles an hour. James looked up at the grey sky as they turned out of the mews of the inn. Foul weather would impede their progress even more.

To James's delight, he found Leah to be even more good-natured in real life than he had imagined in his secret daydreams. Her reaction to him placing his hands on her rump and pushing her up into the carriage had been better than expected. Instead of an angry rebuke for his overfamiliar handling of her body, he got soft giggles. Giggles which had his mind immediately thinking about where else he would like to touch her.

Leah was temptation. She got to him in ways he was only beginning to understand. The next few days held the promise of more delightful discoveries and of struggling to keep his lustful body under control.

Thoughts of her smile sat in his mind long after they had quietly settled side by side on the driver's bench and left the inn.

A little way out of town, Leah turned to him. "Yesterday, you said you were going back to Derbyshire. Was it in order to visit Caroline and her new husband at Newhall Castle?"

"No. I was going to paint. My father has agreed to support me in my endeavors to become a professional landscape artist. I have two large pieces of work which I am hoping to complete and sell in the next few months. If I can find a buyer for them, then I won't have to go back to university. I have some preliminary sketches, but I need to go back into the woods in order to get the right sense of light for the paintings themselves."

She fell silent for a moment, then placed a hand on his arm. "Could you please pull over to the side of the road?"

With a gentle tug on the horse's reins, James guided the carriage over to the grassy edge where they came to a stop. When he looked at Leah, he saw that her face was set in a perplexed frown.

"James, if you come with me to Cornwall, there is a good chance you won't be able to reach Derbyshire before the roads become impassable due to the winter snows. By trying to help me you are putting your career in jeopardy," she said.

The moment he decided to chase after Leah in central London, James knew he was risking more than just incurring the wrath of Guy Dannon. He was putting his love for her ahead of his dreams of being a painter. "I suppose you could put it that way, but I don't regret coming after you. As I see it there will likely be other ways for me to make my art pay, but there was only ever going to be one chance for me to come to your rescue."

Leah sat; head bowed. "You are not who I thought you were, James. I am beginning to think I may have misjudged you."

Her words added another spark to the burning flame he already carried for her. He had long suspected she wasn't the pliable little miss Guy thought he was marrying. He'd seen clear evidence she was a young woman with a spine. There were deeper more intricate layers when it came to Leah. She was much like Caroline in that they both had substance about them, but Leah had a certain warmth that Caroline did not. Her concern for him and his future held a kindness which went straight to James's heart.

He had never met anyone like Leah before, and he doubted he would ever find another woman who made him feel the way she did.

"I think we may have both misjudged one another in the past. I, for one, am glad of the opportunity for us to get to know each other a little better. Who knows where that might lead?" he replied.

She patted his arm. "Yes, I think you are right in it being a time for the both of us to reevaluate our opinions. At least we are starting out as friends. Who knows what will happen between here and Cornwall?"

What did happen was the arrival of a tempest which blew in from the North Atlantic and across the English coast. The gods of fair skies had abandoned the travelers. By day's end, James and Leah had wasted hours sheltering from the fierce rain and winds of an early winter storm. Leah spent her time huddled under her cloak. Their horse did not take kindly to the weather either, which meant James had to carefully handle him the whole way. It was a long and arduous day on the road.

By the time they reached the small village of Mere, it was almost night. The plan of them staying somewhere more out of the way was quickly set aside. James, the horse, and Leah were all exhausted and wet.

When the white Tudor period George Inn appeared in sight, James's shoulders sagged with relief. "I don't know about you, but I need a hot bath and a comfortable bed. We shall just have to hope that if anyone is following us that the weather has also impeded their progress."

"Agreed. I need to get out of these wet clothes and eat a hot supper. I hope they do a stew. The one last night in Salisbury was absolutely delicious," replied Leah.

"And buttered bread," he added.

They both sighed with longing. There was nothing better than buttered bread dipped into a hearty stew, all washed down with a crisp ale or cider.

When the carriage drew to a halt in the yard, James handed the reins over to a stable boy and jumped down. Leah held out her hands to him and let him catch her as she dropped to the ground.

The innkeeper of the George Inn was a tall, gangly man with a wisp of a beard. He gave James and Leah a suspicious once-over as they stepped inside. His gaze dropped to Leah's hand and then to James.

An unmarried couple arriving on an innkeeper's doorstep in the middle of the night might not be the sort of custom that was welcomed in this neck of the woods. The look was not lost on James.

"My wife and I would like a room for the night. Your lad has already taken our carriage and horse around into the stables," said James.

Leah once again proved herself to be in possession of a sharp mind. Instead of countering James's lie, she simply slipped her hand in his and smiled sweetly at the innkeeper.

The aroma of roasted pork drifted in from the nearby kitchen. "Are we still able to procure some supper? That smells like the best roast in the county, doesn't it, darling?" she said. James nodded to her.

The innkeeper's demeanor changed. The question of whether his newly arrived guests were married or not, was quickly set aside as the man showed his obvious delight at hearing Leah's words of praise.

"My wife does do an excellent bit of roast pork and crackling, if I do say so myself. If you fine people would like to get yourselves set in your room upstairs, I shall see to getting you some food. I take it you would like roast potatoes and buttered bread with your supper."

James and Leah looked at one another.

"Yes, please."

Chapter Twenty-Eight

"Are you sure I cannot tempt you with the last piece of roasted potato?"

Leah waved her hand at James. She was so full, from all the wonderful food that she half expected to roll off the bed as soon as she lay down. "Thank you, James, but I am struggling to breathe as it is. I do love a good roast."

The room at the George was fortunately larger than the one they had stayed in at Salisbury, but that didn't take much. James was able to open his travel trunk properly and while the innkeeper was unable to provide a full bath, a bowl of hot water allowed him to shave and clean up.

Leah was happy to also avail herself of clean water and a strip wash while James was downstairs seeing to their horse and making preparations for their onward journey in the morning. Unlike James, however, she didn't have a full bag of possessions from which she could draw. A simple linen nightgown and three plain day gowns were the sum total of her wardrobe. All her beautiful gowns, coats, and shoes remained in London, still packed and ready for the move to what would have been her new home with Guy. What her mother would now do with all the possessions Leah had left behind, she dreaded to think.

I don't expect I shall see any of my nice things ever again.

The new gowns were likely to not fit her by the time she returned to London anyway. At the rate James was feeding her, she would soon be back to her old size. Her day gowns currently hung limply from her frame, but a few more days of stews and roasts, and her familiar curves would begin to return. While her cheeks were still sunken, she already felt less haggard than she had in weeks.

The innkeeper's wife had brought them up their supper after they had both washed away the dust and grime of the past two days of travel. Leah had changed into one of her clean gowns and was now seated across from James at a table under the window in their room.

"I was certain I could have eaten the whole pig when my nose first caught the delicious smell of the roast, but like you, I shall have to concede defeat. I blame the three roast potatoes for my downfall," replied James.

"You ate four potatoes," she said, before teasing him with a smile.

For the first time since she had left London, Leah felt the tension ease in her shoulders. Her heart was beating at a steady rate. It could have been that her body was too busy trying to digest all that wonderful food to remain in its previous near constant state of fear, but she had found herself beginning to relax long before they reached the inn.

James may have been Guy's best friend, but they were quite unlike one another in their nature. Where Guy was all for grand gestures and carefully measured words, it was the little spontaneous touches that gave James his power. A brief brush of his hand here, a kind word spoken there. They all added up to frame the picture of him she was slowly painting in her mind.

She watched as he finished the last of his ale then slumped back in his chair, hands resting on his full stomach. He looked for all the world like a young version of John Bull. And she imagined that if they kept eating such enormous suppers, he would eventually resemble the famous character.

Leah put a hand over her mouth and tried to stifle a mischievous laugh.

"What?" he asked.

"You need a waistcoat if you are going to be John Bull," she chortled.

His gaze settled on his rounded stomach and he chuckled. "I won't need to eat for days; and I expect to be asleep within the hour."

On the road, they had shared an afternoon of talking about almost everything as they sat side by side up on top of the carriage. The only topic of conversation which Leah did not want to discuss further was James's aborted trip to Derbyshire. Guilt sat uneasy in her mind over his selfless act.

Something else sat in the forefront of her mind and this topic was something which could not be avoided. Her grandfather. The question of exactly what they would say to him when they eventually reached Mopus Manor had to be addressed.

"My grandfather is a good man, a kindly man," she ventured.

James's gaze lifted to meet hers. He nodded. "I was wondering when we would get to the matter of Sir Geoffrey. I expect he will have one or two questions when he finds us on his doorstep at the end of the week."

Us. She had been pondering that same word for most of the afternoon. They weren't an *us*, or a *we;* they were travelling companions which made them . . . Leah couldn't quite think of a suitable word to describe the connection between her and James. It was the bones of a friendship at the moment, but it was changing by the hour.

What she didn't want was for whatever they were to be something of a millstone around their necks. James had done more than enough already to assist her; he had made sacrifices which she suspected would cost him dearly.

James should not be the one standing in front of her grandfather having to explain matters when the time came. She had made the decision to run away, not him. The weight of that choice should rest on her shoulders alone. "I was thinking that perhaps you and I could part before we reach my grandfather's house," she said.

It made sense for her to be arriving alone at Mopus Manor. She would already be a disgrace in the eyes of her family; why should James have to bear part or all of the blame for her actions?

The frown lines which immediately appeared on his face were accompanied by a loud huff of displeasure, and a loudly snapped, "No."

"If you would just listen," she implored.

"No. I am not taking you most of the way and then abandoning you at the end. If your father is waiting for you at Mopus Manor and I leave you to face him, then all this will have been for naught," he replied.

There was a firmness in his speech that quickly gave her pause. It told her in no uncertain terms that she would not be winning him over with her proposal for them to part. James was determined to see the journey through to its end.

"I just don't want you getting the blame for what I have done," she said.

He huffed a second time and the frown lines on his face grew deeper. She had secretly wondered what he would look like in full anger, and now had a horrible suspicion she was about to find out.

He got to his feet, and a chill ran down her spine. She had sat through enough of her father's tirades to know when someone's temper was about to explode. Leah held onto the arms of the chair, her fingers going white with the force of her grip. Holding her breath, she braced for impact.

But it never came.

Instead of the usual ranting and loud bellowing which her father was so adept at delivering, there was silence. Instead of the hot sting of a slap against her cheek, there was the warmth from the fireplace.

When she finally lifted her head, she met James's sad, puzzled gaze.

"Leah?" he said.

Her fingers remained locked hard against the chair; the habits of a lifetime not easily changed. She had seen her father approach anger from many different angles. All of them ended in the same way—with her curled up on the floor, pleading for mercy.

With careful, measured steps, James approached. He held his arms limply by his sides, showing that he posed her no threat. Leah remained unable to move; it was as if she had suddenly been cast in stone.

Her eyes tracked his movements, her brain registering the contrast between James's soft unthreatening manner and the hard violence that was the hallmark of her father in one of his full rages.

James bent down and knelt beside her, placing a hand lightly on top of hers. "I won't hurt you, Leah. I would never do that. You are safe with me," he murmured.

She focused on his voice and believed his words to be true. Still, she remained in her prison of silence, unable to respond.

James left his hand in place, his thumb softly brushing over the back of Leah's fingers, gently coaxing her to return to him.

She eventually managed a brief nod. Feeling came back into her body. His entreaty had succeeded. Her breathing slowly returned to normal as the barriers of her self-defense were lowered. Her mind finally convinced her body that she was safe once more.

"I didn't mean to speak so harshly to you," he said.

She shook her head. "You didn't. The reaction is somewhat ingrained, and I have little control over it."

She could name the various levels of heat and volume in a voice, from the cool, sweet sound that usually accompanied endearments, right through to the blazing intensity of soul-destroying wrath. She knew them all, some better than others.

"Deeply embedded, from the way you reacted so quickly. I'm sorry if I frightened you. I am only beginning to understand how things have been for you, Leah. In time, I hope that you will come to trust me enough to tell me more," he said.

A little understanding was all she could ever give to James. The rest of her history would remain as it always had—buried deep.

Chapter Twenty-Nine

Leah hadn't said much in words, but her silence spoke volumes. James cursed himself for having thought her troubles had only begun with her forced engagement. Watching her flinch at the slightest raise of volume in his voice gave him all the heart-breaking evidence he needed to understand why she had not stayed in London and faced up to her father.

One of the few unfortunate things that came from having had a happy and loving upbringing was that he wasn't fully prepared to deal with situations of family cruelty. The *ton* was strict in many of its rules, some of which he considered unfair, especially toward women. Rights he took for granted were often not afforded to the fairer sex. But very few families were outright wicked to their children.

Having a tyrant as a father and living under that yoke day after day all your life was so foreign to him. He honestly didn't know what he could say to her. *Sorry* was such a pitifully inadequate word to use in this situation. Would she even wish for him to say it?

Leah shifted in her chair. Her face brightened. "We were discussing my grandfather and how he is to be approached."

She spoke as if the interaction of the past few minutes had never happened. James decided to let it rest in the hope that at some point she would feel able to discuss her family with him.

And while Leah appeared determined to move on from the deeply uncomfortable exchange, James made his own decision. No matter what happened before or after they reached Cornwall, he would make certain that Leah never had to go back to living under her father's roof. His family had enough power and influence to protect her, and he would see it done.

He wondered how much Guy knew of Leah's family history. Was her former fiancé aware of what Leah had suffered? A chill rippled the hairs on his arm. The notion that perhaps Guy had specifically chosen Leah because she had already been broken by her family sickened James to the core.

"Then we do as we have already discussed. I shall endeavor to discover who is in residence at your grandfather's home, then decide on what is to be done," he said.

"No. I want a say in this and what is to happen. It is my future we are discussing here, much as you wish to be involved in helping me make decisions about it," she replied.

"Well then, may I suggest that I find out what the lay of the land is at Sir Geoffrey's house, then return to the inn at Mopus Passage and let you know. If your father is not waiting for you, we can then travel together to Mopus Manor. But if your father is . . ."

"I will go far away. I don't care where. A boat to France would be a perfectly acceptable option. Anywhere but back to London," she interjected.

It was comforting to know Leah had a spine, that her father had not managed to crush her soul completely. Still, they needed a proper back-up plan in case Tobias Shepherd was waiting for his daughter's arrival.

"I was going to say, if your father is at Mopus Manor, then I suggest you and I leave for Scotland immediately. My Uncle Ewan is the Duke of Strathmore, and my family can offer you protection. You may stay at Strathmore Castle for as long as you wish," he said.

Scotland would offer Leah at least some protection from English law. Her father couldn't just march up to the gates of Strathmore

Castle and demand that the Duke of Strathmore hand his daughter over. James stopped and thought about it for a moment, worried that his knowledge of cross-border law was not strong enough. The last thing he wished to do was to cause further scandal or outrage to the Radley family. He already had enough explaining to do to his father and uncle as it was.

If he and Leah did end up making a run for the Scottish border, he would be stopping in Edinburgh on the way and securing the services of a good lawyer. One that could find some ancient law to protect Leah from her family.

A priest would do the job. If he married her, she would be forever out of her father's reach. She would no longer be a Shepherd; she would be a Radley. *Offer her marriage.*

It was tempting to suggest such a thing, but the time was not right. A forced marriage was exactly what he was helping her to escape. She had the right to choose whom she married. He did not want Leah agreeing to marry him purely out of desperation. Only if and when he was certain that he held her heart would he ask her to be his wife.

"Scotland sounds nice, and something we should seriously consider if it comes to it," she replied.

But. There was a definite *but* hanging on the end of that sentence. He waited.

"But there are some other more pressing matters to consider," she added.

"Such as?"

"Such as what we are to do about sleeping arrangements. It is all well and good to be posing as a married couple outside our room, but you cannot sleep in an uncomfortable chair every night. Your back will be a mess of knots by the time this journey is over if you do that, so we need to find a solution that leaves us both satisfied," she replied.

He stopped himself just in the nick of time. The thought of offering to share the bed would likely get him a hard slap across the face.

Long nights he had lain awake thinking of her, imagining how wonderful it would be to hold her naked in his arms. How it would feel to run his hands over her body, make love to her, and watch her face as he brought her to completion.

James dared not say anything of his thoughts aloud, but his lust-filled body was screaming. If only Leah had not mentioned the word 'satisfied'. He fought in vain, but his cock hardened.

He struggled to his feet, turning quickly away from her. The evidence of his arousal was plain before him. "I just remembered I need to speak to the landlord about the horse. Hold that thought and I shall return shortly," he said.

He staggered out of the room with undue haste, closing the door behind him. The bulge in his trousers was not the least bit amusing. He chided himself. He wasn't a callow youth; he should be able to maintain his dignity around a woman.

Taking a deep breath, he closed his eyes. "Egbert, Aethelwulf, Aethelbald, Aethelbert, Alfred the Great . . ."

Reciting the long list of English monarchs was an effective trick handed down to all schoolboys upon experiencing the first unwelcome signs of puberty. As his body softened and came back under his control, James gathered his thoughts.

Last night he had been too tired to worry about his physical reaction to being close to Leah. Now he had a real problem on his hands. If he was to continue sharing the bedroom with her, he was going to have to deal with his lust. He had to come up with a new plan. One which didn't involve her seeing the bulge in his trousers.

He had only just managed to get Leah to somewhat trust him; he didn't need for her to start thinking he was a sex-starved blackguard.

A bright idea dropped into his mind. Since the innkeeper already thought they were a young married couple, it wouldn't take much for James to convince the man of the need for him to sleep on the floor. Many a husband had been made unwelcome in his bed by an unhappy wife. That was a plausible enough excuse for him to ask for a spare mattress and blanket.

He was halfway down the stairs to speak to the innkeeper when a second idea struck him.

"Much better," he muttered.

Chapter Thirty

"Y ou told them I was with child and you had to sleep on the floor because I felt nauseous. Really? Was that the best idea you could have come up with?" said Leah.

James had returned to their room with a soft mattress slung over his shoulder, and a blanket tucked under his arm.

"The other option was to have told them we had a row, and that you refused to sleep with me. I thought that might be a tad embarrassing for us when we had to face them at breakfast tomorrow," he replied.

Leah rolled her eyes. Now she would have to deal with being fussed over by the innkeeper's wife in the morning. Men and their pride.

"I had to give the innkeeper some reason to hand over this mattress and blanket," he said.

By rights, as an unmarried woman she should have been well pleased not to be sharing a bed with a man. Not to be lying beside James's warm, hard body. Not to suffer the indignity of him draping his muscular arm around her waist, nor of listening to his deep breathing as he slept. And especially pleased not to be taking in the heady scent of his cologne. All those things she now found herself secretly craving.

She cautioned her heart. She had just escaped one near disaster—

she shouldn't go racing toward another possible one. Allowing a tender spot for James to form in her heart would be a foolish thing and could only result in having it bruised, or worse, broken.

"You did the right thing, James. And tomorrow morning I will make sure I am a little tired and unwell if any kind soul asks. There is one thing which would make our story more plausible," she said.

"Yes?"

"I need a wedding ring." Her gaze settled on his signet ring. The amber flames from the low burning fire were reflected on the gold band. The signet was black onyx inlaid with a gold horse and three stars: the Radley family crest. A reminder of his family's powerful, ancient heritage.

He nodded, then removed the ring from his finger. With a smile, she held out her hand, and James slipped the ring onto the third finger of her left hand.

"With this ring," she said, then softly chuckled. Their gazes met. James leaned forward toward her, and for a moment, Leah imagined that he was about to kiss her.

"Good night, wife," he said.

A lump formed in her throat as he pulled away. He had called her his wife. With an odd sensation in her stomach, she turned and climbed into the bed.

James plopped the mattress down on the floor next to the bed and after taking off his jacket, he lay down. Within minutes, the sound of his soft snores could be heard in the room. Leah turned over and much as she fought it, fatigue finally caught up with her. They both slept the sleep of the exhausted.

After the second night, they fell into an easy pattern. Each morning they would rise early and make as much headway as they could during daylight before seeking a village off the main road in which they could stay. By the fifth day out from London, they were close to the tiny hamlet of Mopus Passage where Leah's grandfather lived. A small stone marker on the side of the road was the first and only sign of their destination. From the few other travelers they had passed on the road, James began to wonder just how small the village really was.

"How many people live in Mopus Passage?" he asked.

"A handful. The inn was built only a few years ago, along with a half dozen houses. That is the sum total of Mopus," replied Leah.

At least there was an inn where Leah could wait out of sight while James went on to Mopus Manor to speak with Sir Geoffrey. "Will you tell me why your father and Sir Geoffrey are not on speaking terms?"

She nodded to him. "Things had been bad for a number of years, but the final straw was a little over two years ago when my sister got married. My grandfather thinks that she was forced into marrying a man just like my father. And to be honest, I would have to say I agree with him. Your friend Guy, my brother-in-law, and my father were all unfortunately cast from the same mold."

"So, Sir Geoffrey would likely be inclined to take your side if he knew the truth of what happened with your betrothal?" he asked.

"I hope so. He is the only person I can turn to right now. If he fails me, I have no one else whom I can trust," she replied.

He could have argued that point with her but decided on leaving her remark unanswered. Today was a day for unity and giving Leah as much support as possible. From the way she kept wringing her hands, it was obvious she was nervous about what lay ahead for them.

"Once we reach the village, I shall go into the inn and secure us a room. After we have you safely tucked away, I will head over to Mopus Manor and do a sortie of the house. If I find any sign of your father or Guy being in residence, I shall return immediately to the inn and we can discuss alternate plans. If they are not, I shall make myself known to Sir Geoffrey," said James.

"Agreed. And I will stay in our room until you return," replied Leah.

A little more than an hour later, they turned off the old Malpas Road and into the stable yard of the Mopus Passage Inn. Leah had pulled up the hood of her cloak and covered her face the same as she had done when setting out from London. James helped her down from the barouche before handing the reins over to the inn's stable hands.

"Don't bring my trunk inside yet; we may not be staying tonight," he instructed them. If Guy Dannon or Tobias Shepherd were waiting for them at Mopus Manor, he planned to take Leah and find an inn in the larger town of Truro which was only a few miles away. After that, they would be headed to Scotland as fast as possible.

The inn was a narrow two-storied slab stone building of recent build. From the look of the rest of the houses in the village, Mopus Passage was a new settlement. Leah caught his questioning gaze.

"During the war against the French, a number of small ports were established along the southwest coast to support the British navy. Smaller ports like this one took the bulk of the minor shipping traffic away from the major ports, enabling the navy to move its larger ships in and out of the south coast with ease," she explained.

"That makes sense."

Once inside the inn, they made their way upstairs. They locked the door of their room behind them and politely refused the offer of tea and locally baked pasties.

"Mopus Manor is farther along this road, only a half mile from here. You cannot miss it. The main house sits on a bluff overlooking the convergence of the Tresillian and Truro rivers. The road leading up to the house has a small dip in it. A narrow track which runs around to the rear of the house strikes out from the eastside of the dip. If you take your horse up the track, you can approach the house without being seen. That will give you a view of the stables before you arrive," said Leah.

The stables would hopefully give James a clear picture of who was at the manor. Guy's fancy travel coach with its gold striped details and red curtains would be easy to spot, although he doubted his friend would make the effort to follow his wayward bride to Cornwall. Leah had given James enough of a description of her father's coach for him to be able to identify it if it was in the yard.

The moment of truth had arrived. A nervous bubble sat in his belly, caused partly by his secret wish that the others were indeed waiting for them at the manor. If Leah could not reach her grandfather, then the only road left open to them would be the one which led to Strathmore Castle in Scotland.

James would avoid knocking on the front door of Mopus Manor, and in doing so would keep Sir Geoffrey out of the family squabble. Instead he would return to Mopus Passage, pack up Leah and their things, and make all due haste to the Great North Road and Scotland. Once they were in Scotland, he could turn to the task of wooing Leah and then making her his wife.

Just remember, Radley. You may want to marry her, but she has to accept your marriage suit of her own volition.

He dusted off his coat, checked his pistol, and after making certain that Leah was comfortable and safe, he headed for the door. "Make sure you keep this locked until I return. I won't be long."

His hand was on the door when Leah hurried over to him. She rose up on her toes and placed a hurried kiss on his cheek. "Good luck, James. I shall be waiting here for you."

After stepping through the door and onto the landing, James heard the door close behind him and the key turn in the lock. His hand settled on his cheek, right at the spot where Leah had just kissed him.

"Well that was unexpected," he muttered.

He made his way down the stairs, the heavy clump of his boots matched by the loud thump in his chest.

What he would give for her to be kissing him every day.

Chapter Thirty-One

James tied the reins of his horse to a clump of bushes and started to climb his way up the side of the rise which led to Mopus Manor. The low coastal shrubbery along the road afforded him little cover, so Leah's plan for him to sneak around the back of her grandfather's house was unfortunately not such a sound one. He would have to venture up the hill by foot and hope he could stay low enough to reach the top of the bluff and still remain unseen.

He finally managed to make his way up and around to the side of the manor house without being disturbed. He could see the stables but needed to get closer in order to see what coaches and carriages were inside. He had just decided on how he could best make his way through the low bushes when the *click* of a pistol being cocked stopped him in his tracks.

"This area is well known for smuggling, so we do tend to keep an eye out for unwelcome visitors," said a voice from behind him.

James put his hands up in surrender.

Fuck. I knew I should have kept my pistol in my hand.

"Now turn around slowly. Don't make any sudden moves, otherwise you might find yourself with a hole in your head."

He did as he was told. His plans for the day did not include getting shot.

When he finished turning to where the voice had come from, his gaze settled on a tall grey-haired gentleman holding a pair of pistols. Both pistols were cocked and pointed at James.

"You are not very good at this secret agent lark, are you, young man? For a start, the handle of your pistol is showing in your coat pocket. Now, carefully reach into *that* pocket and pull it out. Slowly. Then throw it over into those bushes," said the pistol-wielding gentleman.

James did as he was told, silently praying that he would live to watch his former spy cousins, William, and Bartholomew, fall about laughing when he told them of this embarrassing encounter. He put his right hand back up in the air, alongside his left.

"Now that I have done as you instructed, may I ask you a question?" ventured James.

The gentleman raised an eyebrow. "If you wish to play it that way, please go ahead. But I would not make any sudden moves as you speak; these pistols have hair triggers."

"Are you from Mopus Manor, and if so, does Sir Geoffrey have guests staying with him?"

A frown greeted his question. "That was two questions. But to hurry things along, I will indulge you. In answer to your first question, yes, I am from Mopus Manor. As to your second question, no, I don't have visitors. I cannot recall the last time I did."

James's shoulders sagged with relief, and he dropped his hands. A pistol shot rang out, and with a panicked cry, he quickly raised his hands again.

"Bloody hell!" he cried.

"The next one won't miss," said Sir Geoffrey.

"My name is James Radley. My father is Hugh Radley, the Bishop of London. I have your granddaughter with me," he replied hastily.

Many times, he had resented hearing people note that his father was the Bishop of London. Yet the first time he found himself in any real danger, he had invoked the name of his father. If he managed to somehow not get shot today, he intended to be angry with himself.

A trickle of nervous sweat slid slowly down his back. His heart was pounding like a drum in his chest. One of the pistols was lowered. Unfortunately, it was the one which Sir Geoffrey had already fired.

"Which granddaughter?"

"Leah."

Sir Geoffrey looked behind James, his eyes full of mistrust. "I don't see her. Nor did you leave her with your horse. What have you done with my granddaughter?"

James summoned up his courage. "If you could please stop pointing your pistol at me, we might be able to discuss this a little more civilly."

The loaded pistol remained pointed at him. "I shall be the judge of what is civil and what is not," said Sir Geoffrey.

James sighed. "I have her hidden someone safe. She fled London to avoid being married off to someone she did not wish to wed. I was the best man for the wedding and accompanied her here. I was trying to ascertain as to whether her father or the jilted groom were waiting for her at your home."

A soft chuckle carried to him on the wind, and to his immense relief, the second pistol was lowered and un-cocked.

"I don't think you can still call yourself the best man if you have stolen the bride."

James's brain was too frazzled with fear to laugh at the obvious jest.

"So, what you are trying to tell me is that you intend to deliver my granddaughter to me. And you, being a sensible young man *and* the son of the Bishop of London, decided to do a quick sortie of the area surrounding my home just in case that arse wipe Tobias Shepherd had beaten you here."

James nodded. "In a nutshell, yes."

"Well then, you had better come with me and we shall go and collect Leah."

"How was I to know he was a decent young chap? He was hiding in the bushes over yonder. He should be grateful I didn't shoot him on sight. The shot I let off was aimed wide; he has nothing to grumble about."

Leah peered out the window of her grandfather's study and gave James, who was sitting outside in the garden, a look of pity. Poor James. It had taken several hours for the color to return to his face after the incident with her grandfather.

James, fortunately, had recovered his humor, and after retrieving both the carriage and Leah from the village inn, he was now sitting in the afternoon sunshine, enjoying a second glass of spirit-restoring French burgundy. Leah had already apologized a half dozen times for her grandfather's gun-wielding greeting. And while he had accepted each one of her apologies with good grace, she still felt terrible over the thought that not only had two pistols been pointed at him, but one had actually been fired.

James took a sip of his wine before setting the glass down. He had retrieved one of his sketchbooks from his travel trunk and was now patiently drawing an outline of the low rock wall which ran along the edge of the garden.

With his jacket lying on a nearby chair and his shirtsleeves rolled up, she was granted the sight of his strong muscular arms. The pencil held in his long fingers moved over the paper with comfortable ease. James was in his element.

There was an odd sense of sadness in them having reached their destination. The days spent on the road with James had seen her come to view him in a new light. In her mind, he had confirmed himself as a kind and decent man. What the sight of him now did to her body was an entirely different matter.

An aching desire for him stirred within her.

Sir Geoffrey came and stood by her side at the window. She smiled at him, relieved that after weeks of planning and an at times frightening flight from London, she was now here at Mopus Manor. When the knock had eventually come at the door of their room at the inn, it had startled her. Her heart was all aflutter when she'd heard Sir Geoffrey's voice on the other side of the locked door.

Tonight, she would be able to lay her head on a pillow and hopefully not wake in the middle of the night fearing that her father was downstairs talking to the owner of whatever inn they were staying at and inquiring about a young woman traveler.

"Your James is a good man," said Sir Geoffrey.

Leah found herself not wishing to correct her grandfather's take on the current state of hers and James's relationship. "I am grateful for everything he has done. He has gone beyond the call in helping me to reach you safely."

"You know your father won't let this matter rest. If he doesn't come here himself, he will write and demand that I give you up if I am harboring you," he said.

"Yes. I expect it will only be a matter of time before his gaze turns this way," she replied.

The trail of breadcrumbs she had left behind in London pointed to her fleeing to another part of the country, but her father was no fool. Once he had exhausted the obvious places that she could be, his attention would no doubt focus on Mopus Manor.

"We shall deal with your father when the time comes. But what are you going to do about that young man? I expect he has burned a few bridges in bringing you here," he said.

James was a very large question in Leah's mind. Helping her to escape from marrying Guy Dannon would likely have cost him that once close friendship. There was also the question of his career as a painter. As far as she was concerned, being her hero had already cost James more than enough.

"He was headed to Derbyshire before he found himself following me out of London. His father has given him six months to create a series of artworks and sell them. I expect he will be keen to resume that journey now that I am here," she replied.

Sir Geoffrey slowly shook his head. "I have seen the way he looks at you. And I think you and I both know that he will not be going anywhere anytime soon."

Chapter Thirty-Two

❧❦❧

"How did you sleep?" Leah asked.

"Well. A proper bed was a nice change from a thin mattress on the hard floor. How about yourself?"

James was sitting outside in the garden on a large stone step. He liked this particular step; it afforded him an uninterrupted view of the Tresillian River which lay far below. The warm morning sunshine was a balm for his tired body.

The trip from London had been mentally draining for him. The horse and carriage he had hired, had been easy to manage. But the fear that Tobias Shepherd was lying in wait for them just around the next bend had made every day of travel long and stressful. The constant rain had not helped. He was grateful for the clear skies of Cornwall.

He sipped at his tea, his gaze fixed on the blue and grey waters down below. Farther to the right, he could see a constant swirling of water where the Tresillian and Truro rivers met. The sun danced across the water, sparkles of light reflecting off its surface.

Leah came and sat by his side. She held a half-eaten piece of toast in her hand. It was good to be someplace where the hard and fast rules of London society could be set aside. They could sit and spend time together without those worries.

"I slept well enough; it was nice to sleep in a proper bedroom. Though I missed hearing your breathing in the room during the night. I kept waking up and wondering where you were," said Leah.

The tea in his mouth caught in his throat at her words, and he fought to keep from choking. If only she knew how many times, he had looked over at the bed in whatever inn they were staying at and smiled as he lay listening to her breathing as she slept. It was nice to think that they had both experienced the same feelings of comfort from knowing the other was close by.

She nodded toward the rivers. "It is so beautiful here. My greatest wish is that my father decides I am too much of a bother and having me stay far away from London suits his purposes. If I have any say in it, I will never go back to London," she added.

More than once James had thought the very same thing about never going back. Mopus Manor was an oasis of calm. "I can see why. The view from here is stunning. I was actually thinking of making the trek along the river and seeing what other places of interest there are so I could get some more sketches finished."

James had already made several drawings of the river landscape. They would be a welcome addition to his portfolio once he started working in earnest on his paintings. His plans to return to Derbyshire had been quietly shelved for the moment. In the meantime, he would have to rely on his sketches and memory to begin work on the *Derbyshire Twins*.

His father would not be happy with the change in plans. Hugh Radley was a man of habit and structure. He didn't like people making sudden alterations and disturbing his world.

He would be especially disappointed when he discovered that James had not only *not* gone to Derbyshire, but that he had fled to Cornwall with Leah. But James would deal with his father when the time came. Right now, he had other priorities which concentrated his mind. Winning Leah's heart was what truly mattered.

"Why do you have to make sketches?" she said.

He turned and gave her a shy smile. Many people assumed that painters just started working on a blank canvas without any preliminary work. Sketches were an integral part of the process. "It helps to have drawings to refer to when you are creating a piece. Especially landscapes. I struggle with getting things into the right perspective and composition when I am first creating a new piece of work."

"Have you always wanted to be a painter?" she asked.

"In my heart of hearts, yes. I undertook some art classes at school, but never got to work under a true master. Most of what I know I have learned from books or watching other painters," he replied.

"But your father wants you to follow him into the church? Claire told me that there had been some ongoing tension between the two of you," she replied.

James hesitated. He did not want to say unkind things about his father. Hugh had relented on his demands and agreed to support James in his efforts, but it had not been an easy task. "I understand my father's point of view. He wants me to be able to make my way in the world. To have a profession that will enable me to support a family. He worries that painting will not allow that," he replied.

"I see. But . . ."

"But what?"

Leah turned to him; quiet determination showed on her face. "But what if you could? There have been plenty of painters and artists in the world who have made a living from their work. What is the worst that could happen if you didn't sell enough paintings? You may have to find paid employment. But at least you would have tried," she replied.

He reached out and placed a hand over one of hers before giving it a gentle squeeze. Her support of his work meant the world to him. "Thank you. Very few people understand the passion of wanting to be an artist. I have tried to explain what it feels like to hold a brush in my hand and set paint to canvas, but most people just give me an odd look."

Leah pointed toward a collection of neat buildings which sat at the front of the estate. One small building stood apart from the others, close to where the path from the steps ran. "If you wish to paint while you are here, I could speak to my grandfather and see if he will allow you to use the old cottage which overlooks the water. It has a better view than from here and you would be able have your things with you and work without being disturbed. I don't think anyone has used it since my grandmother died."

The idea of being able to set himself up and paint caught James's full attention. If he was able to complete some works before the inevitable journey home to London, he would be in a stronger position with his father. And if he could secure a buyer for those paintings, it would finally put paid to the notion of his going back to university. "That sounds wonderful. Could we please take a look at the cottage, and then go and talk to Sir Geoffrey?"

Leah got to her feet. "Of course. And if you think it would suit, I know a shop in Truro that sells artist supplies. I take it you will need some canvases."

The cottage proved perfect for James's needs and Sir Geoffrey readily agreed to allow him to make use of it. Sir Geoffrey also confessed to a long-abandoned painting pastime, after which he showed James the two large easels which had been stored away in the attic.

The easels were soon moved and set up in the cottage. A quick trip in the barouche into the nearby town of Truro saw James returning with new pieces of canvas, frames, and some linseed oil.

He was almost beside himself with excitement at the prospect of having a small, though temporary, painting studio at his disposal. It also added weight to his decision to remain at Mopus Manor for as long as possible. James was biding his time before he would speak to Leah about any plans for the future.

When Leah came and called him for supper later that evening, James was standing, grinning at the fresh canvas he had set up on the easel.

"You look like the cat who has got the cream," she said.

He laughed. "I feel like all the cats who have got the cream. I can't believe I have a painting studio."

Leah stood beside him in front of the blank canvas, a hand held under her chin. She tilted her head, as if inspecting an artwork. "So, what are you going to call this piece? 'Blank canvas without paint?'" she teased.

He loved it when she was playful. It took all his strength not to haul her into his arms and kiss her stupid.

Picking up a brush, he quickly mixed a little dry paint and oil together, then handed the brush to Leah. "Here. You make the first stroke."

"Really?"

"Yes."

Leah set the brush to the canvas where James directed; she began to make small strokes up and down. When she looked at him, he nodded.

"That is good. Keep going."

He watched as she added the first patch of dark blue to the painting.

Then, picking up a fine brush, he mixed in a little white paint and after following the outline of where Leah had painted, a wave began to appear on the canvas.

"Oh, James," she murmured.

It was some time before they finally headed in for supper.

Chapter Thirty-Three

Each morning when she drew back the bedroom curtains, Leah could see that James was already down in the cottage, hard at work. She suspected that if he could fit a bed in the room, he would sleep in the stone building which had once been her grandmother's favorite place to sit and watch the boats come up river from the North Sea.

Having had James all to herself on the journey down from London, she now found herself missing his company during the day. He ate breakfast long before she rose most mornings. His noon meal was taken down to him at the cottage, and by suppertime, he was usually so tired that he took himself off to bed after staying with her and Sir Geoffrey only as long as was polite. Twice, he had fallen asleep at the supper table.

By the end of the fourth day, Leah was feeling a tad jealous of the paint and canvas. She poked her head inside the doorway of the cottage. "Are you busy?"

James was kneeling in the corner, mixing a new batch of paint. He greeted her with a grin. "Come in. Mind where you step. I have some pieces laying out to dry on the floor. Oh, and watch out for the linseed oil rags. They will stain your gown."

The smell of oil and paint in the room was strong enough that Leah felt her head spin. How James could stand to work in among the fumes was hard to fathom.

"You should open a window or two. You don't want to faint from the tainted air," she said.

James frowned, then took in a deep breath. His face registered surprise. "I hadn't noticed the odor until you mentioned it. And now that you have its all I can smell. It is rather strong." He got to his feet, swaying just a little. "Perhaps I need to go and get some fresh air. I will open some windows when I return."

It was the opening she needed. She yearned for them to spend some precious time together. To be able to prize him away from his paintings. To simply walk and talk. She found herself thinking about him a lot of the time. She wanted to know whether his thoughts ever turned to her.

"There are some old sea caves I could show you a little way along the coast. They might make a good subject for one of your paintings. It would get you out into the fresh air. I could ask cook to pack up a small picnic and we could eat it while we are out," she said.

His eyes lit up. "That sounds like a perfect idea. Let's do it."

The caves were farther along the beach than Leah had remembered, and it took close to two hours before she was able to find them. As they walked, she worried constantly that James would call a halt to their march and ask that they return to the manor. She was pleased when he did not.

The unexpected comfort she found in being in his presence had her mind mulling over a number of issues. Foremost being, how long did James plan to stay at Mopus Manor? He had set himself up nicely within the cottage, but she knew it was only a matter of time before he announced his intentions to leave.

The prospect of watching him climb into his carriage and drive away filled her with a sense of dread. She didn't want him to leave, fearing she would never see him again.

While James picked up stones from the beach and tossed them way out to sea, she stood with hands tightly held together. She dared not ask him to remain, fearful that if her father did finally come to Cornwall, his wrath would come crashing down on the man who had tried to save her.

Yet she knew that if she said nothing and simply let James go, she may never get the chance to be alone with him again. Her father would make certain of that.

James picked up the picnic basket and pointed to a small patch of dry sand a little way along the beach. It would make the ideal place for them to sit and eat.

"Did you want to eat first and then explore the caves? That looks a good spot," said James.

"Yes, that way we can leave the basket at the mouth of the sea cave and not have to carry it with us. The rocks can be slippery, and you will need to steady yourself," she replied.

To her delight, James held out his hand. She hesitated for a moment but took it. The warm feeling as she slipped her fingers into his gentle grasp had her turning her head away.

She had missed his touch over the past few days. The brush of his hand on hers as he passed her bread when they sat and ate supper in their lodgings. His steady, protective hold whenever they rounded a bend in the road, and she shifted in her seat.

And those special moments whenever she tried to climb into the carriage. James standing behind her with his hands placed about her waist to lift her up into the driver's seat. A moment which was always followed by him having to put his hands firmly on her backside and push, all the while both of them giggled like small children. James would then climb up beside her and grace her with that silly lopsided smile of his.

That was the best moment of them all.

Chapter Thirty-Four

He had missed her. Missed the simple pleasure of being alone with Leah. The instant she suggested the walk to the sea cave, James had silently scolded himself for having spent much of the past days in the painting studio. After having been together on the journey from London, he had wanted to give Leah some space. But in his eagerness to set brush to canvas, he worried now that she may have felt neglected.

There was an unmistakable note of longing in her voice that only a fool would have failed to hear. He could only hope he was not a fool in love.

They took up a spot on the dry sandy beach away from the rocks. Leah smoothed her skirts, then she dropped down beside him. James's spirits lifted. There was a whole beach on which she could choose a place to sit, but Leah had decided to sit within touching distance of him.

Not that he expected her to be touching him. But still, a man never knew when his luck might change. From the stories he had heard of courtship and love within the Radley family, he knew Cupid was good at rewarding those who took a chance at helping love spark and grow. He shifted a few inches closer to her.

He looked inside the picnic basket, smiling when he saw its contents. There were freshly baked scones wrapped up in a clean cloth, along with pots of fresh Cornish cream and strawberry jam. When he unwrapped the still warm scones, a heady aroma filled his senses with delight. He couldn't remember the last time he had tasted scones.

He broke one of them open and, taking a spoon from the basket, scooped up some of the clotted cream. He was about to put it on the scone when Leah gasped and took hold of his wrist.

"James Radley, don't you dare! This is Cornwall; jam goes on first, then the cream. Don't you be bringing any of those odd Devonshire habits into this county. My grandfather will have you drummed out of the village," she said.

She took a knife from the basket and quickly added strawberry jam to the scone. When she was done, she nodded to James and he contritely placed a dollop of cream on top before handing half to her.

"I'm sorry. I didn't realize the depth of my crime," he said.

Leah gave a *tsk*. She grinned at him before biting into the soft dough.

Taking that as his having been forgiven, James set to work on eating his piece.

"Hmm, these are the best. You can have all the scones you like in London, but nothing is like having them baked here in Cornwall and being able have a large dollop of fresh clotted cream heaped on top." Leah turned and looked at him. "You have some jam on your face."

James put a finger up to his cheek, searching for the errant spread but failing.

With a soft smile, Leah reached out and wiped at a spot on the corner of his mouth with her finger. "There, that got it," she said.

James swallowed deep as he watched Leah lick the jam from her finger. If she had any idea of the effect it had on him, she hid it well. If in fact she had the slightest notion of what being near her at any time did to James and his heated blood, she was keeping it to herself.

He was constantly looking for the signs that she might be harboring feelings for him. He had put the kiss Leah had given him before he'd set off to find Sir Geoffrey down to nerves.

He turned his attention back to the picnic hamper. A bottle of Sir

Geoffrey's home-made ginger ale sat invitingly at the bottom of the basket, along with two small cups. After pulling the cork from the bottle, he poured them both a drink and handed one to Leah.

She raised her cup in salute to him, then downed the contents with one long gulp. "Thank you. Grandfather's ginger ale has always been the perfect drink for washing down scones and cream."

They sat for a time, eating, and drinking to their hearts' content. After three scones and an accompanying number of cups of ginger ale, James felt the need to lie down on the sand and have a snort nap.

Leah pulled out two small apples and handed one to James.

He sat and looked at it, uncertain as to whether he had any room left in his stomach. "Remember the huge supper of roast pig from our second night on the road? I am beginning to feel that full again," he said, patting his belly.

Leah laughed. "Yes, that roast pig was marvelous. But these are Cornish breadfruit apples; they are so sweet you will not be able to resist them. Even just a bite will have you finding room alongside the scones and ale," she said.

James forced himself to take a bite, surprised to discover that when he did, the apple tasted like a strawberry. He stared at it for a moment.

Leah chuckled. "I told you they were good."

He looked at her. The past few days had seen her cheeks begin to fill out once more. The cheeky sparkle in her eyes had returned. Being at her grandfather's house agreed with Leah. But then again, James suspected that anywhere away from her father would see Leah blossom.

"This is a marvelous place. I have never been to this part of the country before," he said.

The sandy beach and beautiful blue water of the River Tresillian stretched out before them. He could imagine that in summer, it would be a wonderful place for long evening walks. His imagination stirred. Long evening walks with Leah, her hand held within his as they shared secrets and stopped every so often to steal a kiss.

"I thought you had travelled a lot in England, what with your father being so high up in the church. I am surprised you have not made it to this sunny corner of the kingdom before," she replied.

James shrugged. All his life, he had been treading the same well-worn paths up and down the country. Every Christmas, it was to Strathmore Castle in Scotland. Back and forth to Cambridge when he had been studying. Only the occasional trip to a friend's estate in the country had seen his familiar routine broken. He had unknowingly become a creature of habit. "I do travel a little. After my trip to Derbyshire, I went to Brighton when Caroline and Lord Newhall decided to elope."

She raised an eyebrow at his comment. "Can you still call it an elopement when you bring the Bishop of London with you?"

James chuckled. "That was at my Aunt Adelaide's behest. She was prepared to let Caroline and Newhall forgo the full St Paul's cathedral wedding as long as they took my father with them to conduct the wedding service."

"It sounds like it was a fun adventure. Not that you could really say Brighton was far to travel from London. My family are always moving up and down the road to Brighton whenever the Prince Regent decides he wants to spend time by the seaside. My father never likes to be out of touch with the royal court for long," she said.

Knowing Tobias Shepherd and his political machinations, Leah's comment was no surprise. Even Guy had started following the court of the future king as his political ambitions steadily grew.

Leah took one last bite of her apple, then tossed the core into the nearby seaside bushes. A scatter of seagulls quickly descended where the apple had landed. The squawks of birds filled the air as they jostled over who was to get the heaven-sent bounty.

She got to her feet and began to hitch up her skirts. James forced himself to resist temptation and turned away.

"You are going to have to look at my boots at some point, James. I can't have my skirts soaked when we venture inside the cave. I didn't take you for being such a prude," she teased.

He turned back to her, his gaze firmly on her face and away from her raised skirts. "I am not a prude. I have just been raised to treat women with the utmost of respect," he replied.

Leah walked over to him and bent low. She lifted his chin and leaned in close; their lips were almost touching. His heart swelled at the prospect of an unexpected kiss. While she gifted him with the most innocent of smiles, he caught the sparkle of mischief which shone in her eyes. "James Radley don't try to tell me that you did not have disrespectful thoughts every time you took a firm hold of my arse and pushed me up into the barouche," she said.

She was right, of course, which was no surprise. Every single time he'd had his hands on her rounded rump, he had felt himself going hard. He delighted in the knowledge that Leah had figured out that his manhandling of her was not entirely respectable. He suspected she had also come to the realization that he had thoroughly enjoyed it.

He dreaded to think what Leah would say if she ever discovered the extent of his disrespectful thoughts about her. Not to mention what he would dearly love to do to her if he could get his hands on not just her naked arse, but her whole naked body.

His focus at this moment was on a single part of her body. Her soft, full mouth.

Please. Please kiss me.

She released his face and pulled away. A stab of disappointment hit his heart as he watched her set about packing up the remains of their picnic. They had been so close. He should have just reached out and taken the opportunity to kiss her.

He tossed the rest of his half-eaten apple into the low bushes, close to the place Leah had thrown hers. His appetite for something sweet was now focused entirely on the woman who was walking toward the entrance to the cave.

James got to his feet and raced after her.

Chapter Thirty-Five

T he sea caves had always been one of Leah's favorite places.
They were where she could allow her imagination to run riot.
The legend of King Arthur had been set at Tintagel Castle
on the other side of Cornwall, facing out to the Celtic Sea, but in her
mind, she imagined him sleeping peacefully within the caves along the
Tresillian River.

She had always kept that piece of fiction to herself, not even
sharing it with her sister when they were children. Her mythical hero
was hers alone. His resting place was forever locked in her heart. Now,
a different hero had stepped into her life.

James followed close as they traversed the slippery rocks at the
entrance of the cave. He slipped at one point, his boot landing in a
deep rock pool with a loud splash.

"Bloody . . ." he muttered.

She laughed. "You don't need to mind your manners around me,
James Radley. I might be gentle born, but I have heard enough foul
language in my time for it not to offend me."

Offering a hand to him, she helped James climb back out of the
rockpool and up onto the relative safety of the rocks. He stood for a

time, shaking the water from his boot, and muttering further foul oaths under his breath.

"Come with me. There is a bigger space farther inside. You can take your boot off and wring out your socks once we reach it," she said.

With his boot still waterlogged, James squelched after her.

Leah was enjoying James's company. It was wonderful to be able to spend time with him and reveal all the secret places from her childhood. She finally had someone with whom she could share them.

She didn't use the word wonderful very often but being with him was just that. *Wonderful.* A bubble of joy bounced around in her stomach along with the scones, sweet apple, and ginger beer. She had almost forgotten what happiness felt like.

The low, tight entrance finally opened up into a much larger space. They stepped into the heart of the sea cave.

"Oh!" he gasped.

A grinning Leah remembered the first time she had seen inside the cave, and her reaction had been the same as James's—pure wonderment.

"Leah, this is amazing! I could never imagine this being here. What a fantastic sight!" he exclaimed.

The sea cave was its own magical world inside the earth. The tide had been out for several hours and a patch of dry sandy beach was visible along the side wall of the cave. Many times, during her summer holidays here as a child, Leah and her sister would take off their boots and stockings and dig their toes deep into the soft sand.

In the middle of the cave was a series of small rockpools. Leah crossed over to her favorite one and looked down. It was studded with colorful sea anemones. To her surprise, there was also a fish inside the pool.

"Poor thing. I hope that when the tide comes in you get washed back out to sea," she said.

James ambled over; the soft squelch of his sea-soaked boot echoed in the cavernous space as he walked. When she looked down at it, he shrugged. "This is a marvelous place. I'm glad you brought me here. Though my boots and wet feet are not so appreciative of the adventure. I fear that they will be making squishy noises all the way home in protest."

Leah looked away, trying to hide her smile. James was attempting to be gruff, but he was failing at it so badly she could only find it endearing. She hadn't known many nice men in her life, but she sensed it would take a lot to get him riled up past the point of simply being a little cross over anything which vexed him. And for that, she was grateful. There was a lot of good things to be said about a man possessed of an even temper.

"Do many other people know about this cave or is this your own secret place?" he asked.

"All the locals know of the cave, though we do tend to keep it a secret amongst ourselves. The folk of Mopus Passage are likely to give wrong directions to day-trippers who bother to enquire, even those from Truro. We like to keep it hidden."

"Why?" he asked.

She leaned in close. "Smugglers. This cave was used for hiding contraband goods during the war against Napoleon. The boats would come in here at high tide, and drop off barrels and casks of banned imports, then the locals would wait until the tide had gone out and retrieve them."

"I take it that it was your grandfather's job during the war to try to catch the local smugglers?" replied James, recalling the comfortable familiarity that Sir Geoffrey had with his pistols.

Leah snorted. "Lord, no. Where do you think they hid most of the smuggled goods? My grandfather's cellars were full of the stuff—he was one of the chief smugglers. He and the local magistrate were up to their eyeballs in it."

She was a delight. James could not fathom how he could have allowed himself to hide away from Leah for those first few days after their arrival. Drawing and painting were his passion, but Leah was, well, she was something else.

His art stirred his heart, no doubt about it. But Leah held his soul in her hand. His very essence of existence danced in the light of her presence. He had never understood the whole notion of love, but if this feeling was love, it was the most powerful force he could ever have imagined.

Their gazes met and James found himself lost in a heaven of blue eyes. One slow blink of Leah's long brown eyelashes and he was gone. He stepped forward, closing the gap between them, before capturing Leah's lips in a soft, lingering kiss.

At first Leah didn't respond, but slowly, surely, her mouth softened, and his tongue swept past her lips. He tried to deepen the kiss, but she pulled back. He sensed her hesitation and waited for her to break contact, but she continued to move her lips against his, staying within the kiss. Their tongues glided over one another once, twice.

A hand pressed against his chest. It was barely a push, but it was enough to give him a clear message. He drew back and broke the kiss. Leah's eyes were cast downward; she would not meet his gaze. *Damn.*

He had misread her signals. Pushed when he should not have. In the unsettling silence, he sensed her fear. She was alone with him, exposed and vulnerable.

"I should not have done that. Pardon my misjudgment; it was wrong of me to take such liberties with you," he said.

"I think it is time we returned to the manor." Leah stepped past him and headed for the entrance to the cave.

After collecting the picnic basket, they headed back to the manor in silence. The whole way, James wracked his brains, trying to think of anything he could say that could undo the damage he had just done.

He came up empty.

On the long walk home, Leah thought about the kiss. It had been even better than the first time. James was skilled when it came to tender, warm kisses. She could never grow tired of the heady sensation of his lips on hers.

But why was he kissing her? That was the question, *and* the reason why she had made him stop. His swift post-kiss apology had cut her like a knife. It had confirmed her worst fears. James had kissed her because he felt an obligation to make some sort of effort. If he had actually wanted her, then he would have declared his love.

He feels obliged to marry me. That's why he kissed me.

They had been alone together on the road down from London. It made perfect sense for marriage to be the outcome her grandfather, and perhaps even her family, would come to expect of hers and James's little adventure.

And marriage to James would be a very different proposition to that which she knew had been set out for her with Guy. James was a good man. He would no doubt in time do what was expected of him and offer for her hand in marriage. But he deserved more. He deserved to be in love with the woman he married.

As they began to climb the steep, winding steps back up to Mopus Manor, Leah chided herself. She had been a fool to nurture the affection she'd felt for James. Every day she spent with him, it continued to blossom and grow stronger. Leah could no longer keep it at bay.

She was in love with James, but she had to let him go.

Chapter Thirty-Six

Late one afternoon, James was finishing the final cleanup of his paintbrushes in readiness for closing the cottage for the night and returning to the manor. He had taken to hiding out in his painting studio for the best part of each day, ostensibly to get work done, but in truth, hiding from Leah.

She had made the task a little easier for him by busying herself with the management of the manor house and helping to plant new herbs in the kitchen garden. Over the past days, he and Leah had slipped into a polite but distant cohabitation of Mopus Manor. James had taken his cues from her and not pressed his luck. He had made a mess of things at the sea cave and had spent endless hours since then wondering if he had read the signs wrong. He did not want to leave Mopus Manor, but feared that at some point soon, he would be asked to go.

A knock at the cottage door stirred him from his private musings of light, shade, and how he could find a way to reconnect with Leah. He was surprised to see that instead of his visitor being Leah, it was Sir Geoffrey Sydell.

In the ten days since he and Leah had arrived at Mopus Manor, James had not seen Sir Geoffrey anywhere near the cliff-facing garden.

His unexpected appearance at the cottage door set James's nerves on edge.

"Mind if I come in?" said Sir Geoffrey.

James put down his paintbrushes and wiped his hands on a rag. He motioned for Sir Geoffrey to enter. "Please, do come in. This is your house; you shouldn't need to ask for permission to enter any room."

He busied about the cottage, clearing away a few of his smaller easels and making room for his guest to sit down. He then sat on a stool opposite to the chair Sir Geoffrey now occupied.

"Sorry about the sudden visit, but since Leah has not yet returned from Truro, I thought now might be a good time for you and me to have a little chat," said Sir Geoffrey.

Ah.

James had known it was only a matter of time before Sir Geoffrey would want to come and talk to him about Leah. Or, to be more accurate, what was to be done about Leah. The situation for all of them was, at best, a temporary one.

Eventually, Tobias Shepherd would receive word as to the whereabouts of his errant daughter. After which, he was unlikely to sit on his hands and leave her to live out her life peacefully in Cornwall. James was surprised that no one had yet come knocking on the door of Mopus Manor, demanding the return of Leah to London.

James had wondered on more than one occasion as to what was happening in London. What had transpired on the morning of the ill-fated wedding after he and Leah had disappeared? A runaway bride was the sort of salacious gossip on which the *ton* thrived.

His own letter home to his parents had been sent at the beginning of the week. He had said little in it other than that he and Leah were safe, and that he would eventually return to London. He trusted his father to keep his confidence.

Sir Geoffrey was a different matter altogether. He was Leah's family, and was therefore bound by a different set of rules when it came to be keeping, or not keeping, secrets from her parents.

The thought of discussing Leah without her being present sat uncomfortably with James. He had already breached her trust with that kiss at the sea cave. He was not keen to give her any further reason to mistrust him.

"Firstly, I need to make it clear I have only my granddaughter's best interests at heart," said Sir Geoffrey.

Upon hearing those words, James put down his cleaning cloth and sat hunched over on the stool. His hands were tightly clasped. He didn't like the sound of the words 'best interests' one little bit. In his experience, people had an unfortunate habit of using that very phrase when they wanted to wrap up unpleasant decisions and hand them over for others to deal with.

Sir Geoffrey held a hand up and sat forward in his chair. "I can see that you are uneasy, James, so let me clarify what I mean. While nothing should happen without Leah's express permission, the reality of the situation needs to be faced"

"The situation being?" asked James.

"My granddaughter is a gently bred young woman, currently on the run from her family. Her father has legal say over her life at present, and the only thing that can change that fact is marriage. Or her father's death, which considering how fit my son-in-law is, will not likely be happening for many years to come," replied Sir Geoffrey.

James ignored the obvious undertone of disappointment in Sir Geoffrey's voice at the mention of Leah's father. They were back to the problem that had sent Leah fleeing from her wedding in the first place: her father dictating her life, and society's expectations of her doing exactly as she was told.

"And that is where you come into it, young man. Though I imagine you must have already accepted that you would have a greater and ongoing role to play in her life. Only a fool would think of travelling for several days with an unwed young woman and not expect there to be further consequences. From my experience of you, I don't see a dull-minded man."

"Society would expect me to marry her," replied James.

"Society and I demand it," said Sir Geoffrey.

This was sweet music to James's ear. Not that he particularly cared what London high society thought of the matter, but the fact that Sir Geoffrey expected him to marry Leah was most encouraging. Her grandfather's opinion could mean all the difference when it came to the point of convincing her that if she had to marry in order to escape her father, then James should be the one she chose.

"I thank you for your candor, Sir Geoffrey. It heartens me somewhat. To be honest, I had planned to speak to Leah soon about the current situation. The problem, of course, being that I cannot in all good conscience pressure her into marrying me. She must come of her own accord," he said.

Sir Geoffrey snorted. "She must be made to see reason, is more like it. I am prepared to indulge my granddaughter only so far. I run the risk of creating a greater schism in the family if I openly defy her father once he discovers she is here at Mopus Manor. Things are bad enough between my son-in-law and myself already."

He rose from the chair and after placing his hand in his coat pocket, he withdrew a small blue box. He offered it to James.

"This is a family heirloom. It belonged to my wife, Alice, and I know Leah has always had a particular liking of it. My wife was a strong woman, but with a kind and loving heart. Leah is so much like her that at times I have nearly called her Alice," said Sir Geoffrey.

Since the topic of marriage was now being raised, it made sense for James to be honest about how he felt for Leah. If Sir Geoffrey knew James loved his granddaughter, it could only help to further his cause.

James looked at the box he now held in his hand. Sir Geoffrey's blessing meant a great deal. "Her strength of character is one of the many reasons why I love your granddaughter," he replied.

Sir Geoffrey smiled. "I was hoping you had formed a special affection for my Leah. She deserves to be with a man who loves her."

James opened the ring box. Inside sat a thin band of gold, encrusted with alternating small emeralds and diamonds which circled the entire ring. He blinked. It was exactly the sort of ring he would have chosen for Leah if he had been tasked with buying her a betrothal ring himself.

"Thank you," he said.

He put the ring box to one side, intending only to show it to Leah if she agreed to marry him. He would not, under any circumstances, be waving it under her nose as an inducement to get her to accept his proposal.

"There is one other thing," said Sir Geoffrey.

"Yes?" replied James.

"I have written to your father."

Chapter Thirty-Seven

"I bought you some Cornish pasties. I hope they are still hot."

James looked up from the bench he was sitting on outside his painting studio and nodded as Leah handed over a small cloth bag. "Thank you. I am partial to a pasty."

"Just don't tell my grandfather's cook that I brought them back from Truro. She fancies herself as somewhat of a master of the art and might not take too kindly to the knowledge that we have eaten ones from foreign climes."

The day spent in the town of Truro had been a delight. It was the first time she had felt safe enough to venture from the house on her own. Sir Geoffrey had insisted on her taking two burly footmen with her just in case her visit unfortunately happened to coincide with the arrival of someone from her family who had been sent from London to retrieve her.

"You should come over to Truro with me next time I visit. There is a color shop on Boscawen Street that I passed on my way to the baker's. I expect if you need more paint colors, you could purchase some there."

"Thank you. I might just do that. It would be good to spend a day away from the easel and freshen my mind," he replied.

He sat the bag to one side, then patted the space beside him on the bench. "Come and sit with me. We need to talk."

Leah immediately stiffened. There was something in his manner that put her senses on edge. He looked like he was about to deliver bad news. She had seen it enough times in her life to know the warning signs.

"Your grandfather came and spoke to me while you were in town."

"About what?" she ventured, knowing in her heart that there was really only one topic of discussion her grandfather would have wanted to raise with James in her absence.

"About you. About us."

Of course, her grandfather had spoken to James. It irritated her that he had waited until she was in Truro for the day to seek James out. People were always having conversations about her but not actually including her in the discussion.

Leah held his gaze, determined to get a full understanding of what had been said in her absence and, God forbid, what had been decided. She could only pray that James had not made mention of the kiss. Or indeed any of their kisses.

"None of what he said came as a surprise. What Sir Geoffrey stated is the obvious. In society's eyes you are ruined, and I have been the one who caused your downfall," he said.

"But you didn't. I made the decision to run away from my own wedding. You merely helped to see me safely delivered here," she replied.

James sat forward on the long wooden bench and held his hands tightly together. He shook his head. This was not an encouraging sight. "Your grandfather can only protect you from your father for so long. You and I being here at Mopus Manor puts Sir Geoffrey in a difficult position. He has asked that we consider all possible solutions to the problem."

"The problem being me," she replied.

He got to his feet and walked a little way away. Standing with his hands in his coat pockets, he looked out over the river before turning back to her. "You are not a problem for me, Leah. Far from it."

Problem, quandary—it mattered little what he wanted to label her as being. She was still *something* that needed to be solved. To her mind, they were now left facing a difficult situation. Both could see the inevitable outcome that everyone would expect of their time in Cornwall, but neither of them wanted to go through with it. At least not like this.

Leah came and stood by James's side. She could never imagine growing tired of the view down to the Tresillian River and beyond to where it met the Truro River. The dark blue of the waters constantly created white-capped ripples at the point where the two rivers connected.

He turned to her. "You and I have to make some hard decisions. I wrote to my father and explained what happened. I told him about the journey here and a little of why you fled the church. Sir Geoffrey informed me earlier today that he too has written to my father. The mail only takes a day or so to reach London, so by now, people will know where we are."

"What else did my grandfather say?" she said.

He reached out and took hold of her hand, and their fingers locked gently together. She was surprised by how much she had felt the loss of his touch. The simple pleasure of being seated beside one another on the carriage bench each day, the feel of his hard thigh against her leg, was something she could admit to missing. And even now, it was nice to simply hold hands.

"He sees no other option than for you to marry. The decision for you, of course, being whom you will wed." His hold on her fingers tightened just enough to have her lifting her gaze to meet his.

James was in a difficult position; society would expect him to offer for her. But if he did and it was only out of a sense of being compelled, then he and she would simply be swapping places. It would be James who found himself bound to someone he did not love, the same as she had with Guy.

"Thank you for telling me. I am sure that was not what you wanted to hear from him," she said.

"You might be surprised by what I want," he replied.

The sudden gruff edge to his voice had heat pooling in her loins. Her body's reaction to him was not surprising; it had been happening for some time now. Much as she had tried to fight it, she knew he had already stolen her heart. What she would give to be able to offer up the rest of herself to him. For him to claim her. For James to love her.

Leah tried to control the whirl of emotion which being this close to James created within her, but she was powerless against its strength. Instead she was left clutching at her sense of fair play and justice.

James was being put in a position that was grossly unjust to him, and because of that, she could not bring herself to speak to him of marriage. He should not have to suffer the punishment of being made to marry someone he did not love.

But things were as they were, and while love might have failed them, Leah was determined that she would not fail James. She had to push him away, force him to leave Mopus Manor. To give him the chance to make decisions about his future before others made those decisions for him.

"Well then, I suggest you start making plans to leave here and soon. Matters are going to get ugly very quickly once I tell my grandfather that you and I are not going to be wed."

Chapter Thirty-Eight

L eah stood at the window of the breakfast room the following morning while James was seated at the breakfast table, enjoying his second cup of tea for the day.

He looked up from his cup as Leah gasped and suddenly pressed her face to the window. "A carriage is approaching the house. No prizes for guessing that it will be my father."

James rose from his chair and came to stand alongside her. He placed a comforting hand on her shoulder, then peered out the window. "It was only a matter of time."

Leah shrugged off his touch. "You should have left while you still had the chance, James."

Her voice lacked emotion as she spoke, but James suspected it was part of her usual detached way of dealing with her father—a deeply ingrained pattern of behavior which was designed to protect her heart and mind from Tobias Shepherd.

A black travel coach wound its way up the long drive which climbed the hill leading to where Mopus Manor stood.

He held his hand up to shade his eyes from the morning sun, then looked again. For an instant, he thought his heart had stopped. "I'll be damned. That is not your father. That is mine!"

He would know the Radley family travel coach anywhere, even at this distance. The Strathmore crest of the three stars and a rearing horse emblazoned in gold on the side of the coach gave it away.

"What can it mean?" she asked.

James could think of a dozen things that the impending arrival of his father could herald, but he was in too much of a hurry out the breakfast room to stop and consider them. "We shall know soon enough," he cried.

After grabbing his coat, he raced outside, then stood waiting impatiently in the chilly morning air while the travel coach made its final turn up the hill and arrived in the manor's forecourt. He had last seen the coach when he had sent it home from the Gloucester Coffee House on the morning, he'd followed Leah out of London. He had not expected that the next time he saw it, it would be as it rolled along a sandy road in the middle of Cornwall, bringing his father.

When it came to a halt, James quickly stepped forward and opened the door. His father's partly bald head appeared, followed by his red and gold woolen cape of office. James frowned. His father only wore his bishop's garb when conducting affairs on behalf of the church.

"Your Grace," he said, and dipped into a bow.

His father gave him a barely perceptible nod. James righted himself, but kept his gaze fixed toward the ground. Hugh Radley's role as a father was secondary to his role as Bishop of London when he was on official business.

"Ah, Sir Geoffrey, how are you?" said Hugh.

James lifted his head to see Leah's grandfather striding toward them.

Sir Geoffrey stopped and bowed before Hugh. "Your Grace. I never expected to see you darkening my doorstep. It appears Mopus Manor has become quite the meeting place for you and your family," he said.

"Yes, so it would seem," replied Hugh, holding out his hand. His father finally turned to James and gave him a tight smile. "Come. You, Sir Geoffrey, and I have much to discuss."

James followed his father and Sir Geoffrey through the front door. He poked his head back in the breakfast room, but it was empty. By the look of it, Leah had made the smart decision to remain out of sight until she was summoned. From the frosty greeting he had received from own his father, James could not blame her.

They were ushered into Sir Geoffrey's private study, and after the butler was instructed to bring tea and toast, the door was closed behind them.

"Should I go and find Leah?" asked James.

Sir Geoffrey shook his head. "You can talk to her after we have discussed and settled matters."

The stern looks on both Sir Geoffrey and Hugh's faces gave him all the clues he needed; they did not intend to discuss anything with Leah until they had made their position clear with James. After that, he was going to be the one left to convince her of what needed to happen.

"Your Grace, where would you like to sit?" asked Sir Geoffrey.

"I have been sitting for days. I am more than happy to walk the floor for the time being and give my legs a good stretch," replied Hugh, unbuttoning his bishop's cloak.

James wasn't certain as to what he himself should be doing. He went to sit on one of the long battered green couches, but the disapproving frown on his father's face stopped him. Hugh began to pace back and forth in front of the fireplace, his hands clasped behind his back, fingers constantly wriggling.

James stepped to one side, keeping out of his father's way. He let his arms hang at his side as he stood to attention and watched Hugh pace. The sight of his father's feet marching up and down the room had him chewing nervously on his bottom lip. Memories of receiving a scolding from his father as a child surfaced in James's mind. Hugh was a loving and affectionate father, but when one or more of his golden rules had been broken, punishment was sure to follow.

James might well be a fully grown adult, but in his father's mind he was not above being made to pay for his sins. In running away with Leah, he had stolen another man's bride, which James was sure had broken more than one of the Ten Commandments.

The door opened and the butler entered the room carrying a tray with cups and a pot of tea on it. He was followed by the housekeeper carrying a smaller tray with toast and cakes. They set the food down on the tall oak sideboard which sat against the wall, then left the room.

James made a step toward the spread, intent on pouring them all a cup of tea, but a second unhappy glare from his father had him beating a hasty retreat back to his spot out of the way. There he stood once more, hands by his side like a naughty schoolboy. Parents always seemed to have the perfect way of make their offspring feel small.

"We shall talk first, then food," announced Hugh.

"Would you please let me explain?" said James, hoping to get the first word in.

His father shook his head. "I think it best that you understand how things are in London before you offer up any explanations to me."

James fell silent. From Hugh's unusually curt manner since his arrival, James didn't expect that the news he was about to hear would be good.

"What you and Leah have done is to create one of the biggest scandals of the year. I was made to stand in front of the Archbishop of Canterbury and answer some very uncomfortable questions regarding my judgement as a parent. Do you have any idea how embarrassing that was for me?" said Hugh.

"I am sorry your grace," replied James, feeling the heat rise up on his cheeks.

"Oh, and don't get me started on the *very* ugly conversation I had with Tobias Shepherd. Suffice to say he was livid. He was making ready to come to Cornwall and retrieve Leah, but Guy Dannon asked him not to bother," said Hugh.

"How is Guy?" asked James. Leah's father was not someone James honestly gave a damn about. His former friend was more of a loose cannon than Tobias Shepherd.

His father huffed. "Do you really care? I mean, you stole the man's fiancée away from him on his wedding day. You can hardly expect me, Guy, or, for that matter, the rest of all of London to think you give a tinker's cuss about him."

James had hoped the letter Sir Geoffrey had sent Hugh had made the situation clear, but that did not appear to be the case. Everyone thought James had stolen Leah.

"I didn't steal Leah from her wedding. I followed her from the church and only intercepted her when we finally reached Basingstoke," replied James.

"So, you say. But you could have stopped her leaving London, and you didn't. Instead, you helped her travel all the way to Mopus Manor. Tell me, James, does that sound like the actions of a man who doesn't have in mind to steal away a young woman? To betray his friend?"

His father's harsh words felt like a slap to the face. He had been expecting some sort of reproach, but to hear his own sire accuse him of such a dishonest and despicable act truly hurt.

Sir Geoffrey got to his feet. He walked over to the sideboard, and after picking up the tea pot, began to fill the three cups. James had hoped he might back up the version of the story already given him by his granddaughter and James. But it was to no avail.

Anger stirred within James. He was not a child. He would only tolerate so much of a berating from even his own father before he would speak to defend both himself and Leah.

"Leah was desperate not to marry Guy. Her family forced her into accepting his suit," said James.

His anger threatened to boil over. His honor was being called into question, and he was not going to stand for it. Hugh may not like what he heard from his son, but James was determined he *was* going to hear it.

His father accepted the cup of tea offered to him by Sir Geoffrey. He blew cool air over the lip of the cup before taking a sip. He then set it down. James refused the tea he was offered.

"And you travelled alone with her all this way, to ensure her safety?" replied Hugh.

"Yes. I did. I felt honor-bound to ensure that not only was Leah saved from having to marry a man who is a vile, debauched monster, but that she was safely delivered into the hands of someone in her family who *did* care for her. I regret nothing that I have done to help her," he replied.

Hugh looked to Sir Geoffrey. "Good. I am glad to have heard it firsthand from my son. James did exactly what I would have expected of him. So, Sir Geoffrey, I am in complete agreement with your proposal. There really is no other option."

James chanced a look at Hugh and then turned his attention to Sir Geoffrey.

Leah's grandfather was slowly nodding his head. "Do you have the license?"

James quickly looked back to Hugh. The air whooshed out of his lungs as he saw his father produce a document from out of his jacket. The document was closed with an official Church of England seal.

License. Bishops tended to handle only one type of license—an ordinary marriage license. But since neither he nor Leah had been resident at Mopus Manor long enough to be able to avail themselves of church banns or an ordinary marriage license, that meant Sir Geoffrey could only be referring to the *other* type of marriage license.

A special license.

James swallowed deep. Little wonder his father had come dressed in his bishop's cape. He had visited the Archbishop of Canterbury before leaving London and had secured a *special license*. James dreaded to think how much money and favors that had cost his father. He now understood Hugh's filthy mood.

"Yes. It cost me not only a pretty penny, but I am going to be indebted to the Archbishop of Canterbury for the foreseeable future, thanks to the efforts of my son," replied Hugh.

It would take a long time for James to be able to pay his father back. The favors his father had called in, he would likely never be able to repay. His father's financial support of his painting career had been generous enough. He was humbled by the thought of all that his father had gone through in order to save the honor of both his son and his future daughter-in-law.

"Well then, all that needs to be done in order for the wedding to take place is for this young man to convince my granddaughter that he will make her a fine husband," said Sir Geoffrey. He downed the rest of his cup of tea. "I shall leave the two of you to talk and eat."

At the thought of Leah becoming his wife, James's heart filled with an odd mixture of joy and guilt. Joy over the fact that he and Leah would be wed—guilt over his fear that she may not want him.

It was only after Sir Geoffrey had left the room that Hugh appeared to relax somewhat. James stood quietly waiting. His father had just travelled more than two hundred and fifty miles along less-than-stellar roads in order to meet with his son—a fact that James knew would test his love. "I didn't want to say too much about Guy while Sir Geoffrey was still here, and I am grateful that he had the discretion to leave us alone. Guy was obviously angry over what happened with Leah, but it was your betrayal which truly knocked him for six."

James raked his fingers through his hair. His father was right; he had betrayed Guy. The moment he had fallen in love with Leah, James had broken all the bonds of friendship. But now knowing what he did about Guy, and his wicked plans for Leah, any sense of guilt James may have once had over betraying his former best friend was long gone. He would protect the woman he loved, and Guy Dannon could go to the devil.

"I love her. I began to have feelings for Leah some time ago; it was part of the reason why I agreed to go to Derbyshire with Caroline and Francis. I was hoping that time away from her would cure me of that ailment. Instead, being apart and missing her only made it worse," he replied.

His father crossed the floor and placed a hand on James's shoulder. "You have to be honest with yourself and the rest of the world over what has happened. If you wish my full support for your marriage to Leah, I shall expect nothing less than that from you."

James met Hugh's gaze. "Guy Dannon was going to use Leah to seduce other men in order to further his political ambitions. He can claim I betrayed him all he likes, but *he* is the one who was prepared to betray the innocence of a young woman in order to satisfy his lust for power. And Tobias Shepherd was prepared to let him do it. As I said before, I regret nothing that I have done since that day in London and I would do it all again if I had to."

Hugh nodded. "Good. The son I raised to be an honest man has not failed me. You must have known where this would all lead to in the end. I just hope you are prepared to withstand the ramifications of your actions once you and Leah return to London. This has been quite the scandal."

"I will protect what is mine," replied James.

"Then marry her. Put Leah forever out of the reach of her father. Make it certain that Tobias Shepherd can never hurt her again. You and Leah must stand before me and God today and become man and wife."

James's thoughts drifted back to the conversation that he and Leah had shared the previous afternoon. For a moment, she had let him hold her hand, and at the time he had seen it as an encouraging sign of progress. Now he knew he was going to have to rely upon that tenuous moment of connection to get her agreement for them to marry.

"I will speak to her and explain the situation. We have discussed some matters already, so this won't come as a complete surprise to her. Can I ask, have we your blessing for this marriage?" he replied.

For the first time since his arrival, the hard look on Hugh Radley's face eased. The lines of his frown softened. It was with an overwhelming sense of relief that James found his father's arms suddenly wrapped around him. "Of course, you have my blessing. Your whole family will be overjoyed at hearing of your marriage. Your mother sends her love, and your sisters cannot wait to welcome Leah into the family. Now for goodness sake, go and tell that girl that you love her, and you want her for your wife," said Hugh.

James sent a silent prayer of thanks to heaven for the long and loving marriage of his parents. His parents had taught him to believe in love. And with love came sacrifice. He was going to offer up his heart to Leah, lay all his secrets and desires open to her in the honest hope that she would accept him. He would have to trust to his faith in love that in time she might come to feel the same for him.

Hugh gave him one last friendly pat on the back before releasing him. Taking James's face in his hands, he leaned in. "If you love her, then make her your wife. It will keep her forever out of that blackguard's reach. And once you have done that, then you and I will sit down and have a long talk about your plans for the future. You will have a wife to support."

James nodded. He would have that difficult discussion with his father, but it would not be until after he and Leah were wed and returned to London.

He would have a wife, and between them, they would find a way for him to keep his life's passion alive.

Chapter Thirty-Nine

L eah couldn't remain in the house a minute longer while she waited for the men to finish their meeting. It made her blood boil to know that she had been deliberately excluded from the discussion. They were talking about her future, yet no one had thought to include her in the conversation.

"Bloody men," she grumbled. After grabbing a woolen shawl, she wrapped it about her and stomped off down to the beach.

As soon as she stepped out of the low shrubs which dotted the dunes and onto the beach proper, she began to walk. The tide was still on its way out and the sand was waterlogged in parts, which made walking a difficult proposition at times. Keeping to the higher, slightly drier parts of the beach, she made her way toward the sea cave.

James's father had come all the way to Cornwall, which set her nerves on edge. People didn't make the journey from London without serious purpose, especially not the Bishop of London. Whatever Hugh Radley had to say, she was not expecting to like it.

If the surface of the beach had been firmer, she would have made better progress. But with her feet constantly sinking into the soft sand, she had barely made it a hundred yards from the cliff path before James called her name.

She stopped and waited for him. There was no point in delaying the inevitable news. Good, bad, or a mix of the two, she would have to deal with whatever her grandfather and the two Radley men had decided. Not that she was considering any of it to be a *fait accompli,* but having already fled from her family, she knew her options were now somewhat limited.

James finally caught up with her. His face frustratingly gave her no clue as to what had happened or been decided in her grandfather's study.

"Well?" she snapped.

He hesitated for a moment, and Leah felt a rising mix of anger and panic well up inside her. When he reached out and touched her arm, she flinched and stepped back.

"It's not bad news," he said.

Leah held his gaze. She had a life's experience of being constantly told what to think and do. She hoped that James, knowing enough of her recent history, would not be so foolish as to try and attempt to persuade her to accept something which he knew she would find unpalatable. There would be no more going quietly along with plans that were against her wishes, of that she was most definitely determined.

He offered her his arm. "Let us go somewhere and talk. A windy beach is not the place for this discussion. Come back with me to the manor."

The place James had in mind turned out to be his painting studio at the bottom of the garden. It, of course, made sense. It was away from the main house, private, and secluded. They would not be disturbed.

And no one will hear me when I get riled up and start yelling.

Leah followed him inside and closed the door behind her. James offered her a seat, but she was too tense to consider sitting down. Her preference would be to pace the floor, but in the cramped space there was not the room.

"Why is your father here?" she asked.

He met her gaze. "He has a special marriage license which he procured at great expense and trouble from the Archbishop of Canterbury. It has our names on it," he replied.

Leah slumped down in the wicker chair near the door. She clasped her hands together. Her fingers twined and twisted around one another.

"And what did you tell your father and my grandfather?" she asked.

James knelt before Leah. He took her hands in his before untangling her fingers and rubbing his thumb over her knuckles.

She looked down at his signet ring, a tear coming to her eye when she remembered having worn it when they were pretending to be married. No one was pretending any more, and it filled her with sadness.

"I told them I would talk to you," he said.

Her head shot up. "As in, you would talk me into marrying you because you have no other option. Your father would not have come all this way if he didn't think you would need to be convinced of what to do. That is not fair to you, James," she said.

He shook his head. "I told them I would talk to you and seek your opinion. Leah, I have never tried to force you into doing anything, and I am not about to start now. Especially not when it comes to the serious matter of marriage."

Her gaze dropped back to her hands. She had been in a similar position once before with Guy, trusting his words that he would ask her first before speaking to her father, and then having to deal with an unwelcome betrothal. "Are you saying you will give me a choice?"

"Yes."

"And what about you? Marriage is between two people. What do you say of this special license?" she replied.

A gentle smile appeared on his lips, at which a flicker of hope sparked in her heart. Was there a chance that he wanted her too, that perhaps that kiss had meant something to him? His fumbling post-kiss apology still gave her concern.

"I will accept your decision. I will not force you into a marriage you do not want," he said.

She could sense he wanted to say more, but something was holding him back. Leah searched for an opening. "Do you believe in marriage without love?" she ventured.

Her words registered immediately on his face. James was shocked.

Good. If he didn't love her, then he would not press her into marrying him.

"I understand that it is a social necessity at times, but if you are asking me if I would willingly venture into such a hopeless union myself, the answer is no. I believe in love," he replied.

She raised a hand to his face, and her fingers traced the stubble of his beard. She liked that since their arrival at Mopus Manor, James had stopped shaving every day. The touch of his day-old growth set her heart racing. It was time to risk it all. To allow her heart to finally speak its truth. She knew it was a gamble, but this was their future, and she would leave nothing on the table when it came to winning his love.

"So, if I told you that I was in love with you, what would you say?" she said.

James bowed his head and her heart sank. But when he looked up again, there were tears shining in his eyes. She left her hand cupping his jaw before brushing away a tear when the first one rolled down his cheek.

"I would tell you that you stole a little piece of my heart that day at the garden party. From that moment on, I slowly but irretrievably fell in love with you. I was so cut up about you marrying Guy that I took myself off to Derbyshire just to get away from hearing about the wedding. The reason I had the travel coach with me when I came to St George's church, was because I intended to flee London as soon as the wedding service was over."

He screwed his eyes shut, and more tears fell. "I would tell you that I betrayed my friend in order to make sure you escaped having to marry him. And I would tell you that I would do it all again in a heart-beat if it meant spending the rest of my life with you."

It was a statement of love that went straight to her heart. There could only ever be one response to such a soul-deep declaration of devotion.

"I love you, James Radley. Will you marry me?"

Chapter Forty

S *he loved him.* James moved swiftly to give Leah his full response. He rose up on his knees and leaning over her, speared his fingers into her hair. Holding her to him, he captured her lips in a searing kiss. There was nothing tender about the embrace as he plundered her mouth. Tongues tangled and teeth clashed. If Leah had wanted slow and easy, she was not going to get it. He could not hold back. His heart swelled as she met him stroke for stroke in the kiss. Her need was as great as his.

Weeks of pent-up frustration tore through James like wildfire. His only effort at restraint being that he kept his hands in her hair. He knew if he let them drop and allowed his fingers to roam, he would tear her gown open and ravish those full, plump breasts.

"Yes, I will marry you. And you will marry me," he said. Not a request, nor a proposal. A command.

"I am yours," she replied.

The battle between his cultured self and his primal needs reached its peak. His hands slipped from her hair and he roughly pushed her skirts up. He touched the naked, soft skin of her leg, then bent and placed a kiss on her inner thigh.

She opened her legs wider and he set his thumb to her slick, hot opening. He stroked her deep, and Leah groaned. "Have whatever you want, James. I am at your mercy. Take me," she urged.

He lifted his face and lay his forehead gently against hers. His heart was beating at a fearsome rate. Desire for her coursed like fire through his veins, but he had to stop. "Believe me, it is taking all my strength not to pull you to the floor and make you mine here and now. But I will be damned if I am going to have held out all this time, only to cave to my base desires at the last and ruin you before you are my wife."

He would go mad if he didn't touch her. The sooner they were married the better.

By sheer force of willpower, James let his hands drop from her thighs. Sucking in deep breaths, he got to his feet. His heated blood still pulsed hard through his body. The look of disappointment on her face almost had him reaching for her a second time and giving in to temptation.

"Today. We get married today. The special license permits us to marry where and when we wish," he said. He held out his hand and pulled her to her feet, forcing himself to ignore her soft mew of disappointment. Soon enough he would give her what she craved.

"It would seem a waste not to use that special license that your father went to so much trouble in order to procure. And yes, the sooner we get married the better, James Radley," she replied.

James risked another kiss. This time, he lifted her chin and placed a soft, almost chaste one on Leah's lips.

"I love you," she whispered.

"I love you too. You have no idea how much I have wanted to hear you say those three little words," he replied.

"Come then. Let us go and speak to my father and Sir Geoffrey and tell them of our decision."

※

"I seem to be developing a habit of marrying family members in odd places," grumbled Hugh.

James gave his father a reassuring pat on the shoulder. "You shall have to make sure that any gentleman who offers for either Maggie or Claire's hand in marriage agrees to be wed at St Paul's cathedral."

Hugh snorted. "Even London would be a good start. It is a pity your mother is not here today, but with the ongoing unpleasantness as a result of your behavior, she was adamant that someone stay with your sisters. We shall just have to have a celebration once you and your new bride return home."

James keenly felt the absence of family on this most auspicious of days. He had attended enough weddings of his cousins over the past year to secretly wish that they were all sitting in the pews of the tiny family chapel, watching him now take his own leap into wedded bliss. Celebrations, of course, would come once he and Leah returned to London. But in light of the circumstance of their impending marriage, those celebrations would be kept strictly within the circle of his family. Along with the celebrations, there would also be repercussions to face. But first, he and Leah had to get married.

"I shall leave you to finish dressing while I go and make sure all is in readiness for you and your bride," said Hugh.

James reached out and took a hold of Hugh's arm. For a moment, they stood and silently looked at one another. He owed him so much. Gratitude. And love. Love for a father who stood by his children.

"Thank you, Papa. It is days like these that I am humbled to be your son," he said.

His father chuckled. "You should be humble about that every day."

After receiving a final fatherly hug, James went about checking his attire. He looked at himself in the mirror. His black suit was clean and pressed. The bronze-colored waistcoat with brass buttons, which he had worn on the day of Leah and Guy's failed wedding, sat over a white linen shirt with a perfectly tied cravat. Sir Geoffrey's valet had gone to great lengths to make certain the groom was immaculately turned out.

In his waistcoat pocket was a Radley family heirloom wedding ring, part of the collection passed down to his father by his paternal grandmother. It would match perfectly with the betrothal ring gifted to Leah by her grandfather.

The small family chapel which faced the Tresillian River was chosen for the ceremony. Leah and James had politely refused Hugh

Radley's offer of the use of the cathedral at Truro. They had arrived at Mopus Manor in a quiet fashion, and they would begin their married life together in the same way.

Sir Geoffrey escorted his granddaughter down the short aisle, and when they reached where James stood, he placed her hand in James's. Leah wore a pale blue day gown, with some seaside daisies and ribbons threaded through her hair. Her simple, elegant attire suited her better than her first ostentatious wedding gown had done.

James chanced a look at Leah, and they shared a smile.

"I never dared to dream that I would get to make you my wife. This is the happiest day of my life."

She nodded. "You are the happily ever after I have always dreamed of, James Radley. Let's get married."

Together, they faced Hugh Radley.

Chapter Forty-One

J ames held Leah by the hand as they climbed the steps to her
bedroom. As of tonight, it was their bedroom.

Her tight grip on his fingers was the only outward sign of
her nerves. Thank god her mother had given her the talk the
week before she and Guy were due to marry. The conversation had
been somewhat vague, but by the end of it, she had finally got an idea
of what to expect.

He stopped at the door. "Ready?"

She nodded, laughing softly as he picked her up and carried her
over the threshold and into the room. With a well-timed kick, he
closed the door behind them, then set Leah on her feet.

A blush of heat burned on both of her cheeks and James bent and
traced his fingers over the patches of blush. She shivered at his touch.

"Don't be nervous. I will take good care of you. Trust me," he
whispered.

"I trust you. Hopefully the nerves will soon be gone." Leah lifted
her lips to his, offering up her mouth. James hungrily took her lips with
his, kissing her deeply. She slipped her hands around the back of his
neck before running her fingers over his short brown hair. She luxuri-
ated in its softness.

Her fingers eventually drifted from his hair to the buttons of his waistcoat. She flicked them open one by one, softly humming as she worked. She was nervous, but Leah was determined not to be the passive partner in this encounter. She wanted her new husband to know that she trusted him.

James shrugged off his jacket and waistcoat. Then his hands set to work on the buttons of Leah's blue gown.

"This won't suffer the same fate as your other wedding gown," he said.

Leah sucked in a deep breath. James leaned in and kissed her neck, the warmth of his lips sending a thrill of sexual heat down her spine. Her whole body was full of nervous anticipation.

Once laces and buttons were dealt with, and her gown removed, all that remained covering her was her thin muslin shift. She put a hand on James's chest. "You are still in your clothes. Is that fair?"

A wicked smile appeared on his lips and his eyes sparkled with mischief. "Well then, wife, it is your duty to address that problem."

Heat pooled in her loins; this was a duty she was looking forward to carrying out. Sensations Leah had only previously known in the privacy of her own bed now throbbed low in her body.

She set to work on the cuffs of his shirt. James lifted it over his head and threw it on a nearby chair. Leah laughed. "You seem eager, my love."

He took her hand in his and laid it on his chest. The fine dusting of brown hair was soft to her touch. She spread her fingers wide, brushing them back and forth.

"And to think you are all mine," she whispered.

"Always."

James took hold of Leah's hand once more and placed it over the placket of his trousers. The hard evidence of his desire for her jutted against the fabric. She licked her lips before letting a slow breath out. She could do this. She trusted James.

Steeling her nerves, she lay her fingers on his buttons and opened his trousers. His erection sprung free and into her hand. She gave a little startled "Oh!" to which he chuckled darkly and deeply.

Leah looked up, and James met her gaze. His eyes had changed from their usual warm brown into a darker shade, which reminded her of his onyx signet ring.

He teased her with a tender kiss on the lips. "Every inch of me is yours from this night on. Now place your fingers around the head of my cock and stroke up and down. There is a sensitive spot just below the base of the tip if you wish to give me extra pleasure," he murmured.

Leah did as he had instructed; her sex throbbed as James let out a long moan the moment, she tightened her grip and began to stroke him. Within a minute, she had a strong rhythm established, the changes in his breath giving her all the guidance she needed.

The passion on his face as she stroked him was so beautiful, it made her heart soar. To know she could do this for him, to give sexual pleasure to the man she loved was elating.

The depth of his breathing became ragged, and she sensed he was close. James lay his hand over Leah's.

"Enough. I beg of you," he said, his voice rough with need.

She released her hold of him, watching with utter fascination as James closed his eyes and pulled in a deep breath. The knowledge that she had reduced him to a state where he was barely able to maintain control was powerful. She made a silent vow to keep him under her loving power forever.

When he opened his eyes again, his gaze settled on her shift. Placing a hand either side of it, he lifted it over her hips and then over her head. The chill night air kissed her naked skin. Her nipples peaked into rosy pebbles and she shivered, her body reacting not just to the cold but the fact she was now completely naked before him.

James reached out and cupped one of Leah's breasts before running his thumb lightly over her hardened nipple. He then rolled it between his thumb and forefinger, and gently squeezed. She whimpered.

Their gazes met for an instant before James bent and took the tortured nipple into his mouth. He licked back and forth across her rosy bud, every rasp of his tongue making her shudder. When he took the nipple between his teeth and nipped, she gasped. The torture was magnificent.

He dropped a hand to the thatch of hair at the apex of her thighs.

As he slipped a finger into her heat, Leah sobbed. This was heaven. She had touched herself in the dark of her bed many times before, but nothing prepared her for the sensation of James's thick finger stretching her. She clung to his shoulders, struggling for purchase in a world that had suddenly spun out of control.

"That's it, Leah. Give in to what you need. Let me show you it all," he whispered.

He settled her onto the bed, then climbed on next to her. After spreading her thighs wide, he knelt between her legs and dipped his head. Leah tried to sit up and see what James was doing, but the lash of his tongue deep into her heated core had her collapsing back onto the bed with a groan.

Her hips bucked as he licked and sucked her sensitive bud. She could not escape even if she'd wanted to. James held her down, his arms wrapped firmly around her upper thighs. Pleasure that she had never thought possible thrummed through her body. Leah lay back on the bed and let him have his way. She was a willing prisoner of his sexual torture.

Her wild imaginings of the art of lovemaking had not stretched to what James was doing to her right now. He was driving her out of her mind with urgent need. She was desperate to reach the peak and fall off the cliff, but at the same time she never wanted the exquisite sensation to end.

When he did finally release her, Leah clawed after him. James simply chuckled and took a hold of her hand, kissing her fingertips.

"Don't be too greedy too soon, my love. We have a long way to go tonight." A soft kiss was placed on her inner thigh. "Come up onto the pillows. We need all the bed for this part," he said.

Leah scuttled back up the bed until she reached the pile of pillows and cushions which decorated the bedhead. James followed after her, like a stalking tiger. She wanted nothing more than to be his willing prey.

He sat back on his haunches and considered both her and the bed. Leah felt suddenly all too aware that she was fully naked, and he was not. Shyness gripped her and she picked up one of the cushions to cover herself.

James quickly wrestled the cushion away from her and tossed it onto the floor. "Never be afraid to show yourself to me, wife. We will see enough of each other to cure your shyness. I promise you that, my love."

My love. The words made her heart flutter. Leah put a hand to her mouth, fighting back tears.

"Don't cry," he whispered.

"It's alright. They are tears of utter relief and happiness. I cannot believe that it is you and I here tonight as husband and wife. I swear I wouldn't change places with anyone else in the whole world right now. This is where you and I were always meant to be, James Radley," she said.

He climbed off the bed before quickly divesting himself of his trousers and returning. He rose over her, placing a hand on either side of the pillow on which Leah rested her head. "With me is where you belong, Mrs. Radley," he said.

The firm resolve in his voice had more tears springing to her eyes. She knew she shouldn't be crying on her wedding night. James was not the sort of man who made women cry, but happiness threatened to overwhelm her.

He kissed away the tears on her cheeks and when he was done, he came searching once more for her mouth. The sensation of their tongues tangling in a sensual dance made Leah's toes curl. She would never get enough of him.

His fingers slid down her hip and to her thigh. They settled at her knees before he pushed her legs farther apart. James moved into the space in between her legs. His thumb slipped into her wet heat and he began to stroke once more.

If she had thought that her ardor for him had cooled, Leah was quickly disproved of that notion. Within seconds, James had filled her body once more with aching and urgent need. Every stoke of his thumb across her sensitive nib sent shudders throughout her body. Slowly, his skilled caresses brought her back to the edge of madness.

"You are ready for me, Leah, ready for us to become one," he said, releasing his hand. He set the head of his cock to her entrance, then slowly pushed inside. A slight sting as he broke through her maidenhead was all she felt. He held her gaze the entire time. When she flinched, he stopped, only continuing when she gave him a small nod.

"Good?" he asked.

"Yes," she whispered.

He withdrew slightly, then entered her deeply once more. James began to flex his hips, thrusting in and out. Leah silently pleaded for him to take her harder and deeper with his every thrust.

She came in a blinding roar of light. Somewhere in the distance, she could hear herself cry out his name. Then, before she could return fully to the world, he increased the tempo of his strokes, until finally stilling and softly whispering, "Leah."

As James collapsed on top of her, Leah held on tight and took his weight. When he tried to roll off, she clung to him and refused to let go. "Stay," she said.

Sometime later, when she finally, reluctantly released him, James grabbed the bed clothes and threw them over their rapidly cooling bodies. Naked together, they settled under the warm blankets, sharing words of tenderness.

"Sleep, my love. I will wake you when we are ready for a second encounter," he said.

Leah looked over at her husband; James's eyelids fluttered as they closed.

"Mrs. James Radley. Who would have thought it?" she whispered."

"Thank god."

Chapter Forty-Two

Their stay at Mopus Manor had to eventually come to an end. Two weeks after they were married, a reluctant James and Leah packed up their things and made preparations to return to London.

"I shall miss your company. It has been nice having other people at my supper table each night," said Sir Geoffrey.

James turned from watching the last of his and Leah's things being packed into the cart for the trip across to Truro. In the morning, they would take the mail coach back to London. The barouche had sadly been returned earlier in the week; he already missed hearing Leah's giggles as he gripped her arse when he helped her up into the carriage.

"We can never thank you enough for all you have done for us. I understand why Leah chose you as the one person she felt she could trust in all this madness," he replied.

"But now she has you." Sir Geoffrey motioned toward the garden and James followed. Once they stood outside the painting studio, Leah's grandfather stopped. James had spent the previous day packing up his paints and completed works before reluctantly closing the door of the cottage for the last time.

"I don't know what the two of you will find when you return to

London. Knowing my son-in-law, there will be consequences and you must prepare yourselves for them. You must protect Leah," said Sir Geoffrey.

James was under no illusion that Tobias Shepherd was going to make things easy for his wayward daughter and her new husband, but he would deal with it all in good time. Leah was his wife now, and beyond the direct control of her father.

"My family is not without significant influence in London. I doubt Shepherd will want to wage an all-out war against me," he replied.

Sir Geoffrey met his gaze. "No, he won't. Shepherd will find subtle ways to hurt you. Which is why I wanted to talk you. If the two of you decide that London is not for you, I want you to know that you are always welcome to return to Mopus Manor. You and Leah have a home waiting for you here."

The generous offer took James by surprise. He and Leah both loved the place, but the thought of actually living at Mopus Manor on a permanent basis had not been something he had seriously entertained until now. He offered Sir Geoffrey his hand. "Thank you. I shall keep it in mind. If Leah and I had not married, I expect she would have stayed here for as long as possible."

"I want you to seriously consider my proposal. You and I could come to an arrangement which would see you become a land owner and therefore eligible to run for office. I have enough influence to help secure your preselection as the candidate for the local seat. From what I have seen of you, James, I know you are someone who would put the interests of his constituents first."

"Once again, thank you. And yes, I will give your offer some serious thought," replied James.

Sir Geoffrey headed back into the house, leaving James alone looking out over the water. He had never considered a career as a politician, having found Guy's machinations not to his taste. If he did take a seat in the House of Commons as the local member for Truro, he would work hard to represent the people. And then, between parliamentary sessions he could still pursue his other career as an artist.

"Yes, definitely something to consider."

They left Truro the following morning, and three days later, James and Leah found themselves standing in the courtyard of Fulham Palace.

"We are home." He slipped an arm around his wife's waist and drew her in close before kissing her tenderly on the forehead.

Leah smiled up at him. "A proper kiss please, husband."

He set his lips to hers, receiving a warm and encouraging kiss in return. When Leah slid her hand inside his coat and rubbed her hand against his trousers, he nipped at her bottom lip. "Minx. Don't you go getting me all aroused just before I am about to greet my parents."

She gave him an innocent 'what, me?' smile in return.

Their flirting was interrupted by a squeal of delight which rang through the air. From out of the front door, Claire came running to greet them. "Helloooo! Welcome home!"

James held his arms out to her. But she, in typical Claire fashion, raced past him and embraced Leah. "My sister. How wonderful. I am so pleased that you married my big brother. I just knew he would be your hero," she cried.

James frowned. Since when had he become a hero? And what did Claire know?

Claire released Leah from her hug, then came to him. Uncharacteristically for Claire, it was in an almost reverent fashion. As her arms wrapped around his waist, she leaned in. "Thank you, James. Thank you for saving Leah."

He shook his head. "I think you have it the wrong way. She saved me. I don't know what I would have done if she hadn't run out of the church."

Claire looked up at him. "There has been the devil of a scandal over all of this, but to me it was the most romantic love story I have ever heard. Even Papa was emotional when he got home last week and told us that not only were the two of you married, but that you were in love."

A look passed between Leah and Claire, after which Claire nodded.

Leah turned to James, taking his hand. "We have a small confession to make before we go inside. Claire helped with my plans to flee before the wedding. She investigated where the travel coaches left from in London and purchased my ticket for Truro. The black cloak I wore during my escape, and which you slept under that first night, actually belongs to your mother," said Leah.

"It's an old cloak, so Mama does not know it is missing. I don't plan to tell our parents any of this, but as Leah's husband, you have a right to know," added Claire.

James looked to his wife. "At least you felt you could trust one of the Radley family when it came to it. I understand why you didn't feel you could do the same with me. And I agree we should keep this a secret."

He shook his head at Claire but couldn't stop the grin which came to his lips. He would be forever grateful for his sister's meddling. With Leah on his arm, and a happy Claire trailing behind, they headed inside.

The welcome from the rest of the Radley family was as warm as he'd hoped. After giving her new daughter-in-law a hug, Mary Radley turned and gave her son a gentle cuff over the ear. "That is for having run away and gotten married without your mother being at the wedding."

James caught the smile on her face as she spoke. Even the normally dour Maggie managed to rally a smile for the newlywed couple.

His father saved the best for last. "I was wondering if the two of you were ever going to come out of the wilds of Cornwall. I told your new landlord that we were expecting you at the start of the week at the very latest, but never mind."

"What landlord would that be?" replied James.

His father sniffed. "You are married. You cannot expect to still be living under your parents' roof, can you? This isn't Strathmore House with its abundance of rooms where you can have your own apartment. I have taken out a year's lease on a house and servants in Wood Street. It is our wedding gift to the two of you," said Hugh.

James looked at Leah; her eyes were brimming with tears. Their own home. This was most unexpected. And very generous.

"I spoke to Mrs. Shepherd and she has arranged for all of Leah's things to be moved to the new house. They should be waiting for you when you arrive," said Mary.

"Thank you," said Leah.

Wood Street, which was close by St Paul's cathedral, was not the most elegant of addresses in London. Leah had rarely ventured this far east in the city, her usual haunts being the rarified air around Mayfair and the parish of St James.

The town house which James's father had rented for them was a short three-story dirty brown brick building with barely any street presence. It certainly wasn't the lavish town house that Guy had prepared for her to live in close to Grosvenor Square. There would be no expensive furnishings, or fabulous green chinois dining settings for her and James.

But it was theirs, and Leah was determined to make it the happy home she had never had before. She trusted James to make a success of his chosen career, and as his wife, she would do all she could to support him.

As they reached the front door, James swung her up into his arms. Leah laughed.

"Time to cross the threshold of our first home," he announced with a smile.

She was still chortling when James slid his foot behind the door and in one deft motion swung it closed behind them. The smile disappeared from his face, and he gently set her down on her feet.

"Bloody hell," he muttered. Leah saw the cause of James's anger.

Dumped in the middle of the downstairs foyer were her trunks. They looked for all the world like they had been thrown in from the street, with some of the corners of her brand-new luggage caved in.

She blinked back tears as she crossed the floor to where her things lay in a muddled heap. She lifted the lid of the nearest trunk; inside were bottles of her toiletries and perfumes. To her surprise they were all intact, only requiring her to reorganize them back into their right places. While she continued to check the bottles and lotions, James moved the rest of Leah's cases and boxes into some semblance of order.

"There is a note on the top of this one. It's addressed to you," he said, handing her a folded up piece of paper.

She took it, and immediately recognized her mother's handwriting on the outside. She straightened her back and unfolded the note before devouring its contents. A second reading of the letter had her puffing out her cheeks. "No congratulations or anything, but that was to be expected. She says all my things are here and in good order. Guy took back everything that he gave me and has asked that I return the engagement ring forthwith. Oh, and I am to receive her and my sister for afternoon tea at the earliest convenience," she said.

A quick check of the rest of her belongings proved her mother to be true to her word. Leah had not thought she would see any of her personal possessions again. She had honestly expected that her father would have demanded every single thing his errant daughter owned be taken into the rear laneway and smashed to pieces. Everything destroyed. That was his usual way of dealing with those who dared to defy him.

"I am pleased that your things have been returned to you," said James, placing a tender kiss on her lips. She gave him a hopeful smile.

He didn't need to mention that with money being tight for the foreseeable future, they would not have been able to replace Leah's possessions if they had been lost to her.

"Let us take a look at the rest of the house. I need to pick a room in which to set up my studio. The sooner I can get working on my major landscape pieces, the sooner I can start earning money from my paintings," he added.

Until he could make money as an artist or find a patron, he would have to juggle working back as a shipping clerk in Charles Saunders's office, as well as trying to complete more works. He had refused his father's offer to continue funding his painting, citing the strain he had already placed on Hugh's purse.

"When are you going to speak to my father? You have every right to ask for my dowry," said Leah.

The question of Leah's dowry had sat in James's mind for most of the trip back to London. He had never thought to find himself in a situation where he would be needing his wife's money in order to live. It made him question his decision to keep pursuing his painting. "I will speak to him. But we are not going to touch your dowry money unless it cannot be avoided. I should be the one to provide for my family," he replied.

James would do his damnedest to find a way to earn enough money to keep him and Leah. While he was well within his rights to ask for Leah's dowry, he had a sneaking suspicion that Tobias Shepherd would make him beg for it.

Chapter Forty-Three

J ames stood out the front of Guy Dannon's house. A house he had visited numerous times in the past, a house where once he had been a welcome guest. He knew that time was now at an end.

"Let's get this done," he muttered.

Taking the door knocker in hand he rapped it loudly twice, then stood back. Guy's chubby butler finally answered it. James started forward in greeting, following old habits, then stopped. This was not a pleasant social call.

"Mister James Radley to see Mister Guy Dannon," he said.

The butler ushered him inside, but instead of James doing his usual casual amble upstairs and seeking out Guy himself, the butler left him standing in the foyer.

"I shall see if my master is at home to you, sir," he said.

Guy, of course, made him wait.

And wait.

While he stood unattended in the foyer, James toyed with the gaudy diamond ring in his pocket. Leah had handed it over as soon as they were returned to London, begging James to be rid of it. The polite thing to do would have been for her to return the ring in person.

But considering the circumstances of her breaking the betrothal, she and James agreed it would be better if he went to see Guy.

Finally, Guy appeared at the top of the staircase. Again, he took his time in coming down the stairs to greet his visitor. James stood with his hands in his coat pocket, the ring grasped tightly in his fingers.

"Radley. What do you want? Or have you come to steal something else from me?"

James slowly blinked. Guy had never called him by his surname in all the years they had been friends. He held his temper in check. He wasn't going to give Guy the satisfaction of seeing him get angry at his taunt.

"Mister Dannon, my *wife* asked me to return this to you," he said, holding out the ring. A sly grin threatened at his lip. He knew it was beneath him, but Guy's accusation of him having stolen his wife made James want to stick the knife in Guy's pride just a little. Stick it in and twist.

Guy snatched the ring from James's outstretched hand. "So, the little whore had you do her bidding? That is no surprise. May I offer you my congratulations. Not on your recent nuptials, mind you, but rather on how well you kept your duplicity hidden from me. Here was me thinking you intended to be my best man, when in fact you and the bride were planning to run away together. You are a cunning bastard; I will give you that."

James had played out this scene in his mind a thousand times. In every one of those scenes, it always ended badly. He took heart from the fact that Guy was not holding a pistol or a sword in his hand. More than one of James's imagined encounters with Guy had ended with him lying on the floor in a pool of his own blood.

He did, however, have a small speech rehearsed. If he owed Guy anything, it was the truth. "I know you are not the least bit interested, but I did promise myself that I would tell you what happened between Leah and myself. On the morning of the wedding, I arrived at the church to see Leah fleeing. I followed her. She made it plain that she did not wish to marry you. As she was determined not to return to London, I felt an obligation to see her safely delivered to her grandfather. At that point, there was nothing between Leah and me."

Guy snorted and put the betrothal ring in his pocket. He stepped closer to James, his face a study in quiet rage. "You are a fucking liar. I saw you on the night that the two of you kissed. You were in love with her even then; it was written all over your face. Tell yourself whatever lies you need to, Radley, but the cold, hard truth is that you stole your best friend's bride because you wanted her for yourself."

James anticipated that this would be the last time he and Guy ever exchanged words, so it was only fair that Guy knew the full truth. Not that it really mattered. Guy thought him a liar, and there was little, if anything he could do about changing his opinion. "I never set out to steal Leah from you. But yes, you are right. I fell in love with her. I wanted her so much that it burned my soul. The greatest moment of my life was when she confessed her love for me. Leah chose me as her husband, her lover; she never chose you."

"Get out," said Guy.

James no longer fought the smile—he grinned mockingly at Guy. Victory coursed through his veins. "I leave you with this parting thought: I never had to force Leah to my bed. She came willingly. And every night after we have made love, she sleeps safely in my arms."

And with that, he turned on his heel and headed for the door. The stream of foul abuse which followed him out onto the front steps and into the street fell on deaf ears.

The visit with Guy had gone as well as could be expected. James had not been under any illusion as to how welcome he would be. He knew he should have felt some shame at having played the victor in the man's home, but he couldn't bring himself to give a damn.

His next place of call, however, filled him with deep, unsettling concern. He had an appointment with Tobias Shepherd.

As with his visit to see Guy Dannon, James was made to wait. He stood, hat and gloves in hand, in the foyer of the elegant town house in Duke Street. And as with Guy, he knew he was not a welcome guest.

He was eventually shown upstairs and into a drawing room. As he stepped through the door, he found Leah's father standing in the middle of the room, hands on hips.

Tobias Shepherd pointed to a nearby blue floral sofa. "Sit." The command was about as civilized as what you would give a disobedient dog.

For a moment, James was tempted to take a bite out of his outstretched hand. Instead, he took a seat on the sofa and tried to remember his manners.

Tobias picked up a bell and rang it loudly. Within seconds, a footman appeared in the doorway. "Tea."

There was no offer of anything more. Social niceties were clearly not the order of the morning for this private visit.

Tobias took a seat in a wide-backed chair some feet away and crossed his legs, placing a booted foot on his knee. His arms stretched out across the back of the chair in a clear statement of position and power. "I see you did not bother to bring my daughter with you."

James shook his head. He wanted to see what the lay of the land was with her family before exposing his wife to them.

Leah was spending the morning with her new mother- and sisters-in-law, getting better acquainted with the intricacies of the extended family of the Duke of Strathmore. He looked forward to taking his bride to Strathmore Castle in Scotland for Christmas.

"No, I did not, sir. My wife is with my mother this morning," he replied. He calmly held Tobias Shepherd's gaze. Leah was no longer under her father's protection. Neither she nor James were going to live in fear of him.

"Ah. Well at least you are prepared to follow some of society's rules. Just not the important ones," said Tobias.

James held his hat tightly in his hands. He was not going to give Mister Shepherd any excuse to lose his temper. Nor was he about let himself be cowered by a bully. He was not some lowly upstart who had dared to marry above his station. His family had been in the senior ranks of the English nobility for hundreds of years. His father was not only the son of a duke, he was the third most powerful man in the Church of England. Only the Prince Regent and the Archbishop of Canterbury wielded more power than Hugh Radley.

"I have done the right thing. I helped a young woman avoid a marriage not of her choosing. I saw her safely to her family, and then married her in front of my father, the Bishop of London," he replied.

"You can hardly call Sir Geoffrey Sydell her family. That old coot is as mad as a hatter," snorted Tobias.

"But nonetheless, the blood link remains. Leah is, of course, now a Radley by marriage and linked to my own illustrious family bloodline. But enough of that. Mister Shepherd, I came here today to present myself to you as your new son-in-law. I did not come here today to bandy words with you. You are my father-in-law, and as such, you are due the right of my respect," he replied.

Tobias sat back in his chair and began to chuckle, a low, laugh which lacked in humor. When he had finished, he fixed James with a steely, cold glare. "No, Mister Radley, you came here today because you wish me to release Leah's dowry to you."

"Leah is entitled to her dowry upon marriage, but as I said, that is not the reason for my visit," he replied.

The hint of a sneer appeared on Tobias Shepherd's face. He was clearly not a man used to being told he was wrong, and James suspected he had just crossed an invisible line. "Well then, Master Radley, you may pay me your respects."

"As my father-in-law, I would be honored if you would call me James. If that does not suit, then Mister Radley will suffice. I am of age and also a married man. I came to tell you that I have your daughter's best interests at heart and that I intend to provide her with a safe and loving home," replied James.

"But not a home fit for a young lady of her station. You can hardly call a rented house far from the civilized streets where Leah grew up a satisfactory replacement for what she would have had. That is *if* you had brought her back to the church and I had been able to make certain of her marriage to Guy Dannon," said Tobias.

The back and forth was tiring, and to James's mind, futile, but it was clear Leah's father was determined to have his say.

James got to his feet and brushed an invisible piece of dust from his hat. There was no point waiting on the tea. Tobias Shepherd had made his position clear. He did not approve of James and Leah's marriage.

"I have no regrets for what I did, nor for having saved Leah from the miserable life that you had sentenced her to; my only regret is that as her father, you cannot wish her some form of happiness. Good day to you, sir," said James. He headed for the door, doubting he would ever be received in the Shepherd family home again.

Outside in Duke Street, he put on his hat and took a deep breath. It was only as he climbed into his carriage that he let his temper finally get the better of him.

"Bloody hell," he muttered.

Knowing Tobias Shepherd, it would take the best lawyers that the Radley family had at their disposal, and a very long time before he or Leah saw a penny of her dowry.

Chapter Forty-Four

Leah sat back in her chair and looked at James. With his gaze fixed on the last of his supper, he was oblivious to his wife's quiet study of him.

He had come straight into the dining room as soon as he had arrived home late that evening from his work at the shipping office. With a few precious hours of painting ahead of him before bed, every minute counted. He had not taken the time to brush his hair or change from his work clothes.

"I am going to start painting the *Derbyshire Twins* tonight. I have used the sketches in my book to give me the basis for the outlines on the canvas, so hopefully that will be enough for me to get them underway. We will just have to wait until after Christmas to make the journey out to the woodlands in order for me to complete them," he said.

Leah couldn't fault James for his dedication to his craft. He worked long hours at the office, then returned home each night and continued with making his sketches from memory. She had stood and watched with pride as he and two burly footmen had moved the canvasses into place in the main drawing room upstairs.

James's beloved *Derbyshire Twins* were ready to be born.

She was interested in his landscapes, but at this moment she was more concerned with him. His brown hair was ruffled. If she knew James, it would be from having had his hands pushed through his locks as he worked the ledgers. She had seen him do it many times while standing, concentrating at his painting.

She sighed. He was lovely. Her warm, slightly scruffy husband made her all a silly mess inside.

He looked up, smiling when his gaze met hers.

"A penny for your thoughts?" he said.

Leah rose from her chair and came around to where James sat. Pushing his plate of supper to one side, she sat on the table in front of him. He moved the rest of his cutlery and wine glass out of the way.

He lay against her breasts as she rested her head on top of his, gently rubbing the back of his neck.

"I could tell you what I was thinking, but I'm sure you would prefer for me to show you. That's, of course, if you have time for me," she purred.

He lifted his head and whispered, "I will always have time for you, my love."

The fierce desire in his voice was all the encouragement she needed. Lying back on the table, she untied the laces of her gown as James pushed her skirts up around her waist. A soft gasp escaped her lips as he set his tongue to her heated sex.

She would never get enough of this man.

Chapter Forty-Five

Leah hadn't realized how far paint fumes could travel. Even with having the windows of the upstairs drawing room open while James worked, the smell of paint and oil permeated throughout the house. At supper the previous evening, she could have sworn she could taste it in her food. James's assurance that she would get used to it was of little comfort.

"I need the space in which to paint the bigger pieces. They are what will bring in the money that we need and help me to gain a reputation with future patrons." Her husband's words and the kiss that came with them quietened Leah's complaint.

It would take them time to adjust to the reality of being married and back in London. She just had to learn to be patient.

Money was tight. Hugh Radley had gifted them the house and servants for a year, but there were still other bills to be paid. The four days a week that James was working at his uncle's shipping office brought in some coin but left him grumpy and frustrated that he was not able to devote his entire time to his artistic endeavors.

"I am sorry. I know I shouldn't complain," she said.

They were dressing early one morning a few days after James had begun to paint the *Derbyshire Twins*. Their bedroom was on the other side of the staircase to the drawing room, but even at this distance Leah could smell the paint fumes.

James took her into his arms, gently rubbing his hand up and down her back. They both knew why she was out of sorts, and the paint fumes were only partly to blame. With her mother and sister coming to pay their first house call today, they both knew Leah would be held to close scrutiny for how she kept her home.

"Finish dressing and then go for a walk. I always find that a stroll brings my nerves under control," said James.

She had hoped he would offer to take her back to bed and use his fingers and tongue to calm her worried mind. But James had work today, and she couldn't keep him from the one source of income they currently had.

"I shall do one last look around the house and make sure everything is ready for our visitors. Did you tidy your studio before you finished up last night?" she asked.

He screwed up his face. "No, sorry, I didn't, and I don't have time to do it this morning before I leave for work. Could you please explain to your mother and sister that it is a workspace, and that they are not always neat and tidy places? I promise to clean it up when I get home," he replied.

James was always leaving things in the place where he had finished with them rather than putting them back where they belonged. Leah was not used to living in anything other than an immaculately tidy and clean house. Her parents did not tolerate things being out of place.

"If I get time this morning, I will tidy things up as best I can in your studio. If not, I shall just keep the door closed," she said.

He placed a tender kiss on her lips before releasing her from his embrace. "Thank you. I know I am a messy person. I hope you love me enough to forgive my faults," he replied.

She couldn't stay mad with him when he gave her one of his wicked smiles. She reached up on her toes and gave him another kiss. "Of course, I love you. But don't you dare pass on your bad habits to our future children," she replied.

After collecting his hat and coat, James stole a final kiss before leaving the house. Leah went about checking with the servants to make sure everything was in readiness for her guests.

Her mother and sister arrived in the early afternoon, and from the moment they set foot inside the front door, the visit went badly. The stern look which sat constantly on Mrs. Shepherd's face was not the least encouraging. It was almost as if she had decided that the visit called for her to be more miserable than usual. Leah secretly worried that she had been instructed to behave in such a manner. Nothing that her parents did would surprise her.

"What a small house, and so close to the poor people. Your marriage is already the result of a shocking scandal, so I would have thought your husband would be trying to make things better for you. Whatever was he thinking, taking this place?" sneered Mrs. Shepherd.

Leah's sister stood silently beside their mother, her gaze roaming the front entrance. She at least had managed a small smile in Leah's direction upon their arrival.

After a short tour of the lower floor, Leah showed her guests upstairs to the formal sitting room. As they went to sit down, her mother stopped and sniffed the air. "Do you have workhouses nearby? Because I am sure I can smell them."

There were some workshops and a blacksmith in one of the nearby streets, but Leah knew where the smell emanated from. It came from within the house.

"My husband is working to establish himself as a painter of land-scapes. The paint fumes are a little strong throughout the house this morning. I shall go and open a window," she replied.

She hurried from the room and opened the door of the main drawing room which James had commandeered for his work. The smell of the drying paint and linseed oil was strong. Oil-soaked rags lay flat on the floor. She stepped over several of them on her way to the window.

"Leah, what have you got yourself into? What a mess. And the smell. I knew your good sense had deserted you when you fled the wedding, but to settle for this as your future is utterly ridiculous."

She turned to see her mother standing in the doorway, hands on hips. The look of disgust on Mrs. Shepherd's face at the sight before her was heartbreaking. Leah's family would never support her marriage to James.

"James didn't have time to tidy up last night. He worked until the early hours," she said, at pains to reassure her mother that all was not lost when it came to her youngest daughter.

"That is beside the point. Not only have you allowed this reckless man to paint inside the house, but you gave up the main drawing room. There must be a garden shed or an out-of-the-way attic that he can use. It is intolerable that a young woman of your birth should have to put up with this sort of nonsense. I thought he was going to go into the church and secure a proper living. Not this childish . . . whatever you call it. Art," huffed Mrs. Shepherd.

Leah looked at the mess in the room. Her mother had a point. There were canvases, rags, and discarded pieces of sketch paper all over the floor.

She wiped away a tear. "Would you like some tea? Our cook has baked a fruitcake," she offered.

"No, I don't think we shall stay. The smell in this room has already given me a headache. I don't know how you can live like this, Leah. Get your husband to clean up his mess and have it moved elsewhere. You are the lady of the house, and he should know his place."

She followed her mother out onto the landing, where her sister stood waiting. With a nod, Mrs. Shepherd headed for the stairs. Her sister mouthed a "sorry" and trailed behind.

At the bottom of the stairs, her mother turned and announced loudly. "This house and its mistress are not fit for polite society. I shall inform all the best hostesses not to extend any invitations to you, Leah, until you have learned from your mistakes."

The sound of the front door being slammed echoed throughout the house.

Leah quietly closed the door to James's studio and went back into the sitting room. The maid had brought cake and a pot of tea upstairs while she had been gone and they were sitting in the middle of the low table which sat between the floral sofas. She poured herself a cup of tea.

It would have been easy to simply sit and have a good cry. A moment of self-pity could be well worth it. But she resisted the temptation. Tears would give her nothing but a red nose and flushed cheeks. Her private hopes for a pleasant 'at home' with her mother and sister had fortunately not been high; and her mother had not disappointed her.

She considered her mother's harsh words and wished that there was not an ounce of truth in them. But her mother was right about the drawing room; she was also right about the paint fumes. Picking up the knife from the tea tray, Leah carved off an inelegant chunk of the fruit cake and stuffed it into her mouth.

The scandal over hers and James's marriage meant that Leah had a tough task ahead of her to prove that she could be a respectable society wife. That task would be made nigh on impossible if people thought her house stank. No one would want to come for tea if they thought they were going to leave her house with a headache. There was only one solution.

James's paintings had to go.

Chapter Forty-Six

James had lived with women all his life, so he knew when one of them was in a bad mood. Even in his tired state, he could tell from the moment he set eyes on her that Leah wasn't happy.

It was the end of a long, tiring day, and he ached all over. He and Francis had spent hours moving crates of wine from a recently arrived shipment. The stairs at Saunders Shipping were steep and his back was still twinging from lugging the heavy boxes. While his official job was to work the ledgers, whenever the office was shorthanded, everyone was press-ganged into service.

All he wanted to do as soon as he got home was to kiss his wife and find his supper. He was exhausted. But he knew once he had eaten, he had at least three hours of painting ahead of him before he finally found the blessed relief of his and Leah's bed.

His first attempt at kissing Leah was rebuffed. She turned her head away and his kiss landed awkwardly on the side of her neck. When he made a second attempt, she pushed him aside.

"My love?"

"Don't you 'my love' me—today has been an unmitigated disaster," she replied.

He had been about to enquire as to how the visit with her mother and sister had gone, but here he had his answer. He waited, unsure of what to say, or whether he should say anything. From the look on Leah's face, he had a horrible feeling that no matter what he said he was going to be on the receiving end of a good ticking-off from his wife.

"Are you going to ask me how the visit with my mother and sister went, or do you not care?" she said.

James had seen his father and mother conduct an argument enough times to know that the best thing he could do at this moment was to accept whatever punishment was coming his way. He held out a hand to her, and after giving him a filthy look, Leah took it.

"Tell me how things went with your mother, and what I can do to make you happy," he said, pulling her into his arms.

"She said the house was a mess. She refused to stay for tea and cake because she claimed that the house stank so much it gave her a headache. She said it was my fault for letting you take over the drawing room. And worst of all, she was right."

He met her gaze. "I said I would try and keep the studio tidier, and I will, I promise. Apart from opening a window or two, there is not much I can do about the smell of the paint. You know I have to work somewhere."

His painting was his path to a real career, his life's passion. The work had to be completed.

The hard set of her jaw did not soften at his words. Instead, she pursed her lips and began to slowly shake her head. The word *no* was written all over her face.

"You need to move your paintings out of the house. There is a wooden shed in the garden which you can use. It will be just like using the cottage at Mopus Manor. I checked it this afternoon. It will hold the two main pieces you are working on, along with the rest of your finished paintings. All your other clean canvasses and dry paint can be stored downstairs in the house," she said.

"No. I need the light and space of the drawing room," he replied, adamant in his resolve.

"And I need the drawing room. How do you expect me to establish myself as a respectable married woman if I cannot entertain at home?" she replied.

He released Leah's hand and started to walk away. He was hungry and tired. There was no point in continuing the argument.

He turned his back on her, and immediately knew he had made a grave mistake.

"Don't you turn your back on me, James Radley! We are not finished!" bellowed Leah.

He sighed. "Leah, my love. I have had the devil of a day. We can talk about this tomorrow."

She grabbed a hold of his jacket sleeve. "We will talk about this now, or you can go and sleep in the other room tonight."

If there was one thing James did not take kindly to, it was threats of any kind. He could accept that Leah was angry, and he was out of sorts with her at this very moment, but her telling him that they would be sleeping apart was not something he would tolerate.

"I am not moving my paintings out of the house. I have to work on the *Derbyshire Twins* in the drawing room. If I work in the garden shed, it will be cramped and cold. It is nothing like the cottage in Cornwall; it doesn't get any real sunlight," he replied.

Her eyes were ablaze with rage.

"You need to move them," she said.

He understood why she was angry; she had been humiliated by her mother. Her family were rejecting their marriage, and her father was taking his time with handing over her dowry. But moving his paintings out of the house would not solve any of those problems. And even if he did, he was certain that her mother would find another way to make Leah feel unworthy.

From the look of grim determination on her face, he could tell Leah was not about to change her mind. Whether she realized it or not, she had found every single one of his pain points and then pushed hard on them. His simmering anger boiled over.

James threw up his hands.

"Alright! I will move them. But if I catch my death of cold from working out in the garden all day, you only have yourself to blame. I hope you will enjoy your penniless widowhood. If I had known you would resent my chosen calling, then I would have had second thoughts in offering to marry you. Perhaps I should have dragged you back to the church and had you marry Guy. At least his fancy house does not smell of paint!"

His words were spoken in anger, and even as he said them, he regretted it.

Tears shone in her eyes, but he couldn't bring himself to apologize.

"Perhaps I should go back to my parents' house. At least there I wouldn't be a complete outcast," she said.

James shook his head. How had a simple disagreement turned to such a furious battle? Leah was using every weapon at her disposal to hurt him.

"You don't mean that," he said.

"No? Well if I see any of those stinking paintings anywhere near the house after tonight, I shall burn the bloody lot of them. And you are not the only one who is regretting this marriage. At least with Guy I wouldn't be having to watch every farthing," she bit back.

He leaned in close. Mere inches separated their faces. "No, you would just be his whore." James brushed Leah's hand away from his jacket and stormed out of the room. He marched into the drawing room and slammed the door loudly behind him.

Chapter Forty-Seven

J ames was good to his word. While Leah sat in the sitting room steaming over their row, he moved all of his paintings out of the house and into the garden shed. When she retired to bed that evening, he was still moving the last of his things. Leah waited for him to come to bed, but when her eyes finally closed in sleep, James had still not appeared.

Leah woke the next morning to see that James hadn't slept on his side of the mattress, and he was already gone from the house. She lay in bed and stared up at the ceiling. There would be time later that day for her and James to speak and apologize to one another. She was certain that her husband would eventually come around and see that she had been right.

After breakfast, Leah ventured into the now empty drawing room. She walked around for a time, imagining where various pieces of household furniture could be placed. There was a rug in one of the other bedrooms which would go nicely in the drawing room—its rusted red shade matched the color of the curtains.

With the smell of paint and linseed oil now slowly leaving the house, it would only be a few days before she could consider hosting guests in the house. Her first visitors would be her mother and sister once more. She would show her mother that she was taking her role as lady of the house seriously. It pained her to crave her mother's approval.

She headed downstairs and into the garden. The wooden shed where James had relocated his work now appeared much smaller than her recollection of the previous day. After pulling the door open, she stepped inside.

There were a number of smaller paintings stacked against the far wall, but the space was mostly taken up by the two large easels which James had set up for the *Derbyshire Twins*. They were at the back of the cramped garden shed.

"It is nowhere near big enough," she murmured.

Their butler had earlier informed her that it had taken more than an hour for them to carefully move the two large canvasses out of the drawing room and slowly inch them into place inside the shed. James had been at great pains to ensure neither of his precious paintings were damaged in the process.

She stood back from the first of the paintings and examined it. Already, the image of a riverbank and the overhanging grey willow trees had begun to take shape. Through the clever use of various shades of brown and green, James had been able to capture some shadows thrown by an afternoon sun.

Even to her untrained eye, it was clear James's work was not a mere indulgence of a passing fancy. Her husband was truly gifted. Given the right support from his friends and family, James could be one of the greats. Someday these works would hang alongside those of the masters, such as Reynolds and Gainsborough—she was sure of it.

She wiped away a tear, her heart swelling with pride. If she had to make sacrifices in order to see him succeed, she would.

She stepped in front of the second of the two landscapes. Less than a foot separated them in the confined, cold space.

James had made significant progress on the work, his long hours at the easel evident. He had created the soft green and gold canopy of the woodland trees, and the first rough outlines of the lush undergrowth could also be seen. She could just imagine James picking up his paint-brush and adding color to bring the rugged bushes to life.

Her gaze then drifted from the paintings and took in the linseed oil rags which had been laid out flat to dry. If she had thought the paint and oil fumes in the expanse of the drawing room had been bad, in the tiny garden shed they took her breath away.

She sighed. James had been right; this was never going to work. Stepping back into the fresh air of the garden, her victorious mood of earlier that morning was now subdued by reality.

"I am a terrible wife," she muttered.

James had supported her from the moment she'd fled the church. He had allowed her to make her own choices. He had seen her safely to her grandfather's house. Never once had he forced her into doing something against her wishes. And this was how she, his wife, had repaid him. How she had shown him her love.

It was her husband who deserved her loyalty, not her parents. Not the people who had willingly sacrificed her to a life of misery for their own political gain. James loved her. Her parents only cared about status and power.

"Oh, Leah, you stupid, selfish girl."

Little wonder James had refused to come to their bed last night. She couldn't blame him, imagining how disappointed he would have been in her lack of support. How frustrated he must have felt standing in the garden shed, wondering how on earth he was going to be able to complete his work when he barely had room to stand.

A hopeful smile came to her lips. James would be at work until late today. She had time to fix this, to show him that his work was important. That if he succeeded in his efforts as an artist, it would be in part due to a wife who fully supported him. And if he failed, they would cross that bridge when they came to it together. In the meantime, she would do everything to help him.

"I hate morning teas and 'at homes' anyway. They are always full of harridans and their spiteful tongues," she said.

The drawing room was still empty and with the help of the servants, she could set things to right before James got home. She would apologize for her berating of him the previous night. They would get their marriage back on an even keel.

With windows and doors left open during the day, she would find a way to deal with the smell of paint and oil. Hopefully, in time, she would get used to it.

She picked up his sketchbooks and tucked them under her arm. Then she bundled the linseed oil rags together and put them out of the way in a wooden box. This made a clear path which would enable the larger paintings to be moved back into the house. Her husband's paintings would be returned to where they belonged, and James would know his wife loved him.

&

Leah returned to the house and spent the next three hours wandering from room to room. She searched for places in which James could paint in comfort, but which would lessen the impact of the paint fumes.

No other room, however, gave the same light and space as the drawing room. So, she decided to tackle the problem from another angle, eventually settling on the idea of relocating the dining and sitting rooms to another floor of the house. Moving their bedroom to one farther away from the drawing room would also help. With that problem hopefully addressed, she rang for the butler.

"I have decided to bring Mister Radley's paintings back into the house. The garden shed is not big enough. Could you please assemble a working party to help move the two large canvases back upstairs and into the drawing room?" she said.

"Very good, madam," he replied.

Leah pretended not to notice his scowl. His opinion of the goings on between husband and wife didn't matter to her. Leah only cared that James could see that she had accepted the error of her ways and was doing everything to make amends.

Intending to personally oversee the delicate operation of bringing the *Derbyshire Twins* back into the house, Leah headed downstairs.

The smell of smoke greeted her as she reached the bottom of the staircase. She screwed up her nose. Someone must have been burning off rubbish in a nearby yard. London was a haze of smoke at the best of times, but this was close by the house. And with the drawing room windows open, the acrid smell would now add to the odor given off by the paint and oil. She made a mental note to close the upstairs windows once she returned.

Opening the door which led out to the garden, she was met with a sight that set her blood to ice. The garden shed was fully ablaze. Flames licked the walls and a golden glow could be seen through the window.

"The Twins!" she cried.

She raced to the door of the shed and grabbed a hold of the metal door handle. Searing-hot iron touched the palm of her hand, and she screamed. Fighting back blinding pain, she pressed on. She had just set foot inside the burning shed when strong arms wrapped around her waist and pulled her back.

"Mrs. Radley, you cannot go in there. You will die!"

She tried in vain to fight off the butler, determined to save anything of her husband's work, but he was stronger. He dragged her away from the shed and to safety.

Servants came racing out of the house, attacking the flames with brooms and rakes as best they could. The sickening roar of the fire filled the air as the shed was engulfed in thick grey smoke. Flames shot into the sky.

Finally, the butler called the staff away from the shed, saying, "It's gone. There is nothing to be done."

Leah stood, tears streaming down her face, as the shed, along with James's precious paintings, was reduced to ashes. When the pain of loss and her badly injured hand finally caught up with her, Leah fainted dead away in the arms of the brave butler.

Chapter Forty-Eight

J ames had spent the best part of the day breathing the foul air inside the hold of a recently arrived ship. Leah may well have her issues with the smell of his paint and linseed oil, but the fumes from them were nothing compared to the stench of a ship which had carried livestock across the Atlantic from America. For the second day in a row, he and Francis had been dealing with bad-tempered captains and poor paperwork. He could only pray that Leah was in a better mood than she had been last night.

He didn't come in the front door of the house, deciding to go around and enter in through the rear laneway. It had been a long day, and before he went inside the house and tried to make amends with his wife, he needed five minutes alone with his paintings.

He and Leah had both said unkind things to each other the previous night, but they were in love. Forgiveness and compromise were something all newlyweds had to learn.

He smelt smoke as he neared the back garden gate. For a moment, he thought that perhaps the household staff had been burning refuse, but the air was rank with the smell of linseed oil and burnt wood.

His hurried steps faltered as he laid his hand on the gate. The smell grew stronger. He came to a halt inside the garden.

Where once the garden shed had stood, a wasteland of blackened ash now greeted him. His jaw dropped open. Shock reverberated throughout his body. The shed was gone. He struggled to breath. Any moment, he would be sick.

"The . . . Twins," he stammered.

All his work was lost.

Leah had threatened to burn his paintings, but never in his wildest imaginings had he thought that she would actually do it. Before his eyes stood the irrefutable evidence. His wife had followed through on her vow of vengeance and destroyed all his work.

He gripped the top of the gate. If he wasn't going to cast up his accounts, he was certain he would faint.

"Why?"

His gaze now drifted to the house. Upstairs, there was no light in any of the rooms. The sitting room and their bedroom were in complete darkness. His life's work was gone, and so, it would seem, was his wife.

She had made good on both of her threats. His paintings were gone; but far worse than that, Leah had returned to her family. She had chosen them over him. Their marriage had been a lie.

He turned and staggered out into the laneway. The dark of night was his only ally as it hid the tears which streamed down his face. He was struck dumb, his mind a whirl of uncertainty. There was only one thing he did know— he had to get away.

The sun was already working its way up the morning sky when James woke. He was lying under a tree along the banks of the River Thames, a near-empty bottle of whisky still clutched in his hand.

He had staggered in a daze from the house down to his old haunt, *The Riverside*. The irony that he'd chosen to get blind drunk at the exact same tavern that he and Guy used to frequent was not lost on him. He craved the comfort of familiar surroundings and old habits.

Rolling over onto his side, he struggled to his knees. When his head protested at the sight of the whisky bottle, he sat his drink on the ground. The whisky poured out, but he didn't bother to right the bottle.

"I think I hurt enough," he muttered.

The whisky had been his friend in the early hours of the morning, numbing him to the pain of loss, but now it only served to punish him. His head throbbed.

The bustle of busy London went on all around him. Carriages passed by, as did countless people. Everyone was going about their business. Lives continued.

He wondered if it was only his life which had suddenly stopped.

His mouth was dry, and his empty stomach growled. He hadn't eaten anything since noon the previous day.

"Fuck."

He should be at work by now, not nursing a hangover. Francis would skin him if he abandoned him to the task of cleaning up the shipping orders on his own.

All he wanted to do was lay down and die.

"How did it come to this?" he muttered.

A dozen theories spun 'round in his mind. Tobias Shepherd had made Leah burn the shed down. No, Guy Dannon had done it. Both of those ideas, while unpalatable, were still better than the thought that the woman he loved had turned traitor and betrayed him.

He began to walk. One foot painfully in front of the other. After finally making his way up from the river bank and to the street, he stopped.

There were many places he could go at this point. He could go back to the tavern and force himself to imbibe once more, thus waking up under the same tree this time tomorrow. But he felt sick enough, so that held little appeal.

He could hail a hack and arrive in his current disheveled state at his uncle's shipping office, where no doubt he would be told to go home and not return until he was in a fit state.

"Or you could just walk home, sober up, and face reality."

That last option, while being the least appealing, was the obvious choice. James had nothing left to lose.

He went home.

Chapter Forty-Nine

J ames stepped through the front door of the house and was
met by the butler. He had hoped to slip in quietly, go to bed,
and get some sleep before facing up to the aftermath of the
fire and Leah's departure.

"Good morning, Mister Radley. Shall I have cook make you some
breakfast?"

He perked up at the thought of food. He would be able to think a
little clearer after some sustenance. "Yes please."

He had taken a step toward the staircase, when he stopped. There
was no point in delaying the inevitable.

"Has my wife returned to the house this morning?" James asked.

"As far as I am aware, Mrs. Radley is still at home this morning. She
had a difficult night, but her maid tells me she is up and about," he
replied.

Leah was home.

He didn't wait to ask the butler anything further. All that mattered
was that Leah was here. James raced upstairs. After searching through
various rooms, he finally found her in the drawing room.

She was seated on the floor with her back to the wall, staring out
the window. When James stepped into the room, she turned and

glanced at him for a moment, then went back to looking out at the garden. The look of hopelessness on Leah's face was heartbreaking. He prayed for the strength to find forgiveness.

"I was surprised to find you here. I thought you had gone," he said.

"The doctor gave me laudanum last night, so I couldn't have gone anywhere even if I'd wanted," she replied.

Laudanum? "Why did you need a doctor?"

Leah held up her heavily bandaged right hand. James hurried to her side, all thoughts of confronting her over the fire put aside.

"I foolishly tried to take hold of the handle of the door at the height of the fire. My hand is badly burned," she replied. She screwed her eyes closed. Tears began to pour down her face as she sobbed. "I expect you blame me for destroying the *Derbyshire Twins*. But you have to believe me, I don't know what caused the fire. By the time I got to the garden shed, there was nothing that could be done to save them."

"You did threaten to burn them," he said softly.

Leah shook her head. "I was angry when I said that, but you can't think I would ever really do such a thing. Your work means everything to you. And to me."

James dropped to the floor next to Leah. Regret sat heavy on his shoulders. In the cold light of the morning, he questioned his rash decision not to come into the house the previous night. It shamed him to think he had immediately thought the worst of her.

"When I saw that the shed and all my work was gone, I thought you had abandoned me and returned to your parents. I'm sorry I was so quick to judge you," he replied.

Hands came seeking; fingers locked together. For a time, they sat hand in hand in silence. James searched for the words to find a way forward.

"So that is why you didn't come home last night? James, I would never leave you. I love you, which is why the loss of your paintings is so hard for me for bear. Knowing I have caused you such pain, unwillingly or not, is just tearing me up inside," she said.

Leah didn't know what had happened to cause the fire, but James still wanted to get to the truth. To stop it from ever happening to them again.

"What happened yesterday after I left for work?" he asked.

She shrugged. "I realized that I had been unfair in demanding you to move your paintings. I went out to the garden shed and it became apparent quite quickly that there was not enough room for you to work. I had been wrong in asking you to move your paintings. I folded and moved your oil rags into a box, and then picked up your sketchbooks before coming back inside. I spent the next few hours trying to figure out a way to rearrange the house so you could go back to painting in the drawing room, and . . ."

James let go of Leah's hand and shot to his feet. He felt like he had been punched in the head. Facing her, he raked his fingers through his hair.

"You piled the linseed rags into a wooden box? In the garden shed. Oh, Leah, no!"

A look of puzzlement sat on her face. "I didn't want them to be on the floor and in the way of the servants when they moved the *Twins* back into the house," she replied.

James took a deep breath. Leah had just handed him the answer as to what had likely caused the fire. "Linseed oil is highly combustible. The reason I lay the cloths out flat to dry is, so they do not ignite. By heaping them together, you created the perfect setting for them to spontaneously combust. While you were in the house sorting out rooms, the oil on the rags would have heated to a point where it finally ignited."

She gasped. "Which means I did cause the fire!"

"Yes, but you were not to know. I should have warned you of the danger of linseed oil. We were just fortunate that it was only the garden shed and not the house. If anyone is to blame for the fire, it is me."

Leah held out her hand. "James, please come and sit. We need to talk. There is something I want to ask you."

He came back and resumed his seat next to her on the floor. His shoulders were sunk in defeat. Leah reached over and handed James his sketchbooks. He took them and sighed.

"I know this is cold comfort to you right now, my love, but you can rebuild. You have your sketches. If you have to go to Derbyshire now, then so be it. I will be waiting here for you when you return," she said.

James flicked open the topmost sketchbook and began to turn the pages. Leah watched his face as the signs of hope slowly began to return. By the time he closed the book, a soft, tentative smile sat on his face.

"Thank god you saved the sketchbooks. Now, what was it you wanted to ask me?" he said.

"Are you happy in London?"

The question had been on the tip of her tongue for several days now. With her parents being set against hers and James's marriage, and James working himself ragged in order to establish his career, Leah had begun to wonder if London was truly for them.

"I can't say it has been a wonderful experience since we returned from Cornwall. At times I feel like it is you and I against the world. That's why last night was such a blow to me; when I thought you had gone . . ." he replied.

"I want to return to Cornwall. My family are set on making things difficult for us in London. And you are going to work yourself into an early grave if you have to keep the hours you are doing. I don't want living in London to cost us our marriage," she said.

She could quite happily go back to Mopus Manor and live there permanently. If James had not followed her, that had been her original plan.

"Your grandfather did offer for us to come and stay with him, and I have thought about his suggestion that I consider running for office. Truro is a big enough town for us to be able to get whatever we need, and London is only a three-day trip from there. But are you serious about it? I mean, it would involve leaving friends and family behind," he replied.

Leah would not miss London, nor the pressure that living in the city would place upon James to earn enough money to keep his wife and family in the particular lifestyle approved by other members of the *ton*. She did not want that for her husband, nor for their future.

She leaned over and placed a tender kiss on his lips. "Yes. I want us to be where you can pursue your passion, and where we can raise a family. I couldn't think of anywhere better than my grandfather's house."

James pulled Leah to him and kissed her deeply. When he released her from the kiss and their gazes met, he nodded.

"Let's do it."

Chapter Fifty

S*ix months later*

Leah sat on one of the high, dry rocks at the entrance to the sea cave, watching as the tide continued to go out.

A lone male figure appeared on the beach in the distance. She knew it was James from the soft roll of his gait.

She clambered off the rocks and went to meet him. As they drew close, she could see he was beaming.

"Wife! I have missed you," he cried.

Leah leaped into his embrace, and James wrapped his arms around her. Hungry mouths joined in a long sensual kiss. The feel of her husband's touch again after two weeks was magnificent.

"I have missed you too. How was London?" she asked.

"Good and excellent," he replied.

She raised an eyebrow and he laughed teasingly.

"Good in that the dowry is now finally settled. Your father was his usual pleasant self when I met with him at his solicitors to sign the papers. But I was respectful and polite to him," he said.

"And you being polite to him would have annoyed him no end. I am sure he would have much preferred it if you had engaged him in another battle of wills," she replied.

It had taken six months of, at times, blunt correspondence between the parties to finally get Tobias Shepherd to release Leah's dowry. He had been more than a little outraged to discover that she and James had given up London and relocated permanently to Mopus Manor. By refusing to stay and allow him to exact his petty revenge on them, Leah and James were beyond her father's reach.

"So, what is the excellent news?"

He kissed her again. "Francis secured me an audience with the Prince Regent. After I showed him the new miniatures of the *Derbyshire Twins*, the prince immediately decided he wanted the main paintings. They are going to be hung in the royal pavilion at Brighton."

Leah squealed. "You sold two paintings! James that's wonderful. We must celebrate!"

A familiar look crossed his face. One she had been missing for the past few weeks. She went to pull out of his arms, intent on leading him home and to their bedroom, but James refused to budge.

He nodded in the direction of the rocks where she had been sitting.

"Here. Now. I can't wait," he growled.

When they reached the rocks, James took a seat before lifting Leah into his lap. The moment she was settled, he speared his fingers through her long, fine hair. As their lips met, he whispered, "Leah."

Two weeks without waking beside him and having him make love to her felt like an eternity. The longing of those lonely hours they had spent apart was captured in a single kiss. They reached for one another, hungrily grabbing hold of clothing, hair, skin, anything. Neither were prepared to let go.

She gasped as he slipped his hand from around her waist and roughly tore open the buttons on her coat. His fingers touched the soft form of her breast, then brushed over the hardened nipple.

She raised herself up and straddled him. His face was now level with her breasts. She placed a hand on the back of his neck, then slowly rubbed. He lifted his gaze and she met a pair of warm brown eyes clouded with passion. He groaned.

The front of her gown gave little resistance to his hurried attention. Buttons and lacings were swiftly dealt with before he pulled the folds of her gown apart. The instant her naked breasts met the chill of the wind from the river, her nipples peaked, and she craved to feel his mouth on them.

James dragged a nipple into his mouth, sucking hard. She whimpered. Her hand continued to stroke the back of his head as he sucked and laved at her breast.

Tugging on the corner of her skirts, she pulled them free of his lap. She closed her eyes as he delved his hand under her skirts and blazed a trail up her leg. When he reached her hip, she rose on her knees. Leah didn't need to tell James what she wanted. He slipped two fingers inside her and began to stroke. She angled her hips, allowing him full access to her heated core.

He released her breast and his forehead came to rest on her cleavage. The noise of the river and the wind fell silent to her ears. All she could hear was the hard thump of her heart. Her love for this man was all-consuming.

"Oh, James," she murmured, knowing there would be time for talking later.

He continued to work his magic while Leah clung to him, her head resting on his shoulder. He was a master of loving her body. Her sobs and breathing became more ragged the deeper and harder he stroked. When he slid his thumb over her sensitive bud, she sobbed. "James, please."

With his one free hand, he flicked open the buttons of his trousers, releasing his engorged erection. Their gazes met. The look of pure desire on his face reflected her own desperate need.

Taking his hardened length in hand, she guided it to her heated, slick entrance. Slowly, Leah sunk down and took the fullness of him inside her. They sat for a minute, their foreheads gently touching, absorbing the earthy presence of their joined bodies.

Then Leah began to rise up and down, riding James. They held one another's gaze.

"That rock is going to leave marks on your arse," she teased.

"I don't care."

The pace of their coupling increased. She watched the emotions cross his face as she rode his hard cock. The torture of gliding up and down his erection was divine.

He took a firm hold of her hips and pulled her down fully onto him. At the same time, he offered up his mouth to her. She kissed him back, while he held onto her and began to draw her up and down the length of him in an ever-increasing tempo.

"Oh God, James," she sobbed. She was close to completion.

"Lean forward; let me grind against you. I want you to see stars when you come," he ordered.

Leah did as he commanded. His erection ground hard against her sex and she cried out, collapsing against him. He wrapped his arms around her and held on tight.

She eventually pulled out of his arms, smiling at him. She was exactly where she had always meant to be, and he knew it.

He whispered, "I love you."

Their lips met in a kiss that sealed the moment. James closed his eyes as Leah worked herself against his cock. She knew how to bring him to the edge, then pull back before taking him close once more. Loving him with her body was beyond pleasure.

"Fuck me," he muttered.

"As you wish."

With her hands held tight on his shoulders, she rode him hard once more. Gripping her hips even harder than before, he held her in place as he stroked his length deep into her willing body.

On the end of one final frenzied thrust he cried "Leah", then stilled.

Utterly spent, they wrapped their arms around one another, their faces cheek to cheek. The only sounds were the noise of the wind and the slowing beat of their hearts.

When James eventually roused, Leah sat back and looked at him.

He brushed her windswept hair away from her face, then placed a soft, almost reverent kiss on her lips. "It is so good to be home. I don't miss London at all. I used to think that in coming here, we were running away from our old lives. But I realize now that we were, in fact, running toward our destiny," he said.

She took his hand and placed it on the slight bump of her belly.

"No more running, James. My love. We are home," she whispered.

Epilogue

The odd look on her grandfather's face when he saw James pull into the forecourt of Mopus Manor had Leah looking away, trying not to laugh.

"A barouche is not the most practical of things. You will need a driver every time you go to town. And what about the children?" muttered Sir Geoffrey.

"This is purely just for Leah and me when we make short trips into Truro and the surrounds on constituency business. We don't need a driver," replied James.

Leah pretended to ignore Sir Geoffrey's concerns. At some point, he would see her, and James do their little dance as her husband hoisted her onto the driver's bench. What he would make of it was anyone's guess.

All that mattered to her was that every time she and James travelled from the manor and into town, her wicked husband would have an excuse to lay his hands on her body. She also thought it best not to mention the little cove where a barouche could be well hidden from the road by the shrubs. Nor the blanket that they planned to keep in the box under the driver's seat of the new carriage. Sir Geoffrey need never know about any of those things.

Leah was also pleased that her grandfather had the good sense not to enquire as to why it seemed to take forever for her and James to make the short trip in and out from Truro, even when they did use the larger estate carriage. The fact that Leah's hair was always mussed up upon her return home from a visit to town was also never mentioned by anyone.

Some secrets were best kept between the local member for Truro and his good lady wife. In that particular matter of parliamentary business, James and Leah were in firm agreement. They and their two little boys travelled up to London together for each session of parliament but were on the road home to Mopus Manor and Sir Geoffrey at first light the very next morning.

"And it will be useful for me when I have to make the trip over to Brighton to oversee the hanging of my landscape pieces in the Brighton Pavilion. His Majesty, the king, has commissioned another two landscapes to go along with the *Derbyshire Twins*. The new pieces are to be of the Cornish coastline. The barouche will enable me to make the trip in good time and then be back home here with my family as soon as possible," said James.

Leah gave her husband a loving smile as James pulled her into his arms.

Home for them would always be Mopus Manor. Their lives and hearts were entwined with the windswept coastline of Cornwall, and in that, they were two of a kind.

Author Note

Malpas, Mopus and Truro

My husband's family originate from Truro in Cornwall, his grandfather lived in Lemon Street, so I have always wanted to set a book in the area.

Mopus Passage was a tiny hamlet in the area near Truro, but the actual location of Mopus Manor is where the village of Malpas now sits at the confluence of the Truro and Tresillian Rivers.

And if you ask anyone from Cornwall about scones, jam goes on first then clotted cream. Those from Devonshire may however beg to differ...

Linseed Oil

My research for this book uncovered some interesting information about paints and oils. When linseed oil rags are drying, they can spontaneously combust. As the oil oxidizes it generates heat. The rags can act as an insulator, allowing the heat to build to a point where the cloth eventually ignites. If you are using linseed oil to restore furniture etc. be sure to handle clean up rags which have linseed oil on them strictly in accordance with manufacturer's instructions.

Also by Sasha Cottman

The Duke of Strathmore

Letter from a Rake

An Unsuitable Match

The Duke's Daughter

A Scottish Duke for Christmas

My Gentleman Spy

Lord of Mischief

The Ice Queen

Two of a Kind

Mistletoe & Kisses

Regency Rockstars

Reid

Owen

Callum

Kendal

London Lords

An Italian Count for Christmas

About the Author

Born in England, but raised in Australia, Sasha has a love for both countries. Having her heart in two places has created a love for travel, which at last count was to over 55 countries. A travel guide is always on her pile of new books to read.

Sasha's novels are set around the Regency period in England, Scotland, and Europe. Her books are centred on the themes of love, honour, and family. Please visit her website at www.sashacottman.com

Grab your FREE book and get VIP reader exclusives, including contests, giveaways and advance notice of pre-orders. Sign up at www.sashacottman.com

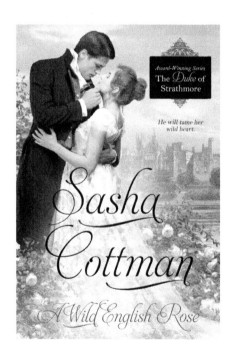

Printed in Great Britain
by Amazon

81155159R00154